ChangelingPress.com

Slider/ Ashes Duet

Harley Wylde

Slider/ Ashes Duet

Harley Wylde

All rights reserved.
Copyright ©2020 Harley Wylde

ISBN: 9798686038516

Publisher:
Changeling Press LLC
315 N. Centre St.
Martinsburg, WV 25404
ChangelingPress.com

Printed in the U.S.A.

Editor: Crystal Esau
Cover Artist: Bryan Keller

The individual stories in this anthology have been previously released in E-Book format.

No part of this publication may be reproduced or shared by any electronic or mechanical means, including but not limited to reprinting, photocopying, or digital reproduction, without prior written permission from Changeling Press LLC.

This book contains sexually explicit scenes and adult language which some may find offensive and which is not appropriate for a young audience. Changeling Press books are for sale to adults, only, as defined by the laws of the country in which you made your purchase.

Table of Contents

Slider (Hades Abyss MC 3)..4
   Prologue 5
   Chapter One...9
   Chapter Two 25
   Chapter Three...36
   Chapter Four...52
   Chapter Five 64
   Chapter Six...91
   Chapter Seven 112
   Chapter Eight...126
   Epilogue 136
Ashes (Devil's Boneyard MC 7) 140
   Prologue 141
   Chapter One...149
   Chapter Two 163
   Chapter Three...174
   Chapter Four...188
   Chapter Five 203
   Chapter Six...216
   Chapter Seven 230
   Chapter Eight...248
   Chapter Nine 259
   Epilogue 277
Harley Wylde...284
Changeling Press E-Books 285

Slider (Hades Abyss MC 3)

Harley Wylde

Vasha: Being groomed for the man who purchased me is the only life I've known. But I want more. I want freedom! My husband-to-be is a cruel, vicious man. I dread the day he claims me. When my bodyguard and friend, Anatoly, arranges my passage to America -- as a mail-order bride -- I hope it means things will be better. I never counted on my husband being so handsome, or so tender. Nor did I know that passion between a man and a woman could be so consuming! He leaves my knees weak and makes my heart race. There's just one problem... He doesn't know we're married! I don't know how it happened, or how to fix things, but it's clear Slider is angry. Leaving was the only thing I knew to do, but it was also the hardest decision I've ever made.

Slider: I'm not even thirty yet, but I'm already tired of the bullshit that comes with easy women. Maybe seeing my Pres settle down gave me a new perspective. Having the same woman in my bed every night is starting to sound more and more appealing. Or guy. I'm not picky. Love is love. What I didn't count on was my ex-lover deciding to "help" me with my problem. When he left a naked woman in my bed, I was pissed... until I realized she was in trouble. She needs me, and maybe I need her too. I always did have a hero complex, but it only takes a few minutes of knowing her before I want to slay her dragons, keep her safe, and show her that not all men are evil. I didn't count on her being my wife. I seriously fucked up and I have to get her back.

Prologue

Vasha

My heart hammered against my ribs. The man in the suit circled me, a pungent scent of tobacco, vodka, and mothballs made my eyes water. I knew who he was, why he was here. And I'd never been more scared in my life. Growing up under the care of Grigori Popov, I'd known fear before, but not like this. This man, Vladimir Bykov, would own me. I was to be his bride, but I knew what that meant. Obeying his every command, letting him touch me, do things to do me... and I'd have no say in the matter. I was an accessory, something to own and play with.

Bile rose in my throat as he trailed his cold, clammy fingers down my arm. There was a stain on his shirt and sparse silver hair peeked from the neck of the button-down. I didn't know how the buttons hadn't popped off his rotund figure. I had nothing against older men, but this one... revulsion filled me. The thought of lying under him nearly made me throw up.

"She's perfect," my soon-to-be husband said. "And properly trained?"

"Vasha! Present yourself to your husband," Grigori demanded.

I swallowed the knot in my throat and sank to my knees, head bowed, hands in my lap. The picture of subservience. It was the last thing I felt. I wanted to scream, to hit them. Instead, I knelt and did nothing. Just the way I'd been taught. Sit quietly, be meek, and take whatever punishments I received without complaint.

"Good," Vladimir said. "And she can take a cock?"

I felt the blood drain from my face, hoping he wouldn't ask me to prove it. Grigori had a woman from a brothel come every week and teach me the proper way to please my husband-to-be -- orally -- by using a ten-inch dildo. I tried not to look at the man's crotch, but I seriously doubted he was anywhere near that big. Not that I wanted to find out. The mere thought of putting him in my mouth made vomit rise up my throat, but I choked it down. If I let it spew across the floor, or the men, there would be hell to pay.

"Of course," Grigori said. "She's been instructed on all your desires and needs."

"Her virginity is intact?"

"Yes. You're welcome to examine her to be certain."

No! I wouldn't, couldn't stand the thought of such a humiliation. I'd already suffered at the hands of a so-called physician checking for my hymen, sticking his fingers inside me while Grigori watched. It was something I'd endured every year since my fifteenth birthday, when my true training had begun in order to prepare me to be a proper wife.

"If she does not bleed on our wedding night, I'll be back for a refund."

"We honor all our transactions," Grigori said. "If the merchandise is damaged, a refund is reasonable."

Merchandise. Because I wasn't a living, breathing woman. Just collateral. Something to be bought and sold. Useless except for providing use of my body and popping out kids. Although, the man purchasing me as his wife couldn't have children. I'd already been informed of that. As well as what would be expected of me to ensure he had heirs. It wasn't common knowledge my husband-to-be was sterile. Instead, I was to spread my legs for his guards, while he watched, until they got me pregnant.

I'd do anything to escape my fate. Anything!

When I was finally dismissed, I practically ran to my room. Anatoly was waiting, his gaze full of concern as I dashed away the tears on my cheeks. It was a sign of weakness to cry, but the situation was so hopeless. I was doomed to a life of misery.

"I can't do it," I said, my voice breaking. "I can't!"

I knew he understood. Anatoly was only a few years older than me, but he'd been my assigned guard since I'd turned fifteen. Before that, I'd considered him a friend, almost a brother. We were still close, but we could never allow anyone to see. They would use us against one another, and we suffered enough already.

"There's only one way out of this. You understand? There's no going back if I do this, help you escape. It would mean leaving Russia, living with a stranger. Would it be better to let Vladimir have you, or to offer your body to a man you've never met in a country you've never seen?"

No one could be as horrible as Vladimir, could they? Being with him would be like having an animated corpse fuck me. It's what he reminded me of... a bloated, disgusting dead body. Except he moved and spoke.

"A stranger would be preferable." At least then I'd have a chance. Or so I hoped.

Anatoly nodded. "I'll see that it's done. Be prepared to leave at a moment's notice, Vasha. We only get one chance at this. One! If it fails, then we're both going to die. Or perhaps you'll only wish you were dead."

I knew this would cost him. I wouldn't be the only one leaving Russia. If Anatoly stayed, once my absence was noticed, then he'd be tortured and eventually killed. It gutted me to think of the sacrifice I asked of him, but maybe a life elsewhere would be better for both of us.

"Do it, Anatoly. I need out of here. I'll suffer anything if it means I don't have to let that man touch me."

He gave a nod and came closer, pausing a moment to kiss the top of my head.

"Rest. I'll set things in motion."

We'd had this discussion before. Several times. There was a website on what Anatoly called the Dark Web. A place where women were bought and sold. He said I'd be a mail-order bride, but I knew I'd likely end up someone's whore. As long as it put me far from Vladimir's reach, I didn't care. Well, I mostly didn't care. The thought of ending up in a brothel somewhere was frightening, but it was a risk I had to take.

Whatever was asked of me, whatever was required, I'd do it.

Even marry a stranger, sight unseen.

I could only hope the man who chose me wouldn't change his mind. If he sent me back to Russia, I'd end up right back with Grigori, then things would become much, much worse for me. He had a wide reach in Russia. Sneaking out would be difficult enough, but the moment I returned I'd be at his mercy again. I'd never been much of one for prayer, but I'd kneel every night and beg God if that's what it took.

Chapter One

Slider

I eyed Surge across the room, noting the way he leaned into the pretty blonde. Looked like he was back to banging the club whores, which was a pity. I'd already scanned the offerings tonight and no one snagged my attention. It wasn't like he and I were in a relationship, but we had fun from time to time, and had been a sure thing the last three weeks. I'd thought he was getting as tired of the club sluts as I was, but it seemed I was wrong. The men we called brothers, the Hades Abyss, didn't seem to care who we fucked, as long as we handled shit when we were needed. Even after I'd been named the club's Secretary, no one had batted an eye at me spending time with Surge. I knew a lot of clubs wouldn't feel the same. But none of that seemed to matter right now. The way Surge's face was practically in the blonde's fake breasts told me he'd already found his hook-up for the night, and it wasn't me.

One thing was for sure. If he thought he was tumbling back into my bed, he'd better get tested first. We'd gone together weeks ago to have that done, and since we'd only been with each other after getting the all clear, not to mention we'd still used protection, I hadn't been worried. But there was no telling what some of those women were carrying, and I liked my dick too much to take any chances with it rotting off. A bit of latex wasn't foolproof.

Pushing to my feet, I ambled through the clubhouse and headed outside. I leaned against the porch post, wondering if I was getting too old for this shit. I wasn't even thirty, but the fact that easy pussy, or even easy ass for that matter, didn't seem all that appealing anymore made me wonder if I was going to fall prey to the same bug that had bitten Rocket and Spider. Was I ready to settle down? And if so, did I want to settle down with a woman or a guy? I was pretty sure my club wouldn't care that Surge and I had been fucking, but would they be quite so accepting if it was a permanent thing? How would it look for a club officer to be gay? Technically, I was bisexual, but to some people it wouldn't make a difference.

Speak of the devil. I smelled Surge's cologne before I saw him.

"We good?" he asked.

"Yep. Just tired of the scene inside."

He shoved a mug of beer toward me. "Here. Drink. Might take the edge off."

I took it and gulped down half. It was more bitter than what I usually had, but beer was beer. At least, tonight it was. Maybe if I got drunk, I wouldn't care that I'd be spending the night alone.

He rubbed the back of his neck and cast a look around before reaching for my hand. He twined his fingers with mine. "I know you want more than what I can give you, and you should have it. I'm sorry I'm not ready to settle down, and I hope things don't get weird between us. I like you, a lot, but I still want to have fun and meet new people. Maybe learn some new things."

I could understand that. He was younger than me. While I'd been partying hard since high school, Surge was only recently experimenting and opening up more. He'd been a bit reserved when he'd first asked to prospect. I gave his hand a squeeze before letting go.

"It's fine. I get it. You were clear up front that we were just having fun. Guess I'm just... envious. I see what Spider and Rocket have, and I think I might want that too."

He looked torn. Before I could react, he pressed his lips against mine in a fast, hard kiss, then took a step back. The way his hand shook belied his agitation, but I hadn't kicked him out of bed. This was his doing. I didn't understand what he was thinking or feeling. Had he just been scared of getting too close to someone?

"This might be overstepping, but there's a gift at your place. All right, so I seriously overstepped, but I think it's what you need. Before you even said anything, I could tell that you were starting to get that itch. I knew that our time was up or you'd start wanting more from me. You've had that look in your eyes almost since the beginning. I've been working on this surprise for over a week."

A week. For a week he'd planning to end things and hadn't given me a fucking hint? All he'd had to do was say he was bored and we'd have gone our separate ways. No big deal. If he'd just talked to me, been honest about what he was thinking and feeling, then maybe I wouldn't be so disappointed right now. I'd expected more from him. Not more as in a relationship that was long-lasting, but I'd thought he was man enough to be up front about shit.

"What the fuck does that mean?" I asked.

"You want someone steady in your life, and that's fine. It's just not something I want right now," he said. "Maybe someday. I don't know. But it doesn't mean you shouldn't have it. All I want is for you to be happy, Slider. Now go check out your gift."

I ran a hand down my face, wondering if there was a way to rewind and undo this conversation. It was weird as shit and getting worse by the moment.

"What the fuck kind of gift is supposed to resolve my relationship status? You better not have hired a fucking stripper." Nothing against those women, or men, but they just didn't do anything for me. I didn't like fake. If someone was with me, I wanted it to be genuine, which was probably why I was so fucking tired of the scene in the clubhouse every night.

He smirked. "Why don't you go home and find out?"

Jesus. I thrust the half empty mug at him, and stepped off the porch. My bike was buried three deep so I decided to walk my ass home. Mostly I didn't want to stand around waiting for everyone to move their rides when I didn't know what the fuck was waiting for me at the house. If Surge had wanted to call it quits between us, all he had to do was say so. I'd known he wasn't in it for the long haul, but this was fucking ridiculous. What the hell kind of gift had he left me?

Swear to Christ if he'd left a woman in my house, some stranger, I might very well kill him. There were times I had to question his reasoning. There was shit in my house I didn't need someone digging through, and I knew enough about women to know they were fucking curious. If I walked through my door and got shot, with one of my own guns no less, I was going to be fucking pissed. Worse, if whoever he'd left inside had stolen anything, I was going to pound Surge's ass into the damn ground.

I stomped up my front steps and threw open the door, not caring if I scared the shit out of whoever was inside. The lights were on, but I didn't see anything out of the ordinary. I went room by room, then closed my eyes and took a calming breath before opening the last door -- the one to my bedroom. Curled in the center of my bed, bare as the day she'd been born, was a small female. I blinked a few times, thinking my eyes were playing tricks on me. Then again, the room did spin a little. Just how strong had that beer been?

Glancing around, I spotted a pile of clothes that looked like they would fall apart at any moment. They weren't the type of worn material that people paid high dollar for, but more the kind you owned when things were really fucking bad. I focused on the woman. I'd seen plenty of beautiful women before, but this one seemed almost otherworldly. She was dainty, and delicate. Her blonde hair was so pale it was nearly white and lay in a wavy tumble across my pillow. Slowly, I entered the room and shut the door behind me.

Any anger I'd felt melted away. It seemed he hadn't left a stripper in my house. I wasn't quite certain what he'd done just yet. But the strippers I'd seen around town wouldn't have been caught in dead in the clothes piled near the bed. I hoped to Christ he hadn't paid some homeless woman to sleep with me. How was this woman a gift? I moved closer and reached out to shift a strand of hair that had fallen across her cheek. It was soft, softer than anything I'd felt before. Kneeling next to the bed, I studied her a moment. The sharp blade of her nose, her prominent cheekbones, the way her lashes lay dark against her pale cheeks. It was a little like discovering the fae were real and one had fallen asleep in my bed. I smiled a little, thinking of *Goldilocks and the Three Bears*, except there was only one grumpy bear in this house, and I was quite content to leave her sleeping in my bed.

What. The Fuck. Everything felt a little fuzzy and strange. What the hell was wrong with me? I'd never had thoughts like this before, and I sure as shit wasn't poetic. It felt like I was swaying, but I'd only had half a beer. The one Surge had given me. Had he spiked it with something? And why? I'd trust him with my life, most of the time, but right now I had to wonder just how well I knew him.

I pulled my phone from my pocket and shot off a text to Surge. It took a lot longer than normal as I kept hitting the wrong keys, but eventually I made two coherent sentences. At least, they looked right to me, but with my brain in a fog it was hard to say if they really did make sense.

Who is in my bed and how is she a gift? And what the hell did you give me?

I waited a few minutes, but didn't get a response, which meant he was probably balls-deep in one of the whores up at the clubhouse by now. Or avoiding me. If he really had drugged my beer, then I'd beat the shit out of him. Tomorrow.

I looked at the woman again. Her breasts were on the small side, but her nipples were the prettiest pink. I caught myself leaning toward her and knew I needed to get away, go sleep on the couch. There was no way I was taking advantage of a passed-out woman, regardless of what drugs Surge had added to my drink. I wasn't a rapist, wasn't the type of man to take advantage. The women I took to bed wanted it and knew the score. This one… this one was different.

Standing, I meant to take a step toward the door. Instead, I found myself pulling off my cut and setting it on top of the dresser. It was almost like my body had a mind of its own as I stripped out of my clothes. Naked, I slid into bed beside the sweet angel sleeping there. My cock ached and I already had pre-cum beading on the head. My hand shook as I reached for her, tracing the curve of her waist and down over her hip. *No! Don't touch!* I jerked my hand back.

My gaze raked over her, and I wondered if she expected to have sex with me. I didn't have any idea what Surge had told her, what deal he'd made to get her naked in my bed. It was wrong on so many levels, and I hoped like hell he hadn't done something awful. The kind of thing we protected women from. She didn't look like a prostitute, but what if she was here under duress?

I hadn't even realized I'd reached for her again until I noticed the way her nipple was hardening against my palm. *Shit.* She was naked, vulnerable, and I was feeling her up while she slept. This wasn't me. I wasn't the type of asshole who took what wasn't freely given, didn't matter if they were male or female. I forced myself to stop caressing her, even though I could have petted her all night, and gathered her in my arms. I didn't know why she was here, who she was, or what the fuck was going on, but the soft scent of her made me want to never let her go.

A protective urge rose inside me. She felt fragile lying against me, and some fucked-up part of me wanted to slay her dragons and claim her. I knew it was the drugs, knew I needed to let her go. I just couldn't seem to do it. There was a disconnect between my brain and my body. What I wanted to do and what my hands kept doing were two different things.

I was going to kill Surge. I'd never felt like this before. My dick was harder than granite, and the woman in my arms felt like... mine. I rubbed my beard against her neck and breathed her in. She murmured something in her sleep and snuggled closer, turning so that she faced me. A soft breath left her, caressing my chest. Her eyes slowly opened and her unfocused gaze seemed confused at first. When she truly noticed me, she stiffened for a moment, then reached up to lightly touch my beard.

"Slider?" she asked, her voice soft but the heavy Russian accent was undeniable, and sexy as fuck.

"Yeah. I'm Slider."

She licked her lips. "I'm Vasha."

I reached up and traced her lips. "Why are you in my bed, Vasha?"

Her face blanked of all expression, except her eyes. They told me a lot. Fear. Whatever had brought her here, she was scared.

"He said you wanted me. Was he wrong?" she asked, her tone uncertain.

"Oh, I want you, *krasotka*." I pressed my cock against her, letting her feel exactly how much I wanted her.

A soft gasp escaped her as her eyes went wide. "You know Russian?"

"Only a few words." Well, maybe more than a few, but I was far from proficient. "Grew up in an orphanage with a mix of nationalities. My hometown was a melting pot. There was a Russian neighborhood. Some of those kids lived with me when they lost their families, or were abandoned. I picked up bits and pieces of various languages."

Her fingers caressed my beard again. "You want me? Truly?"

"Yeah. I want you, but I don't take unwilling women, or those who feel they don't have a choice." I studied her. "I have a feeling you're at least one if not both of those."

She dropped her gaze and trailed her hand from my beard down my chest. She pressed her palm tight against my skin, right over my heart. A strange expression crossed her face before clearing.

"You're a good man. He said so. Said you wouldn't hurt me."

Who had said so? Surge?

"Of course I won't hurt you. I'm an asshole, but I'm not a rapist." My jaw tightened. "Is that what you think of bikers? We're just all murderers who fuck women even if they say no?"

Those beautiful silver eyes locked on mine. "No. I've seen monsters. Lived with them. You're not a monster. But if you don't want me, if you make me leave… then I have to go back to them. There's nowhere else to go."

Shit. I didn't know what she was running from, but I understood a little better why she'd willingly be naked in my bed, want to give me anything I asked of her. She wasn't scared of me, she was terrified of being sent away. Surge hadn't given me a gift. He'd given me a fucking damsel in distress. He knew I wouldn't turn her away. I also wasn't going to fuck her. She could stay without having to sleep in my bed. Not that I wanted to do much sleeping.

"I'm not going to make you leave, Vasha, but I won't treat you like a whore either. You don't have to take off your clothes for me to keep you here."

She bit her bottom lip, indecision on her face. I wondered if I was about to find out why she was running. I wanted her to trust me, to tell me what had her so terrified. I'd slay dragons for her. I wanted to blame the drugs, but her situation was rapidly clearing my head. Hearing that someone might hurt her had been enough to kill whatever buzz I'd had.

"In Russia, I was groomed to be the bride of a repulsive man. He was ugly, inside and out, and cruel.

There was no warmth in his gaze. They taught me the way to please a man, to submit to him in every way. I was scared. Terrified. A friend helped, created a listing your Surge found, then he arranged for someone to pull me out of there. When I came to this country, I had only one order to follow. Be good to you."

She was breaking my fucking heart.

"Vasha. *Zolatka*, I will protect you with my life, and you don't have to give me anything in return, much less your body. You aren't a bartering tool. You honor me with such a gift, but it's not necessary."

"It is," she insisted. "And... I want to."

The effects of whatever Surge had used to dose me were gone now, but I had to wonder if he'd drugged her too. Her pupils were dilated and her heart rate was a little fast. I wouldn't take advantage of her. She needed me to keep her safe, not shove my dick into her just because she was high and thought that was what she wanted.

"Surge drugged us," I said. "You don't really want this."

She nodded. "He did give me something. Because I panicked. I completely lost it and he worried I'd hurt myself. When I was calmer, he explained everything. I'm here because I want to be. He didn't force this on me. Coming here was my choice. Being in your bed was also my decision. He gave me several opportunities even before leaving Russia to back out of our deal."

I wanted to ask about that deal, but I didn't want to push too hard too fast. What she'd told me was more than I'd hoped to get from her.

"Do you not find me pretty?" she asked, her voice a near whisper. "I know men don't have to find a woman beautiful to get hard. It's why I removed my clothes before lying down. I'd hoped to tempt you."

Oh, she tempted me all right. And I felt like an ass for it. She was vulnerable, and here I was wondering how tight she'd be when I fucked her. I wouldn't be that guy. I'd been him before, taking whatever was offered and not thinking about *why* they wanted in my pants. Wouldn't do that ever again.

"You're beautiful. I thought a fae had fallen asleep in my bed."

She smiled a little and her cheeks flushed.

"You can have the bed, Vasha. I'll sleep on the couch. In the morning, we can discuss things. Whatever you're running from, or whoever, I can help you. No payment is necessary." I ran my hand down her hair, cupping the back of her neck. "Don't ever let someone take your body as compensation for anything."

I watched as her eyes filled with tears and my heart lurched. I hadn't meant to make her cry! Before I could apologize, she burrowed into me and held on tight. When women sprung a leak, I always ran the other way. This time, I couldn't. And oddly, I didn't want to.

I held Vasha as she cried, just waited as she let it all out. She hiccupped a few times as she got herself under control, then swiped at the moisture on her cheeks like the salty tracks running down her face offended her. She took a few deep breaths before she seemed to be back under control.

"Feel better?" I asked.

"Yes."

I released her, intent on getting out of the bed and putting some much needed space between us. Rolling to my back, I was about to slide out of the bed when she flung herself at me. My body locked up tight as her small hand wrapped around my cock. It felt like my heart was about to pound out of my chest, and all I could hear was static in my ears.

"Vasha." I put as much warning into my tone as I could, but it didn't do me a damn bit of good.

The flick of her tongue over the head of my cock had me groaning.

"Vasha, stop," I said. My voice was strained even to my ears. "*Nyet!*"

The barked word in Russian caught her attention and she froze, her lips around my shaft. Her gaze locked on mine. She retreated, sitting on her knees, hands in her lap, and her chin tipped down so that she stared at the mattress.

What. The. Fuck.

"Vasha, look at me." She didn't move so I repeated the command in Russian. Her gaze lifted to mine. What I saw in her eyes changed everything. Determination. Humiliation. Lust. Confusion. One emotion slid into another, then cycled back to the beginning. She'd mentioned being *trained* to be a bride. I had a clue what that meant now. My Russian wasn't the best, and I really didn't know much. I could hold a decent conversation without embarrassing myself too much, but that was it. I knew more than I'd told her, but not enough to speak it fluently.

She needed this. Needed me. No, she needed me to take control, to command her to do my bidding. Using only Russian, I barked out another order.

"On your back, hands above your head."

She scrambled to obey. When she was lying in the center, her slender fingers wrapped around the spindles on my headboard, I reached into my bedside table drawer and pulled out the handcuffs I'd gotten recently. I'd intended to use them on Surge, but that didn't matter now. Clicking them around her wrists, I locked her to the headboard. Her pulse fluttered in her neck, but it didn't escape my notice that her nipples were harder.

I leaned over her, bracing my weight on my arms. Her gaze flicked to my chest. She visually traced the ink on my body, then dipped lower over my abdomen and finally to my cock. Her breath hitched and her lips parted. It wasn't fear coming off her right now. It was one hundred percent need.

"Please," she begged.

Leaning down, I took one of her nipples into my mouth, lashing it with my tongue before gently biting. She cried out and thrashed under me, but I didn't stop, didn't let up. I ravaged her breasts, leaving whisker burn on her pale skin. She parted her legs and I knew what she wanted, but I wasn't ready yet. She was at my mercy, and I intended to give her as much pleasure as possible. I licked and kissed my way down her body, taking the time to rub my beard against her once I discovered it made her shiver and moan. She damn near orgasmed when I scraped it across her breasts. I'd never had a woman so responsive before, not one who wasn't faking it anyway.

The way her body flushed, the need in her eyes, and the scent of her arousal proved she was every bit as turned on as I was, possibly more so. It made me feel a little like a god, the way she begged and pleaded, feeling her body arch and twist. When I knew I couldn't take another moment, I finally covered her body with mine and rubbed my cock along her slit, soaking myself in her wet heat.

"Look at me," I demanded.

Her gaze locked on mine and I slowly sank into her. She was so fucking tight! I had to work for it, one inch at a time. Vasha panted, her body tight. I was barely in when I felt the resistance and I gave her a hard stare.

"Something I need to know?"

She pressed her lips tight and I started to withdraw. Vasha cried out and wrapped her legs around me, trying to keep me in place.

"Stay! Don't stop!"

"Vasha." My tone held a hint of warning.

"Please. If it's not you, then who? Who should I give my innocence to?"

I started to tell her it was a gift and should be cherished, and that was enough for everything to click into place in my head. Surge had left me a gift. Fucking hell. He'd known she was innocent. It wasn't just Vasha that was my present, but the fact she was untouched. I was going to kill the fucker.

"I don't care if it hurts," she said. "I want it to be you."

I leaned down and pressed a kiss to her jaw, then down the column of her neck. Rubbing my beard against her tender skin, I tried to distract her. My cock slid another inch into her tight pussy. She was so fucking wet, but it wasn't enough. There was no way to do this without some pain. I was too damn big and she was tiny. I closed my eyes and prayed she'd forgive me, then thrust hard and deep.

Vasha stiffened under me. I murmured words of comfort in her ear, holding still as she adjusted. As the tension in her body eased, I began to move. Short, shallow strokes until I was certain she wasn't in any pain. Shifting my weight, I rubbed against her clit with

Harley Wylde   Slider/ Ashes Duet

every thrust. It wasn't long before she was panting and writhing under me.

"That's it, *krasotka*. Come for me."

She let out a keening sound, and then her pussy clenched down and I felt her release coat my dick. The extra lubrication had me sliding in even farther and I groaned at how fucking incredible she felt. Most women couldn't handle all ten inches, but it was as if Vasha had been made just for me. We fit perfectly. I drove hard and deep, the headboard slamming into the wall as I took what I wanted, what I needed. I roared out my release, pumping her full of cum.

Shit. What the fuck had I just done? My heart was racing and there was static in my ears as I realized I'd just taken her bare. My gaze locked on hers, but she only gave me a tender smile. I had to tell her, let her know what I'd done. She had a right to know there could be consequences, and if she was angry, then I'd let her lash out all she wanted. I'd never been so stupid in my life.

"Vasha, I... I'm sorry."

"It was perfect," she said.

"No, I meant." My gut clenched. "I didn't use protection."

She tugged at the handcuffs and I reached for the key. After I unlocked them, I rubbed her wrists, and realized I was still balls-deep inside her. I withdrew and winced at the streak of blood on my cock. She had to be hurting right now. I got up and went into the bathroom, washing off my dick, then getting a warm wet rag. Vasha still lay sprawled on her back, a contented look on her face. Gently, I cleaned her, then pressed the cloth against her pussy.

She moaned a little.

"Sore?" I asked.

"Some," she said.

"I'll run a hot bath for you."

I hesitated only a moment before I pressed my lips to hers. I felt her fingers wrap around the back of my neck, and it was all the encouragement I needed. Deepening the kiss, I tried to tell her without words that I would take care of her. She wasn't just a one-night stand, not just a random fuck. When I drew back, her eyes were still closed, but her lips curved in a smile.

Before I could do something stupid, like fuck her again, I went to run a bath.

Was this how Spider had felt? Or Rocket? Had they felt this... sense of ownership with their women? Seeing Vasha in my bed, before I'd even known her name, I'd wanted her. Not just to fuck, but I'd wanted to claim every inch of her. Maybe I was a caveman for thinking such a thing, but she felt like mine, and now that she'd given me her innocence, I didn't plan to let her go anytime soon. Maybe not ever.

Chapter Two

Vasha

In all the times I'd contemplated what my first time would be like, I'd never once thought I would enjoy it. I'd thought it would hurt, and it had, but not because Slider was being rough or cruel. He hadn't wanted to cause me pain, and that had made me cry even more than the sting I'd felt as he claimed my virginity. Then that kiss! No one had kissed me before him.

I heard the water shut off and he came back, holding out a hand to me. I'd stayed where I was, not daring to move without permission. In the past, my lessons had been degrading and I'd hated them. When Slider had given me commands, I'd obeyed because it's what I wanted. The thought of Vladimir doing such a thing sent a chill down my spine, but seeing Slider in that role -- all domineering and alpha -- it had made me burn hotter for him.

Maybe there was something wrong with me. Perhaps my time in captivity with Grigori had warped my mind.

I grasped Slider's hand and stood, but once I was on my feet, he lifted me into his arms and carried me into the bathroom as if I weighed no more than a feather. I pressed my cheek against his chest and breathed in his scent. For the first time since my parents died, I felt safe. He'd promised to protect me, even if I hadn't spread my legs for him, and I'd known in that moment that he was different. He wasn't anything like the men I'd known.

And he was mine! Or rather, I was his.

Happiness bubbled inside me as I thought about a future with him. I wondered how many children he'd want. Could I be pregnant already? When I'd felt the hot spurts of his release inside me, I'd wanted to grip him with my thighs and beg for him to do it again and again until we created a baby. In Russia, I'd dreaded my responsibility. With Slider, I wanted to be a good wife and mother to our children.

Slider eased me down into the water, then knelt beside the tub.

"This should help with any pain or tenderness," he said, then reached out to brush the hair back from my face. "We need to talk about the fact I took you bare. I never meant to do that."

My heart nearly stopped. He hadn't wanted to be inside me without a barrier? Was there something wrong with me? Did he not think I'd be a good mother to his children? Was he going to send me back now? Panic crawled up from my belly and I gripped the side of the tub.

"Vasha, do you understand? I didn't use a condom."

"Yes." I felt like I was going numb. "You didn't use one, but you wish you had. I understand. I'm…"

I couldn't continue. It felt like my throat was closing up, but I knew I needed to say the words.

"You don't feel that I'm worthy."

He stared at me a moment, then tipped his head to the side slightly. "What the hell does that mean?"

"Not worthy of being a mother. You wish you had used protection so I don't get pregnant."

"Vasha, we're both speaking English, but I think there's a disconnect somewhere."

I dropped my gaze to the water and skimmed my hand across the surface. I'd been raised to be nothing more than a wife and mother, a trophy, a piece of property. Now that I had someone, a man I could see myself loving, he felt that I didn't deserve him, and maybe he was right. Slider was strong, and so very sexy. He could have his choice of any woman. Why would he want me?

"Vasha," he said softly. When I didn't look up, he said my name again. Harder.

I jerked my gaze to his.

He reached and placed his hand over my belly under the water. "Did you want to get pregnant? Are you trying to tell me you want a baby?"

"In Russia, I was groomed for one thing only. To be a proper wife and mother. I know things are different here, but if I'm not good enough for my only intended purpose, you might as well send me back." I took a steadying breath. "Or just have someone kill me."

"What the fuck? Are you fucking insane, Vasha?"

I felt tears burning my eyes. Now he thought I was crazy. I wasn't making things better, only worse.

"Look at me, *kroshka*."

I forced myself to do as he said.

"Vasha, I was upset that you thought you deserved to die. I'm not sending you back, and I'm sure as fuck not having someone kill you. Having a baby could be a wonderful thing for you, but only if the circumstances were right. We just met. Do you really want a child with me?"

"But you're my husband. Who else would I have children with?" I asked, not understanding.

Slider's expression blanked.

"What?" He removed his hand and stood. "What do you mean I'm your husband?"

"You bought me. Anatoly made sure there were papers, a marriage by proxy, which Surge agreed to on your behalf. You're my husband, Slider. If you don't want children with me, then what good am I?"

He stumbled back a step, then bolted from the room. I heard him slam a door and I wondered what I'd done wrong. It had almost seemed as if... My breath caught. No! He hadn't known we were married? If Slider hadn't signed the papers for a marriage by proxy, then had Surge forged his name? And was our union even legal?

Now that I was no longer a virgin, no one in Russia would want me. Not as a wife and mother. I'd only be good for one thing.

The water started to turn cold, but he hadn't given me permission to get out. Would he come back? After my fingers had pruned and my teeth started to chatter, I got out of the tub, then drained the water. I dried off and put my clothes back on, then cleaned the bathroom. I pulled the sheets from Slider's bed and found the laundry room. The buttons and knobs seemed straightforward enough. I'd never actually washed clothes, but it couldn't be that difficult. Grigori had sent his laundry out so it hadn't been part of my training. I also threw in the towel I'd used. By the time the washing machine was finished, and I'd also dried everything, Slider still hadn't returned.

I remade the bed, folded and put away the towel, then looked around the house one last time. I'd thought I would be happy here. It wasn't a huge house like the one Vladimir boasted he owned, but it had felt like a home. I'd looked forward to celebrating holidays, raising a family, and finally being safe and cared for. I should have known better. Good things never happened to me. Why would this be any different?

I let myself out of the house, and started down the paved street. I vaguely remembered the way to the

Harley Wylde   Slider/ Ashes Duet

front gate. When I reached my destination, a young man stood at attention, watching me carefully.

"I need to leave, please," I said.

"You were the one Surge brought earlier?" he asked.

"Yes. There was a misunderstanding. I'm not supposed to be here. I need to leave so Slider will no longer be angry."

The man's eyebrows rose and he rocked back on his heels. He opened the gate and let me through, then shut it behind me. The sound of the lock clicking felt too final. I glanced back once, then started walking. It didn't matter where I went. I had no money, no way to call anyone, or anyone *to* call for that matter. While I was free and no longer suffering in Russia, I didn't know that this was any better.

My feet ached and the darkness settled around me in an eerie silence. I'd thought the town was this direction, but it seemed I'd been walking too long to not find any buildings or people. Which meant I was going the opposite way. My stomach cramped with hunger. I'd been so foolish, thinking that I could escape, that I'd have a good life if I only left Russia. At least with Grigori, I had regular meals and a roof over my head. My clothes were threadbare, but only because he'd insisted Vladimir would purchase my wardrobe once we were married.

Stupid. I was so stupid. Such a silly girl, hoping and dreaming for something that didn't even exist. Growing up, I'd heard such wonderful things about America, the grand opportunities. Instead, I seemed worse off than before. It felt like I'd walked forever. I could feel blisters forming on my feet, and a town was ahead in the distance. Hardly any lights were on, but I hoped I could find a place to rest for a little while.

By the time I reached the town limits, I was stumbling and about to fall over. I was exhausted, starving, and felt like I'd lost all hope. I saw a wooden bench under a streetlight and I made my way over to it, collapsing once I got there. I couldn't even sit upright. The moment my butt hit the seat, I slumped over and curled into a ball. I don't know if I zoned out or fell asleep, but the rumble of motorcycles jolted me to the here and now. Four shiny bikes stopped in front of me, the men on them looking every bit as dangerous as Surge had seemed when we'd first met.

"Not a good place for a nap, little one," the eldest one said. "Don't you have somewhere else you could sleep?"

I shook my head and forced myself to sit up. "I thought I did, but I was wrong."

The blond one smiled, his eyes crinkling at the corners. "How long have you been in the country?" he asked in Russian.

My eyes went wide, my chest started to ache, and I thought I might pass out. Had someone sent him after me? I'd thought it was a coincidence bikers had found me, but what if I was wrong? What if Slider sent them and they were going to send me back to Grigori? I whimpered and tried to get away, but my legs gave out when I tried to scramble off the bench.

One of them caught me, bringing me tight against his chest. "Easy. We're not going to hurt you. What the fuck did you say to her, Philly?"

"Nothing! I swear. I just asked how long she'd been in the US."

I struggled, trying to break free and save myself, but I didn't have the strength I needed. Hunger and exhaustion had weakened me too much.

"Hey," the man holding me said softly. "No one here will hurt you. Philly is a dumbass. Ignore him. We all do."

The one called Philly huffed and muttered a *whatever*.

"I'm named Kraken, Philly is the shithead who scared you, Titan is our Pres," he said nodding to the first man who spoke to me. "And the one on the end is Stone."

I focused on the leather vest in front of me. I remembered Surge wearing one with his name on it. When I saw the same words -- Hades Abyss -- stitched onto it, I knew that I'd been right to be scared.

"Please. Don't take me back. I'll disappear, I promise," I said.

"Take you back where, sweetheart?" Titan asked.

"Slider didn't want me. He was so angry. I left. Please, I didn't know that he wasn't the one who --" I clamped my mouth shut. Maybe I was giving them too much information.

"You try to trap Slider?" Titan asked.

"*Nyet*! I'd never do such a thing! It was a misunderstanding."

"And if I called our brothers in the Missouri chapter and asked them, would they also say it was a misunderstanding? Or did something else happen? Who are you to Slider?"

I swallowed hard. "I thought I was his wife."

The one called Philly swore. "Motherfucker. Someone bought you, didn't they?"

I nodded. "I was married to Slider by proxy, but when I called him my husband, he became angry and stormed out. He wasn't the one to request me, didn't sign the papers. Please. I can't go back to Grigori. I'll disappear. Slider will never hear from me again, I swear."

"What do you mean someone bought her? What's the marriage by proxy crap?" Stone asked.

"On the Dark Web in Russia, men sell women as mail-order brides. They ship the women out of the country to live as wives to guys who typically can't get laid on their own. Fat, balding, smelly men usually buy the women. How the fuck did you end up with Slider?" Philly asked.

"Surge picked me up when I arrived here. He took me to Slider's house and left me there. I thought I was waiting for my husband. I didn't know that Slider wasn't aware that I existed, or that I was in his house."

Titan cracked his neck. "We can't leave her here. If Slider didn't want her, I doubt he'll be looking for her. Still, keep your eyes and ears open for any word that he's changed his mind. Until then, we'll take her home with us."

"Shouldn't we call them?" Kraken asked.

Titan shrugged a shoulder. "Probably. Don't care right now."

Home with them? They were handsome men, but it didn't mean I wanted to be their whore. I fought again, trying to get free. I'd run, if my legs would hold me. Anywhere was better than lying on my back and servicing whoever paid enough. I'd rather live in the gutter. If I'd stayed in Russia, I'd have endured the touch of Vladimir and his guards, but they were all disgusting and liked causing pain. Having to serve multiple men who at least seemed kind would likely be a better fate, but it didn't mean that's what I wanted. I'd never willingly be anyone's whore.

"You're scaring the shit out of her," Philly said. He switched to Russian when he addressed me. "Calm

Harley Wylde   Slider/ Ashes Duet

down. None of us will hurt you. We're just taking you home so you can rest, get some food, and have a safe place to stay until things get sorted."

I stopped fighting. Could I trust them? Was Philly telling me the truth? Kraken eased his hold on me, but didn't release me completely. I swayed and nearly passed out. He cursed and clutched me to his chest again. Everything was swimming and black dots started to dance across my vision.

"I think we need some rooms for the night," Titan said. "We'll head back home after she's had some food and sleep. I don't think she can sit on the back of a bike in her present state."

Philly pulled out his phone, scrolling and tapping.

"There's a motel two blocks up. The pictures on the website seem decent enough. Old but clean. I'll grab some food and meet you there," Philly said.

"Just get something for her. I'll order pizzas for the rest of us," Titan said. "She probably needs something healthier."

"On it," Philly said, then he swung his leg over his bike.

As he drove off, Kraken led me over to the motorcycle he rode. He hesitated a moment, eyeing me and the machine. With a shrug, he got on the bike, then pulled me down in front of him. He started the bike, then place a hand against my abdomen to hold onto me. Slowly, he eased down the street, going so slow that if there had been more traffic, people would have likely been upset with him. He pulled into the motel right where Philly had said it would be. Instead of getting off, he left the engine running and just held onto me. Probably a good thing since I felt like I was seconds away from passing out.

- 33 -

Titan went inside and came back what felt like hours later. I wasn't entirely certain I hadn't fallen asleep. He handed a keycard to Kraken, and one to Stone. Without a word, he got back on his bike and led the way down to where I assumed the rooms were located. He used his keycard to enter the first-floor room marked 22 and nodded his head to the rooms on either side.

"Kraken, you can either room with Stone and let Philly watch over her, since he knows her language, or you can keep an eye on her and Philly can room with Stone for tonight. Each room has two beds." Titan stepped into his room. "I'll have the pizza brought to my room. Once you're settled, come over and we'll eat."

Stone and Kraken shut off their bikes. I awkwardly tried to get up and couldn't manage. However long I'd walked and been without food, my body had reached the point of no return. I needed sleep and food. Stone picked me up, cradling me in his arms. It reminded me of the tender way Slider had carried me into the bathroom and I almost started crying. It wasn't that I had gotten attached to him in the short time we spent together tonight, but more the idea of everything I'd lost. I'd thought we were married, that we would have started a family. Now I had nothing and no one.

Stone paused in front of the door to the left of Titan's. "Are you staying with her or is Philly?"

"We'll ask him when he gets back. For now, just put her in there. If he wants to stay with her, then we'll take the other room," Kraken said.

I wanted to tell them I didn't need a babysitter, but as weak as I felt they might be right. I must have fallen asleep again because the next thing I knew, I smelled food. Philly sat in a chair at the small table and had a sack in front of him from a sandwich shop. I pushed myself upright in bed and the room spun.

"Easy," Philly said. "I got you a sandwich and some soup. Which do you want first?"

"Soup," I said, knowing that would settle my stomach better. After being hungry for so long, I worried the sandwich would be too heavy first off.

Philly brought over a small plastic bowl and spoon. He handed them to me, but my hands were shaking. Instead, he sat on the edge of the bed and fed me one bite at a time. I hated being so much trouble. The men had been nice to me, so far. I was a bit concerned they would reach out to Slider. Would he be angry and want me returned? I knew he didn't want me, but what if he'd been mad enough to want me punished? It wasn't my fault! I hadn't realized he didn't know about the marriage. It had never occurred to me that Surge had set up the entire thing and never told him. Who did that sort of thing?

I managed to eat all of the soup, then Philly helped me to the bathroom. He shut the door, staying on the other side, while I took care of business. When I was finished, he braced me while I washed my hands, then carried me back to bed. As tempting as the sandwich sounded, I was too tired to even think of eating anything else. I felt the light touch of his fingers across my brow as sleep pulled me under.

Chapter Three

Slider

What the fuck had she meant I was her husband? I would damn sure remember getting married, and I hadn't seen her before I'd found her in my bed. Which meant Surge had something to do with this shit. I'd tried to find him at the clubhouse without any luck, and the fucker hadn't been at his house either. I blew up his phone with texts and calls, but he refused to answer.

I didn't know what else to do, so I called Wire over at the Dixie Reapers. I didn't think Surge would have pulled off something like this without a little help, and since Wire was a fucking genius, it had his name written all over it. I worried he wouldn't pick up, but after a while he answered.

"It's late and Lavender needs her rest. You woke her up so what the fuck do you need?" he asked.

"Sorry for waking your woman. I think Surge did something he shouldn't have, and I was wondering if you knew anything about it."

Wire sighed. "Slider, I presume?"

"Yeah."

"Your wife was listed on the Dark Web, for sale to the highest bidder. They had it dressed up like a mail-order bride ad, but those women never end up in a good place. Surge said you wanted a wife and kids, so I helped him get her over here. The two of you were married by proxy."

Fuck. "So it's a legitimate marriage?"

"About as much as anyone's is around here. But yeah, as far as the government is concerned, she's here legally… as your wife."

"Thanks for telling me."

I hung up the phone and wanted to slam my head into a wall. What the hell was I supposed to do now? Pinching the bridge of my nose, I tried to hold off the headache I felt forming between my eyes. I knew I needed to go back home, talk things over with Vasha, and figure out what the fuck we were going to do. I couldn't divorce her or she might be sent back to Russia. Did I really want to stay married to a woman I didn't know? Yeah, I'd fucked her, taken her innocence... shit. She could be pregnant even now.

I wandered the compound for a while -- hours in all honesty -- just trying to clear my head, then went to the clubhouse to drown my sorrows. I didn't know how much time passed before I went back home. The house was eerily silent. I didn't see Vasha in the bedroom or bathroom, but I noticed the bed was neatly made and the sheets smelled like detergent. Even the towel I'd left out for her was laundered and put away. But where the hell was she?

After scouring every square inch of the house, I realized she wasn't here. Was that why Surge wouldn't answer? Had Vasha gone to him? Anger simmered in my gut, even though it was ridiculous. Why should I care if she ran to him? He'd created this mess and he should help clean it up. Since Vasha wasn't here, and Surge wasn't home, had he taken her to a hotel?

I tried calling him again, and this time he answered.

"It's about fucking time you pick up," I said.

"Shouldn't you be fucking your wife?" he asked.

"Fuck you!" Wait. "You mean she's not with you?"

Surge was quiet a moment. "I really hope that's a bad joke. Of course she's not with me. I left her in your damn bed."

I narrowed my eyes and held my phone out to glare at it before putting it back against my ear. "You'd better not have seen her naked."

"What I should have said is that she was going to wait for you in your bed. No, I didn't see your wife naked. Why are you calling and texting me so damn much?"

"And you didn't answer!"

He snorted. "Yeah, because I figured you'd be pissed if you were blowing up my phone that much, but your wife is gorgeous and she's exactly what you need. Now what the fuck do you mean is she with me?"

"Vasha is missing," I said. "I was angry and left, went to find you actually. When I came back home, she wasn't here."

I heard rustling and a soft murmur in the background, then his booted steps across a hard surface.

"I'm on my way. Call Fox and Bear. Get them over to your place. It's really fucking bad that she's missing, Slider. You have no idea the shit storm she left in Russia. Those men won't let her go easily. If she's out there on her own, she's vulnerable."

My throat tightened. "Surge, I didn't use protection. What if she's already pregnant?"

"Don't do anything stupid. I'm on my way."

The line went dead, and I quickly called Fox and Bear, telling them I had an emergency. I didn't get into the details over the phone. The fact Surge had done this behind everyone's back wouldn't look good. I didn't know how the VP would react when he heard the news. I couldn't cover for Surge this time. He'd not only done something like this without the club's knowledge, but he'd involved an officer. Me. Fox was going to lose his shit, and I had a feeling Bear would be pissed too.

Now we had an innocent Russian woman roaming around, and Surge seemed to think the men she'd left in Russia would be coming for her. I paced my house while I waited. I heard all three bikes at the same time. Fox came through the door, followed by Surge and Bear. I could see the panic in Surge's eyes, but I didn't know if he was worried about his own ass or Vasha. Maybe it was both.

"What's going on?" Fox asked.

"My wife is missing," I said.

Fox and Bear shared a look, then stared at me. I knew they wouldn't ask, but they needed to know.

"Surge bought me a mail-order bride from Russia."

"Is that why the two of you were spending so much time together lately?" Bear asked. "Because we all just thought the two of you were fucking. Not that we care either way. I'm with Fox, though. What's the emergency? Just go get your woman."

I looked at Surge, giving him the chance to redeem himself. The idiot wasn't even paying attention. Instead, he was fiddling with his damn phone. What the fuck? He's the one who told me Vasha could be in danger, and now he was what? Playing Candy Crush or some shit?

"What the fuck are you doing?" I asked him.

Surge jerked his gaze up to meet mine. "I was reaching out to our friends in the area to see if anyone saw Vasha."

"Maybe we need to know exactly what we're getting into," Fox said. "Can one of you start from the beginning? Because none of this makes any fucking sense. For one, why did you have to buy a woman, Slider? They fall at your fucking feet."

"That was my doing," Surge said. "I knew he wanted to settle down. I saw an opportunity and I took it. Wire helped me get Vasha here, and helped arrange her marriage to Slider by proxy."

"Jesus fucking Christ," Bear muttered.

"The men who are after her… who are they?" Fox asked.

Surge tapped on his phone, then turned it toward us. Two men filled the screen one. One was fit, but his features were hard and cruel. The other had a rotund figure, jowls that reminded me of a hunting dog, and eyes that were devoid of any warmth. No wonder Vasha had risked everything to escape. I hated the thought of either of those men touching her. She'd been a virgin, but that didn't mean they hadn't put their hands on her.

I studied the men, committing their images to mind. If I saw either of them, they were going to die a slow and painful death. What they'd done to Vasha was inexcusable. For that matter, I hadn't been much better. I'd run out of here, angry, and she'd disappeared. Had she thought my anger was directed at her? It wasn't. I'd been furious with Surge, but never her. She was an innocent in this mess.

"Find my fucking wife!" I growled at Surge. "This is your damn fault! If you'd just told me up front what the hell you'd done, then she wouldn't be out there alone! She probably thinks I'm mad at her, but it was you that I was pissed at."

Fox's phone chimed and he pulled it from his pocket, his eyebrows climbing high. "Anyone know the Mississippi chapter was in the area?"

"No. What the hell? Shouldn't they have given us a heads-up?" I asked.

"Usually. I'll find out why they didn't at another time. Right now, it seems they have your wife. Titan said they're in a motel a town over from here. Found her walking around over there."

What. The. "Are you shitting me? How the fuck did she get all the way over there? It's miles from here!"

"Let's go find out. And we can ask whoever is on the gate why the hell they let her leave," Bear said.

I looked down at myself and realized I'd thrown on the clothes I'd worn to the clubhouse earlier. If I was going to get my wife, I didn't want to go smelling like cigarettes and cheap perfume. I waved a hand at my brothers and went down the hall to my room. I stripped off my clothes, then got in the shower, giving myself a quick scrub. When I got out, Surge was sitting on the foot of the bed.

"Seriously?" I asked, walking past him naked. It wasn't like he hadn't seen it before. Before today, I'd have teased him about doing a lick test to see if I'd gotten my dick good and clean. But right now, it just felt wrong that he was in here while I was getting ready. Thanks to him, I was off the market.

"I'm sorry I didn't tell you about Vasha. I worried you would say no, and I knew she needed help."

I jerked on my boxers, then my jeans, tucking my underwear so it didn't bunch under the denim. It didn't escape my notice that Surge was watching my every move, his heated gaze lingering a little too long on certain parts of my anatomy. At one time, I'd have gotten off on him watching me dress. Hell, I'd have gladly undressed for him, before he'd put Vasha in my bed. Whether I'd asked for it or not, things were different now.

I grabbed a black tee out of the dresser and pulled it on before sticking the end down into my pants. The zipper gave me a fight, refusing to close. I growled as I jerked on the damn thing.

"Need some help?" Surge asked.

I glared at him and finally managed to fasten my jeans, and I made a mental note to toss this pair out later. Who the fuck had time for troublesome zippers? As for Surge's offer of help, I'd deal with him later. Right now, I had a missing wife to find.

After threading a belt through them and fastening it, I slipped on my cut and my boots. Surge followed me out of the bedroom and I stomped my way through the house, still pissed as fuck at him. Fox and Bear were out front, sitting on their bikes ready to go. We drove through the compound and stopped at the gate. Jack was at the gate, and while he was usually diligent, I was about two seconds from tearing into him for letting Vasha out of the compound.

Surge placed a hand on my arm to hold me in check. It took a great deal of effort to bite my tongue and let Fox ask the questions. The last thing I wanted to do was terrify the kid, but at the same time, maybe he needed a good scare.

"You let a woman out of here earlier," Fox said.

Jack snorted. "No offense, VP, but I've let a ton of women in and out of here tonight. The clubhouse looks like it's at capacity."

"This one wasn't a club whore," I said, my tone biting. "She's my fucking wife and now she's missing."

So much for letting Fox talk. The VP shot me a look, but I shrugged. It wasn't like I was tracking down a pissed-off teen or something. Even though Vasha and

Harley Wylde   Slider/ Ashes Duet

I hadn't shared our ages, I did know Surge well enough to know he wouldn't have married me to someone underage. So at least there was that. It didn't change the fact I needed to find her, and I needed her right this damn minute. This was a woman who was in trouble, could have gotten hurt, and I wanted to know how the fuck she'd gotten out of the compound and who had taken her to the next town. I couldn't keep her safe if I didn't know where the weak spots were.

Jack opened and shut his mouth about five times. "I'm sorry, Slider. I didn't know. She said something about you being angry and that she needed to leave. I thought maybe she'd tried to ask too much or something and overstepped."

"Wait." Fox lifted a hand. "She mentioned Slider specifically, and when we asked about a woman leaving, you gave me some smartass comment about there being a lot of women here tonight? You obviously knew who we meant."

Jack's back stiffened and he threw his shoulders back. "Sorry, VP. I didn't mean any disrespect. Honestly, the woman looked like she was about to start crying. I felt sorry for her. If Slider was pissed and going after her, I just…"

Jesus Christ. I slammed the heel of my hand against my forehead. Was I such a jackass that the Prospect thought he had to protect a woman from me? And the way she'd run off… I'd known she thought my anger was directed at her. There was no other reason for her to leave. Hearing Jack confirm it fucking hurt. I hadn't meant to do that to her. Maybe there was a reason I hadn't had a steady girlfriend or boyfriend. I apparently sucked at this shit. Hell, Surge had thought he had to buy a woman and cheat to marry the two of us.

- 43 -

Maybe I needed to re-evaluate a few things, but first I needed to get Vasha home, where I knew she'd be safe. Then I wanted to know more about the men who wanted her. I hoped they didn't know she'd come to America, that they wouldn't be able to find Surge's purchase and trace her here. He was good, but he wasn't the best. I could only hope that Wire had set everything up so that shit didn't come back to bite us in the ass. Or more importantly, place Vasha in danger.

"I know where they have her," Fox told me. "Let's get your wife and we'll settle all this later."

We rode through the gates and hit the highway heading out of town. It wasn't until we were on the open road that I realized I never asked Jack how Vasha had gotten so far from home. Someone had to have picked her up. But who? Surely she hadn't walked that damn far.

I opened up the bike and took lead, roaring down the road as fast as I dared. If Vasha was with our Mississippi chapter, then I knew she was all right. I still wanted to see for myself that she hadn't come to harm. More than that, I wanted to clear the air and let her know I'd never been angry with her. I hadn't reacted well when she'd claimed we were married, and that was on me. I could admit my part in her running off, but I was still pissed as fuck that Surge hadn't given me a heads-up and that Jack had let her leave.

By the time we reached the next town and I found the motel, my stomach was knotted up and I worried that seeing me might upset Vasha even more. I'd been an ass. My gaze scanned the lot and I frowned when I didn't see any other bikes. We circled the building and still couldn't find anything but cars and trucks.

"This is the right place, isn't it?" I asked.

Fox nodded. "Yeah. This is where they said they were staying."

The sun was peeking over the horizon and I wondered if we'd just arrived too late. Had they already gone home, taking Vasha with them? I glanced at Fox and he pulled out his phone, making a call. I assumed he was reaching out to Titan, but he must not have gotten an answer by the aggravated look on his face.

"I'm heading in to see if the manager can tell me anything," I said, driving back to the front office and parking outside the glass door. I heard my brothers following.

An elderly woman was at the desk, knitting what looked to be a baby blanket. I pushed on the glass door and stepped inside. She smiled when she heard the bell over the door jingle, then a cautious look crept across her face when she saw me. It was the cut. I damn well knew it, and it pissed me off that there were assholes who gave the rest of us a bad name. I'd never hurt a woman or child, but this lady didn't know that.

"If you're looking for your friends, they took off when the police were called," she said, her voice thin and reedy.

"Police?" I froze mid-step. "Did something happen? The woman with them. Is she all right?"

The lady eyed me up and down. The way her lips pressed together, I knew she didn't want to tell me shit.

"Please," I said, softening my tone. "She's my wife. I've been trying to find her all night and was told to come here. Did she leave with a group of men? Did she look like she was okay?"

The woman relaxed a little and beckoned me closer. I walked up to the counter, laying my hands on top so she'd see I didn't have a weapon. At least, not in my hands. There was a nine millimeter at my back, but she didn't need to know that. If she had information of Vasha's whereabouts, then I wanted to hear it. If anything had happened to her, I'd never forgive myself. If I hadn't lost my damn temper, hadn't made her think I was angry with her, then she'd have never left. She'd be safe.

"Something was wrong with her. Could barely stand up, looked drugged or something. One of them tossed her across his lap and they rode out of here like the devil was nipping at their heels."

Right. Because someone had called the cops. Dammit!

"Did you see which way they went?" I asked.

She pointed down the highway, farther away from the Hades Abyss compound.

"Cops chased them for a bit, but I don't know if they caught up to them."

I thanked her and went back outside. Fox was still frowning at his damn phone, and the others were waiting patiently. Unfortunately, I didn't have a damn thing to tell them, other than our brothers weren't here and neither was my wife.

"Titan still isn't answering," Fox said.

"The lady said she called the cops. I think she was under the impression they were going to hurt Vasha. Instead, they tossed her over one of their bikes and rode out of here, but the woman said Vasha couldn't stand on her own and appeared drugged." I wanted to put my fist through something. "Where the fuck did they go? They knew we were coming, right?"

Fox nodded and tapped at his screen.

"I'll call Wizard," Surge said.

I'd damn near forgotten the Secretary for the Mississippi chapter was a computer genius like Surge. Well, calling Surge a genius was a stretch, but he knew a lot more about computers than I did. While he made the call, I walked down to the street and looked in the direction our brothers had supposedly taken. It wasn't like I really expected to see them waiting just down the road, but maybe some part of me had hoped for a clue.

I was about to turn and head back to my bike when I heard the rumble of a Harley. It could have been anyone. It wasn't like only clubs rode. Someone could have been driving to work, or just out to enjoy the morning. Either way, I turned and watched, waiting to see if it would be someone I recognized. When Stone pulled to a stop two parking lots over, I ran to my motorcycle.

"It's Stone. Come on," I said, turning the engine over and roaring through the lot. I pulled onto the street and went to meet him. I heard my brothers at my back, but as we got close, Stone pulled out onto the road and went back the way he'd come.

We stuck close, following in hopes he'd take us to the others. Or in my case, I was hoping he would take me to Vasha. The town limits came and went, and still Stone kept going. I started to worry we were in for a long-ass ride, and my bike needed gas soon, but I'd go wherever the fuck I needed if it meant getting her back.

After another thirty minutes, I saw a sign for a gas station and motioned that I would be getting off. I pulled ahead of Stone so he would see me exit the highway and I stopped right by the pumps. I filled my tank and Fox did the same while the others waited at the edge of the lot. Within ten minutes, we were back on the road. I seriously hoped we weren't driving all

Harley Wylde   **Slider/Ashes Duet**

the way down to Mississippi. If Vasha couldn't stand on her own, what the hell had happened to her? And how was she handling being on a bike for so long?

Finally, Stone pulled off. We'd been riding for hours and had crossed into Arkansas. The little town that came into view looked like it came straight out of a 1950's sitcom, but I could see the appeal. Stone stopped at a motel on the main strip and shut off his bike. We did the same and followed him to a room on the first floor. He did a complicated knock and Titan opened the door.

"It's about fucking time," the Pres muttered.

I entered the room and my legs about gave out. I rushed to the bed, where Vasha lay deathly still. My hand shook as I reached for her, but I ran my fingers through her hair before pressing them against her throat.

"She's alive, but she's been through hell," Kraken said.

I could see that. There were purple smudges under her eyes and she seemed even paler than before.

"What happened?" I asked.

"We were hoping you'd tell us." Titan folded his arms over his chest and glared. "We found her on the outskirts of that town, looking half dead. She could barely stand, was about to pass out, and hadn't eaten in a long-ass time. So what the fuck happened?"

"It was a misunderstanding. I was pissed, but it was at Surge. I think she assumed I was angry with her, so she ran. Do you know how she got there?"

"Walked," Philly said.

Walked? They had to be fucking with me. There was no way. Was there?

"Are you telling me she walked from our compound to the next fucking town down the

- 48 -

highway? Alone? At night?" My heart hammered in my chest as I thought about all the things that could have happened. She could have been hit by a car, picked up by someone who would rape and murder her, a starving coyote or rabid animal could have attacked. Vasha was so small, so helpless. And I'd made her feel like she had to leave, to face all that on her own.

My knees hit the floor next to the bed and I took her hand in one of mine. The moment I'd seen her in my bed, I'd felt like she was mine. I'd never been possessive of someone before. At the time, I'd thought it was the fact Surge had drugged me, but now I knew different. It didn't have anything to do with the beer I'd had. It was just Vasha. She made me want to keep her safe, and I'd failed her.

"I'm so sorry, *zolatka*. I never meant for you to leave," I murmured, pressing a kiss to her forehead. "Come back to me. I'll make it up to you somehow."

"She can't go anywhere yet," Titan said. "Not on a bike at any rate. We wouldn't have even left if it weren't for the crazy lady at the other motel calling the cops."

Fox leaned against the wall and stared at Titan. "Why did you go so far? One town over would have sufficed."

Titan rubbed at the scruff on his jaw, and I didn't think he would answer. His gaze held mine, and I saw the anger simmering inside. Then he looked down at Vasha and his features softened. It seemed she'd gotten to the Pres. I could understand it. Beautiful women had a tendency to make men do stupid shit, like try to take someone's wife all the way to another fucking state.

"I was taking her home," Titan said. "She trusts us and Philly speaks her language. Since it seemed she'd been unwanted by Slider, I thought I'd give her a place to stay until she figured shit out."

I snorted, knowing that was bullshit. He'd known I was coming for her. But I wasn't about to argue with the President, even if he wasn't over my chapter. Didn't matter. Either way, he outranked me. Last thing I needed was to piss off Titan and then end up on Spider's bad side.

"You don't have to stay," I said to the room in general. "I'll keep watch over her until she's able to travel. Then I'm taking her home."

"What if she doesn't want that?" Philly asked.

"It's my hope that she'll understand and forgive me once I explain things." I rubbed my thumb over the back of her hand. "I was angry at Surge for doing something without saying a fucking word to me. Then I realized Vasha was missing, and none of that mattered. I just knew I needed to find her, keep her safe."

Kraken barked out a laugh. "He's already fucking falling for her. I think she's in good hands, Pres."

"Fine. We'll head out, leave her with your crew, but if she ever wants to leave and needs a place to stay she's welcome in Mississippi." Titan gave me one last glare before he turned and walked out.

"I'll take care of the room situation," Fox said, stepping outside.

One by one, my brothers cleared the room, leaving me with the woman who had turned my world upside down with just one look. Maybe Kraken was right. Maybe I was already falling for her. As long as she gave me another chance, then I was perfectly fine with that. If she kicked my ass to the curb, it was going

Harley Wylde **Slider/ Ashes Duet**

to hurt like hell. No less than what I deserved. I'd take whatever she threw my way. Within reason.

I just had to get her well and back on her feet.

Better yet. Get her back into my bed. There was already a chance she was pregnant, but if I made sure of it, then she'd have no choice than to stay. Might make me an asshole, but I wasn't letting her walk away without a fight.

Chapter Four

Vasha

Everything was a bit of a blur. I remembered meeting Philly and the other bikers, vaguely recalled him feeding me soup. Anything after that was hazy. Waking up to find Slider on the bed next to me was enough to make my heart start racing. He'd found me! I just didn't understand why he'd want to. Was he so angry that he'd tracked me down in order to punish me? I lifted my hands and saw that I wasn't shackled to the bed. He must not have been worried I would escape, but his arm draped across my waist was heavy enough to hold me in place. Perhaps he'd thought that was enough.

"You're awake," he said, his voice husky from sleep.

It was so unfair! He was sexy in the morning. My body betrayed me, reacting to his nearness. I shouldn't want him! He was no different from the others. I'd thought he was, but I'd been wrong. Hadn't I? The tender way he watched me conflicted with the anger he'd displayed when I'd last seen him.

"You need anything?" he asked. "Water? Need to use the bathroom? Are you hungry?"

I blinked, not sure how to respond. Did he really want to get me something? Or was it a trick? Grigori had done that before. If I misbehaved, he'd offer me something I really wanted, then slap me around and remind me I didn't deserve to have anything. Before his reaction to our marriage, I'd thought Slider would never do something like that. Now I wasn't quite so sure.

He lifted his arm and used his finger to trace the bridge of my nose. "I'm so damn sorry, *kroshka*. It

Harley Wylde   **Slider/ Ashes Duet**

wasn't you that I was angry with. It was Surge. I didn't mean for you to leave, much less walk all the way to another town."

"You're not angry with me?" I asked, my accent thicker than usual. Even I could hear the difference.

"Never with you, *zolatka*."

I looked around the room and didn't see anyone but the two of us. What happened to the men who had helped me? Were they in trouble for giving me assistance? Had Slider hurt them? I felt so confused. I wanted to trust him, to believe that the tenderness I'd seen in him was real, but I was scared. Men had never been trustworthy. Not in my world. I wanted him to be different, *needed* it.

"I had Surge go pick up a few things for you. I had to check the sizes on what you were wearing now." Slider sat up, then got out of bed. He walked over to the dresser on the far wall and lifted two plastic bags. "It's not much, but there are few changes of clothes from the skin out, as well as some bath products I thought you might like. I ordered everything online so he just had to pick it up in the nearest big city."

"You didn't go get them?" I asked.

"I didn't want to leave you. It's been two days since I caught up to Titan and the others. You've been asleep most of the time, and muttering in Russian. I picked up enough to know you were upset with me, and scared of Grigori and Vladimir."

I turned away from him.

"Surge showed me pictures of the men who hurt you in Russia. I don't think they can find you here, Vasha, but if they do, I won't let them take you."

"Why?" I asked, wincing when my voice broke.

"Because you're mine," he said softly.

I wanted to believe him. No one had ever wanted me as anything other than a broodmare. I just didn't understand what had changed.

"Why?" I asked again. "I was yours before and it didn't matter. Why does it matter now?"

He set the bags down and came closer, sitting on the edge of the bed. He didn't reach for me, didn't try to touch me. Slider stared at the floor, the lines of his body hard and tense. At first, I thought he wouldn't answer, but it seemed he'd only been gathering his thoughts. Or maybe he'd been trying to decide what I wanted to hear.

"The night I found you in my bed, I'd decided that I was tired of casual hook-ups. I wanted an actual relationship, something that could last." He grimaced and glanced my way quickly before turning away again. "You should know I haven't just been with women. I like men too. I know a lot of people don't understand that, or find it disgusting, but if I'm going to ask you to stay, to be mine, then I think you need the full truth."

Of course I knew there were men who preferred men, and those who liked both, but I'd never had someone come out and admit it. The fact he seemed worried how I would react told me a lot. Someone had hurt him at some point, badly, for being different. I hesitated only a moment before reaching for him. I placed my hand on his thigh and waited to see what else he'd say.

"Surge and I..." He stopped and audibly swallowed. "We were together for a few weeks. Nothing serious, but we were exclusive during that time. He knew I wanted more, and he didn't. So, he found you online, bought you, married you to me by proxy and thought he was giving me what I wanted and needed."

As much as I wanted to harden my heart toward him, it broke a little. Someone he'd trusted, invited into his bed, had betrayed him like that. I was grateful to be out of Russia, to not be married to Vladimir, but I didn't like that Slider had been hurt in the process. I could understand his anger now.

"If you come back home with me," he said, "then I'll spend the rest of my life making it up to you. Unless the fact I've been with men is a deal breaker. I didn't mean to take my anger out on you. It was Surge who had pissed me off by not telling me what he'd done. Even worse, he'd lied to you too. You didn't know that I had no clue we were married. And I checked. Wire told me that the marriage is real, at least as far as the authorities are concerned."

"You'd let me leave?" I asked.

He opened and shut his mouth, then gave a humorless laugh and shook his head. "No. I want to be that guy, the one who understands and gives you what you want, but that's not me. I'd fuck you every chance I had, make sure you're pregnant, and then you'd never be able to leave. So I guess I'm a rotten bastard, just like all the other men you know."

I wanted to know more about him. Needed to know more. If I was going to remain with him, be his wife and the mother of his children, then I needed to know who he really was, not just on the surface but deep down. The fact he admitted he'd do what it took to keep me from leaving meant he was at least being honest with me. It was more than most men had given me.

"You said you grew up in an orphanage."

He nodded.

"Do you remember your parents?" I asked. I couldn't remember mine anymore, not as well as I once had. There were bits and pieces that stuck with me. My mother had hair like mine and bright blue eyes. I knew that much. Sometimes, if I focused hard, I could almost remember her voice. I'd forgotten my father for the most part.

"I never knew them," he said. "My mother dropped me on the doorstep of a fire station with a copy of my birth certificate and a note that she couldn't raise me. Surge did a little digging for me once, with the help from some other guys like him. All I know is that she was Egyptian and had been here on a student Visa. He found a record of her attending a college near the place I'd been abandoned, but she didn't finish her degree. She was killed in a robbery."

"I'm sorry."

He shrugged a shoulder. "Shouldn't hurt when I never even knew her. But it does. My father was listed as unknown so I have no idea who he was, but I'd guess either a student or professor where she was attending school. For all I know, I'm the product of a one-night stand at some frat party."

"My parents died when I was young. I used to think of them often, but now I barely remember my mother and I've mostly forgotten my father. I do remember they were kind to me, but that's all. Maybe your mother thought you'd have a better life if she gave you up."

"Guess I'll never know."

I did have an idea of how he could find his father's family, but I didn't know what he'd think of it. When I'd first arrived in America, I'd had to wait for Surge to arrange my transportation to Slider's home. I'd spent a few days just watching TV in a hotel room.

There had been a commercial that played several times a day about a DNA test. One of the people in the ad said they'd found family they never knew they had. Could Slider do the same and find his father? I didn't really understand how any of it worked.

"What about one of those DNA kits?" I asked.

He paused and looked at me. "Like the family tree shit they advertise?"

I nodded.

"I guess I could think about that. Not sure I'm too crazy about someone having my DNA where anyone can access it." I didn't understand and he smirked a little. "Vasha, I'm part of an outlaw club. We don't always do things the legal way. If we did, then you wouldn't be here right now. There are things I've done in order to protect the Hades Abyss, and having my DNA floating around out there probably isn't the best idea."

"Because it might be used to link you to a crime?" I asked. It didn't seem possible. He was being so kind to me, was better than the men I'd known back home. Shouldn't criminals be evil? No... No matter what he said, I didn't believe him. He was a good man. Kind. Nothing like a criminal.

"Yes. I'm not a good man. I've done things..." He sighed. "I have blood on my hands, *kroshka*. But I swear that I will do everything I can to keep you safe, and I will never raise a hand to you in anger."

"Never?" I asked skeptically.

He leaned closer, his nose nearly brushing mine. "Maybe not quite *never*. I bet your pretty little ass would pink up nicely if I were to spank it. But I don't think that's a punishment you'd mind too much."

My body heated at his words and I felt myself grow slick between my legs. Thinking of his hand cracking against my ass shouldn't turn me on, but it did. I licked my lips and my breath quickened. Slider's eyes dilated as he stared at me, then his mouth was pressing against mine. His kiss was hard and demanding, his tongue thrusting between my lips. He groaned as he devoured me. As much as I loved his kisses, I gave him a gentle nudge to back off.

When he pulled away, I placed my hand over my mouth. My cheeks warmed in embarrassment. I'd just let him kiss me like that and I hadn't brushed my teeth in… I didn't even remember when. He tasted like coffee, even though he'd been sleeping when I woke, but I worried that my kiss had been gross to him.

"Right. No kissing," he muttered and stood up.

"Wait. It's not that."

"Then what, Vasha? You just shoved me away."

I pressed my lips tight together. "My breath stinks."

He stared for a long moment, then burst out laughing. I didn't see what was so funny. I'd been told often that I needed to always make sure my teeth were clean and my breath was fresh, or I would upset my husband. Granted, Grigori had meant Vladimir, but I figured the same would be true for any man.

"Surge picked up toothbrushes for both of us and some toothpaste. Come on. You can brush your teeth if you're that worried about your breath." Humor danced in his eyes. "For the record, I didn't mind in the slightest."

I swung my legs over the side of the bed, then braced myself on the nightstand as I tried to get up for the first time in days. My legs felt weak and trembled a moment, but they held me up. Slider moved toward me, but I held up a hand.

"I'd like to try on my own."

He nodded and gave me some space. I managed to walk to the bathroom counter and brushed my teeth, then splashed water on my face. My hair looked oily and gross. Slider slipped past me and set out some things in the shower, then stacked some women's clothing on the rack above the toilet and set out a towel.

"Think you can handle a shower? The way you stared at the tub I figured you wanted one."

"Maybe," I said.

"Would you be all right with me showering with you? Then if you start to fall or get lightheaded, I'll be there to catch you."

It wasn't like he hadn't already seen me naked. I let him help me undress and get into the shower. The water was steamy and felt divine. When he joined me, I couldn't help but stare at his abdomen and chest. He was just as beautiful as I remembered. I don't know how long I stood there staring at him, but Slider didn't seem to mind. He reached for the knobs to adjust the water and I realized it had already started to cool.

"Would my beautiful wife permit me to wash her?" he asked.

Beautiful. Me? He thought I was beautiful. I'd heard men compliment me before, but usually it was for being quiet, docile, obeying instantly. Not many commented on my looks, and the few who had, had only made me shiver in a not-so-good way.

"Vasha. Are you all right?" Slider asked and I realized I hadn't answered him.

"I'm fine, and yes, you may wash me. Thank you, Slider."

He paused mid-reach for the soap. Had I done something wrong?

"Slider?"

"My name's Upton. Upton St. Clair. When we're alone, you can use my real name." His gaze narrowed. "If we were married by proxy, how did you not already know my name?"

I felt my cheeks warm. "I was nervous and not paying attention. They had to prompt me four times to repeat my vows."

"There's something you should know," he said. "The marriage in Russia? It's not legally binding. Or it wasn't at the time. I think you were only asked to go through with it so you would feel better coming here. Thanks to some magic with a computer once you arrived in the US, our marriage became legal. According to my government anyway."

"So... we weren't really married in Russia, but we are now?" I asked, feeling a bit lost and confused. He'd mentioned something earlier, but I still didn't understand. If saying my vows hadn't made it legal, how could a machine?

"Yes."

"And your name is Upton, but I can only call you that in private?"

He nodded.

I wasn't entirely sure I understood, but I would eventually learn the ways of this country. Slider washed me, his touch gentle and more than a little arousing. My nipples hardened against his palms as he washed my breasts, and I shifted restlessly, wanting to ease the ache between my legs. He took his time, every stroke of his hands only making me want him more.

"Easy, *Zolatka*. You're still weak. I don't think shower sex is a good idea right now."

I whimpered, then bit my lip to stifle the sound.

"I'll wash quickly, then you can rest while I find us something to eat." He leaned closer and kissed me, a brief press of his mouth to mine. "You need to regain your strength. It's a long ride back home, and I don't want to worry about you falling off my bike."

"I didn't think I went that far," I said, which was apparently the *wrong* thing to say. Slider's expression darkened and his jaw went tight.

"Yes, we'll be having a discussion about the danger you could have been in while *walking* to another town."

I bowed my head. "Yes, sir."

I could feel the change in the air. Slider growled and pressed me up against the wall. My heart hammered in my chest, but I didn't dare meet his gaze. Would I always be afraid of men? Would I always wonder when Slider would lash out, when he'd show me the side all men seemed to have? I felt his hand tremble as he gripped my chin and forced my gaze to meet his.

"What the fuck was that shit?" he asked, his voice low and deadly. "Is that what they trained you to do? Obey like a lap dog? Say 'yes, sir' and 'no, sir' as if men are better than you?"

I licked my lips but didn't answer. Did he really want to know? Didn't he expect my obedience like Vladimir would have? Like Grigori had demanded? I'd thought all men were like that. Anatoly had been my friend, and had been sweet to me on occasion, but I'd been certain he was different with the women in his life, just as hard and cruel as Grigori and Vladimir were with me. Had I been wrong?

"Answer me, Vasha."

"Y-yes."

"Tell me, exactly, what they expected of you. I want to know every damn thing those bastards did. You were a virgin, so I know they didn't rape you."

Could I tell him the things that had been forced on me as part of my education? I'd never seen someone angry on my behalf before. Not even Anatoly. It started slow, just a few words, and then I couldn't seem to stop. I told him about having a dildo forced down my throat so I could learn to properly please my husband, about being trained to bow and kneel, to not hold eye contact with men for more than a few seconds. Everything poured out.

With every word, I saw Slider's face darken more, anger simmered in his eyes by the time I'd finished. The shower had grown cold, so he shut off the water and gently dried me. I pulled on the clothing he'd purchased, running my hands down the soft leggings and shirt.

"I'm not angry with you, Vasha," he said. "I want to murder Grigori. No one should treat you the way he did. I'd like to burn his house to the ground, and fry anyone inside who helped in your mistreatment. Don't ever be afraid to tell me what you're thinking or feeling. I'm not them. I won't hurt you or degrade you."

I gave him a quick nod, still unable to believe a man like Slider existed, then went to sit on the bed and wait for him. I heard his fist slam into something several times, and I winced, hoping he wouldn't hurt himself.

When Slider came out, he only had a towel around his waist. He pulled out one of the dresser drawers and grabbed some underwear. The towel fell to the floor and I looked my fill as he got dressed. Unless he'd planned ahead and packed a bag, it looked like he'd bought clothes for himself as well as me. He picked up his keys off the dresser, then came to give me a kiss.

Harley Wylde **Slider/ Ashes Duet**

"I'll be back soon. The guys went home, but they sent a Prospect to help keep an eye on you. We didn't know how long you'd be out of it." He pointed to the wall behind the TV. "Knock on that wall if you need something before I'm back, or if you get scared. Teller is a good kid. You can trust him."

If Slider believed that Teller wouldn't hurt me, then I'd knock on the wall if I needed something. Slider left, the door automatically locking behind him, and I turned on the TV to pass the time. I wasn't quite sure what to make of my new husband. He'd been angry at my training, or rather angry with Grigori for forcing that on me. Only Anatoly had ever cared about me before, and even then he hadn't been able to show it or we'd both have suffered. Slider was different from anyone I'd ever met, and I was so thankful that Surge had found me and placed me in Slider's bed that night. I was starting to think he might be the best thing that ever happened to me.

Chapter Five

Slider

A week had passed since I'd chased down Vasha, and we were finally back home. Except, as I looked around, I realized this place hadn't really been turned into a home but was just a resting place for me. I had the basics and not much else. Since she'd washed my sheets the last time she was here, she must have looked around a bit. There wasn't a lot of house here to justify a tour, but I wondered if I should still show her around.

"I'll just put my things away," she said, carrying the sacks I'd crammed into my saddlebags down the hall to the bedroom.

I watched her walk off, admiring the sway of her ass with every step. I hadn't fucked her again, not since that first time, and I was starting to get a serious case of blue balls. Waiting had seemed like the right thing. It was clear that she wanted me, the way her gaze tracked my every move, and I'd caught her staring at me multiple times. There wasn't a lack of heat between us, but we'd gotten off on the wrong foot, and I felt like I needed to make amends.

After hearing more of what she'd suffered, I'd realized that my little Vasha had been more sheltered than I realized in a lot of ways, and had been subjected to one too many horrors. If I ever got my hands on Grigori, I'd find the biggest fucking dildo I could, jam it down his throat until he gagged, then I'd shove it up his damn ass. I'd strap him down and instruct him on the proper way to spread his legs, just the way he'd done to Vasha.

Knowing he'd seen her naked, had touched her, forced a damn toy down her throat, was enough to make me want to go on a murder spree. Thankfully, her tormenters were far away in Russia. If they ever stepped foot on US soil, the only way they'd be leaving was in body bags, but more than likely, I'd cut them into little pieces and scatter their remains.

I heard a knock at the door and went to answer it. Philip stood on the other side, three large boxes at his feet. I'd made sure to order more clothes and shoes for Vasha, hoping I timed it right for them to arrive today. It seemed I'd been right. I jerked my head letting Philip know to bring them inside.

"Down the hall. Take them to the bedroom."

Philip carried the first two together, then came back for the third. There was a flush on his cheeks and his head was bowed. It made me curious so I followed along, only to find Vasha bent over, putting things into the bottom drawer. The leggings she wore hugged her, cupping her ass and leaving little to the imagination. No wonder Philip looked a little warm. Poor guy had gotten an eyeful without meaning to. I already knew he'd never look at my wife in an inappropriate way. Although, if Vasha weren't taken, I had no doubt he'd have been all over her.

"Vasha, *zolatka*, we have company."

She jerked upright and spun toward me. Her gaze flitted over to Philip and I saw the nervous twitch in her fingers. Her body tensed and white bracketed her lips. His presence scared her, and I hated that. None of the men here would ever harm her. She was safe, and I needed her to know that with absolute certainty. The bastards in Russia had made her fearful of any men, and it pissed me off.

"Vasha, this is Philip. He's a Prospect."

"Ma'am," Philip murmured, not holding her gaze for long.

I saw amusement flicker in her eyes.

"Ma'am?" she asked. "How old are you?"

"Twenty-four," he said.

Her lips twitched as if she fought not to smile. "I'm six years younger than you. You may just call me Vasha. If that's all right with Slider?"

"Whatever you want them to call you, as long as they remember you're mine." I winked at her so she'd know I meant the words teasingly. Sort of. Anyone looked at her in a way I didn't like, I'd pound them into the ground -- after Vasha was out of sight.

Wait a minute. Six years younger? She was only eighteen? We hadn't discussed our ages. I was ten years older than her, but it didn't really matter. Not to me anyway. Spider and Luciana were happy together despite the age gap, and same for Rocket and Violeta. I didn't know what Vasha thought about it, though. She didn't appear to care one way or another. She had to know I was older than her. Then again, the pictures Rocket had shared meant that older men were the norm for her. She'd been expected to marry a man who looked as old, if not older than Spider.

"I should get back to the clubhouse," Philip said and beat a hasty retreat from the room. I heard the front door slam and smiled.

"That's funny?" she asked.

"He wanted to give us some space. Or maybe he noticed the way I look at you. I don't think he wanted to be here if our clothes started coming off."

She eyed me up and down, sucking her lower lip into her mouth. She'd tried more than once to get into my pants while we were gone, but I'd wanted her to take the time to rest and heal. The more time I spent with her, the less angry I was with Surge. He'd saved her, and that was what mattered. The fact he'd married us without even letting me know hadn't turned out to be a complete disaster. Vasha was sweet, and more tempting than any woman should be. And she was mine.

I tried to keep hold of my caveman tendencies so I wouldn't scare her. Or maybe it was more that I didn't want her to lump me in with the other men she knew. The thought of her believing I was every bit as evil as Grigori and Vladimir made my stomach twist. For her, I wanted to be better. I'd used plenty of women in my life, but she made me regret those moments. Not the ones I'd kept around for a while, even though those had been few and far between. I even regretted the random guys I'd hooked up with when I was younger.

For her, I'd be willing to wipe away the majority of my past, if only such a thing were possible. The brothers who stood with me would help protect her, and the blood on my hands would never wash clean, but I'd kill again in a heartbeat if it meant keeping her and them safe. The violence wasn't what bothered me. It was the fact I might have hurt someone vulnerable. What if any of those men or women had been through something similar to Vasha? What if they'd been groomed to submit, to accept whatever happened to them? No one deserved that kind of life, and I wished I could change the world and make it a better place so that innocents like Vasha would never know cruelty or abuse.

Then again, a Utopia would never exist and I'd have better luck finding a magic lamp.

"Are you still going to insist I need more time?" she asked.

"Guess that depends." I crooked my finger and she came closer. "If my controlling side comes out, are you going to have a flashback to your time with Grigori? Will you slip into that mind space he made you create? Or will you stay present with me?"

She took so long to answer I worried she never would. Finally, she huffed out a small breath and gave a nod.

"I'll remain with you."

"If anything I do hurts you, or makes you feel uncomfortable in any way, you need to tell me," I said. "I want you to feel safe with me, Vasha."

She reached out and took my hand. "I know you will never hurt me, Slider."

I arched an eyebrow and stared her down, making her cheeks flush.

"Upton," she corrected.

I'd never cared for my name, but I liked the way it sounded on her lips. It was the only thing my mother had given me, other than a letter of apology, and maybe that's why I'd hated it so much. That and it made me think of preppy boys from the private school I'd grown up near. The orphanage couldn't afford to send us to the school up the street so we'd all attended public school. Didn't mean the boys from that fancy, expensive school hadn't walked by our home and thrown out taunts every chance they had. Until the nuns chased them off.

Vasha reached up and ran her fingers down my cheek, then lightly tugged on my beard. I needed to trim it down a bit.

"What are you thinking about? It's like you went somewhere in your mind just now," she said.

"Sorry. My name reminds me of my mother, which in turn makes me think of my time at the orphanage and the places I went after that."

Vasha led me to the bed and sat, pulling me down next to her. "Tell me about it."

"I had a few friends who lived there with me. I told you about the one who taught me Russian. Another came from an Italian family who had only been in this country a few generations. His entire family was killed in a house fire, but he'd not been home that day. He was the only survivor and went into the system. And then there was Mack." I smiled faintly, remembering the huge redheaded kid. Everyone had been afraid of him because of his sheer size, but he'd been a giant teddy bear. "He had a bit of a reputation, but it was undeserved. Great guy."

"Do you keep in touch with any of them?" she asked.

I shook my head and looked off, not really seeing anything. I traveled back to the day I'd left, placed in foster care with a family. It was the first of many, and each was worse than the last. I had no idea what had become of the boys I'd known back then. Maybe one day I'd look them up, but I was almost afraid of what I'd find.

"I'm glad you had friends," she said. "I had Anatoly."

My hand clenched into a fist. I hadn't brought up Anatoly, but she'd murmured his name in her sleep more than once the last few days. I'd wondered just how close they were. Obviously they'd never slept together since she'd been a virgin, but had she cared for him as more than a friend? It was ridiculous for me to feel jealous over someone she knew long before me, but I had to admit that was exactly how I felt.

"Tell me about Anatoly," I said, wondering if I needed to track the guy down and kick his ass.

She smiled softly. "We were friends when we were younger, but he was several years older than me. One day, he began training. When I became old enough to be considered as a potential bride, Anatoly was assigned as my bodyguard. He had to ensure that I not only didn't escape, but that no one touched me inappropriately."

I almost didn't want to know, but I had to ask.

"Was he in the room during your lessons?"

She shook her head. "Grigori made him wait in the hall. But he was outside the door and heard everything. I was embarrassed the first few times, but Anatoly took my hand and said that I was brave for enduring everything they did to me."

He was right. She was one of the bravest people I knew. Even though I had a feeling she didn't see herself that way. It had taken guts to leave the compound when she'd thought I didn't want her here. She'd known no one in the area, had no place to go, and yet she'd set off anyway. I wasn't happy that she'd disappeared like that, but I had to admire the courage it took.

"As the time drew closer for Vladimir to claim me as his bride, Anatoly saw what it was doing to me. He placed an ad on the Dark Web for a Russian bride. As you know, your Surge found me and here we are."

"And Anatoly?" I asked.

"He came to America with me, but we parted ways. Surge sent someone for me and once Anatoly handed me off, I guess he thought his job was done. I don't know where he is now, or how to even contact him."

"Surge might know, if you'd like to speak with him." I might not like that she said his name in her sleep, but I owed the guy. He'd saved her and gotten her away from Vladimir and Grigori.

"No. I think it's best that chapter of my life stay closed. Perhaps one day I'll run into Anatoly somewhere, but I won't seek him out actively."

I placed her hand on my thigh and traced her slender fingers. I found myself holding her hand as often as possible. There had never been a man or woman in my life who made me want to touch them as often I craved the feel of Vasha. Whether it was running my fingers through her hair, holding her hand, or just sitting close enough that our bodies touched, I needed that contact with her as much as I needed air.

There were times when I watched her it was as if I'd known her my entire life. Some part of me just seemed to know that she was mine, that I needed to protect her. Maybe it was a throwback to the times of Neanderthals, but the possessiveness I felt with Vasha was unlike anything I'd ever experienced.

"I want you to meet my family," I said. "All of them."

"You mean your club?" she asked.

"Yes. They're my brothers. I don't really have a blood family, so they're the closest thing I have, and in a lot of ways, they're better. They're your family now too. You can also meet Luciana and Violeta. You might like having women to talk to about stuff."

"You mean you want me to meet them *now*?" she asked, her eyes going wide.

I looked at the clock by the bed. It was still early enough there wouldn't be a party at the clubhouse. I shot off a text to Spider, letting him know that I wanted to introduce my wife to everyone. Then I realized I'd never told him I was married. I had a feeling Surge hadn't said a damn word. Fox knew, and as VP he may very well have told Spider.

What wife?

Then again… I responded quickly. *Can you just call everyone to clubhouse? I can explain later.*

I didn't get an answer, but a few minutes later my phone went off.

Every last fucker wearing club colors better get your asses to the clubhouse. Rocket, bring Violeta.

Eloquent as ever. I snickered, then noticed Vasha was stiffening next to me, and going deathly pale. "They won't like me," she said. "They won't think I'm good enough."

I made sure I had her attention, then lightly brushed my lips against hers. I'd noticed that kissing her seemed to calm her down, or at least redirect her thoughts. "They will love you. You're mine and that's all that will matter to them."

She gave me a slight nod and stood. "I should change."

I leaned against the headboard and watched her flutter around the room.

"Vasha, open the boxes."

She turned to face me, frozen for a moment, then scurried over to them. She pulled off the tape and gasped when she saw the contents. It didn't take her long to pick a deep purple dress and a pair of black heeled boots. I admired the lines of her body as she stripped off her clothes and pulled on the new things. I didn't know the first damn thing about women's fashion, but I'd bought items similar to what I'd noticed Violeta and Luciana wore, hoping Vasha would like them.

From where I lay, I could see her as she ran into the bathroom and started brushing her hair, her teeth, and even when she stared at herself hard. There was panic flashing in her eyes and her chest rose and fell rapidly. If she didn't seem so upset or worried, it would be cute that she cared so much what my family thought of her.

"You're beautiful," I called out. "Stop worrying, *kroshka*."

She chewed at her bottom lip and I stood up, knowing I needed to distract her again. I walked up behind her, placed my hand on her stomach and pulled her flush against me. Her gaze met mine in the mirror and I leaned down to rub my beard against her neck before kissing her gently on the column of her throat, then her shoulder. Didn't hurt that I had a perfect view straight down the front of her dress and could admire her breasts. She sighed and tipped her head back.

"You're mine. Remember that. No one will take you from me. No one will call you names or sneer. Anyone who hurts you in any way will answer to me. Understood?"

"Yes, Upton."

I ran my hand up and down her bare arm. "You look beautiful. If anything, I should be the one worried."

Her startled gaze met mine. "Why would you worry? I won't do anything I shouldn't! I won't even talk to another man."

"You misunderstand, *kroshka*. My brothers may flirt with you. They will know you're mine, but they'll delight in trying to get a rise from me. If I feel the need to knock their heads together, I don't want you to think badly of me, or fear me."

She turned in my arms and placed her palms on my chest. "I'm not afraid of you. You've been so kind

Harley Wylde   Slider/ Ashes Duet

to me, so sweet. No one has ever treated me as well as you do."

I disagreed, but after her previous experiences with men, I could see how she might feel that way. I kissed her brow, then tugged her from the bathroom. If I didn't get her out of here, I'd be tempted to flip up her skirt, and then we'd be really late. I needed her to meet the others and realize that she had more than just me. My family was her family now. I knew that Luciana and Violeta would welcome her, and my brothers would watch over her whenever I couldn't.

It was important to me that she realize she wasn't alone. After everything she'd been through, I wanted Vasha to feel welcome here. More than that, I needed her to realize that there were people she could rely on. Her days of isolation and fear were at an end. I'd do whatever it took to give her a happy life. The idea of keeping her, of staying married to a woman I didn't know, should have me running the other way. But every time I held her, or just watched her, there was a part deep inside that knew she was right where she belonged. I didn't know what made Surge look for her, or what led him to her, but I was grateful. Not only would she no longer suffer at the hands of Grigori or the man who had planned to marry her, but I had a feeling that having Vasha in my life would be a good thing.

"Time to go meet the family," I said, kissing her quickly, then leading her out to the bike in the driveway. If I didn't get out of the house, I'd end up taking her to bed.

I stared at the machine, then eyed her dress and knew I couldn't ask her to ride on it. It looked like I would need to buy a truck or SUV in the near future. I didn't even know if Vasha was able to drive. But if she

- 74 -

couldn't, then I'd still need a vehicle to take her places when a bike wasn't practical. Not to mention she could very well be pregnant already. I wanted to ask when she'd know, but I wasn't certain how she'd take the question.

My home was far enough from the clubhouse that I didn't want to ask her to walk, especially since she was dressed so nicely. Pulling my phone from my pocket, I shot off a text to one of the Prospects, telling him to bring an SUV to my house. It didn't take long before Jack pulled into my driveway. He left the engine running, hopped out, and started walking back the way he'd come. I helped Vasha into the vehicle, then got behind the wheel and drove to the front of the compound. We passed Jack and Vasha gave me one of those looks only women seem to have perfected.

"What?" I asked.

"You left him walking."

I snorted. "Yeah, and after he let you walk out of here he should be grateful that's all I've done to him. You could have died walking to the next town, not to mention you exhausted yourself enough you slept for days."

She kept quiet as I pulled into a spot in front of the clubhouse. I frowned at the line of bikes and lack of other vehicles. I'd thought that Luciana and Violeta would be here already, but it seemed we'd gotten here first. I hoped that Vasha wouldn't be overwhelmed with nothing but men inside. She opened her door and I narrowed my eyes at her.

"You'll wait until I get over there. I'll open the damn door, Vasha."

She cast me a startled glance, and I realized that no one had probably ever offered her such a courtesy. It would take time for her to adjust to her new way of

Harley Wylde   **Slider/ Ashes Duet**

life, and the fact that not all men were assholes. Well, maybe that wasn't entirely true. All men definitely had the ability to be assholes, and even I was one when the occasion called for it. I led her up the steps and frowned at the loud music blaring from inside. What the hell? I'd thought we'd have a relatively quiet gathering so everyone could get to know my woman, not an all-out party.

We stepped inside and I froze. Not only were the old ladies not present, nor their men, but club whores paraded around the place barely clothed. A few were giving blowjobs out in the open, and I felt Vasha stiffen. This was the last fucking thing I needed. One of the regular women, Christa, came rushing toward me, pressing her bare breasts against me as she flung her arms around my waist.

"You're here!" She squealed and bounced a little.

I could feel Vasha retreating, physically and emotionally, and I knew I had to stop this shit immediately. I shoved Christa, not caring if I was gentle or not. She could clearly see the woman standing next to me. What the fuck?

"Back the fuck off, Christa. I didn't give you permission to touch me."

Vasha took another step away from me, and I knew I was fucking this up. I needed to put Christa in her place, but at the same time, I didn't need Vasha to lump me in with men like Grigori. What the hell was I supposed to do to defuse the situation? With club whores, I'd found that being direct, and even a bit mean, was the only way to get my point across. Hell, some of them even got off on being treated like shit, which I'd never understand. Vasha didn't know that, though, and I didn't want her to think badly of me. I'd fucked up enough with her already.

Harley Wylde   Slider/ Ashes Duet

I decided to ignore Christa and focus on my woman. Maybe she'd get the fucking hint and disappear.

"Vasha, it's not what you think."

"Who is she?" Vasha asked, her voice barely discernible over the music and laughter around us.

"Christa is a club whore." My woman paled and I cursed myself. "Not that kind of whore! She's here voluntarily. Christa and women like her are here for sex. They'll sleep with anyone in a cut, even multiple guys a night. None of them have to be here, they aren't paid for services rendered. It's one hundred percent their choice."

Christa tugged on my arm, trying to get my attention, but I was tired of her shit. I kept my gaze locked on Vasha, willing her to understand. I didn't need this to cause a problem between us, not when we were finally getting to be in a good place. She glanced at Christa, then looked around the room. Her features were pinched and she was still too pale, but I could tell she was trying to view things from a different perspective. She studied the inhabitants of the room before sighing and looking up at me.

"They're not forced?" Vasha asked.

"Slider, who is she?" Christa asked, her whining tone grating on me.

"Vasha is my old lady. Now get the fuck away from me, Christa!"

She gasped, her eyes going wide as she stared at Vasha and took a step back. Other people nearby were starting to notice that I was here, with Vasha at my side, and the room was growing quiet. I was fucking pissed. They were supposed to be here to welcome my woman, not fuck anything with a pussy. Why the hell were the club whores even here?

I felt a presence behind me and turned to see Spider and Luciana. The Pres narrowed his gaze on the room and I heard him growl. Yeah, I wasn't the only one pissed off at the turn of events. I reached for Vasha, pulling her against my side, as Spider moved farther into the room, his wife trailing him with a disgusted expression. It was no secret that Luciana detested the club whores and would gladly banish them from the compound, but that would never happen. At least, not as long as we had single men.

"What the fuck is wrong with you?" Spider yelled. "Anything here with a pussy that isn't patched better get the fucking hell out of my motherfucking clubhouse! Now!"

The women scurried into their clothes and ran from the clubhouse. Spider stalked forward, reaching back to grab his wife's hand. I led Vasha farther inside, stopping at the table Spider was sneering at. A Prospect rushed forward and started wiping it down, as well as the chairs. Probably a good idea. Who knew what had transpired in here already tonight, or when the last time was this place had been scrubbed.

Spider sat and pulled Luciana into his lap, and I did the same with Vasha. Rocket and Violeta showed up a few minutes later. The snarl on his face told me he'd seen the club whores outside, probably lingering in hopes they'd be allowed back inside. Once everyone at the table was settled, and a Prospect had brought over beers for the guys and bottled water for the ladies, I introduced Vasha to Luciana and Violeta.

I wanted to tell her they'd both suffered at the hands of men and would understand what she'd been through, but it wasn't my story to tell. If they wanted her to know, they'd share the details of their pasts. Or at least let her know she wasn't alone. It was my hope they'd become friends.

"I'll make sure everyone has some extra work to do this week," Spider said. "Present company excluded. I can't believe those fuckers had those women in here after I said I wanted everyone present. Guess I needed to spell shit out more clearly for the dimwitted in the bunch. How the fuck did they misconstrue the type of meeting I wanted? What part of you getting an old lady spelled out 'bring in the club whores'?"

"How did you meet Slider?" Violeta asked.

Vasha looked up at me, uncertainty on her face. I didn't know if she was embarrassed over her circumstances, or if she wanted permission to tell them. I gave her a slight nod, hoping it was what she needed or wanted from me. I felt her body relax as she leaned against my chest, and I tightened my grip on her waist.

"Surge made arrangements for me to leave Russia," Vasha said, then fell silent. I pressed a kiss to her temple and decided to give them an abbreviated version to save her from having to speak about it.

"Surge knew I was thinking about settling down. Vasha needed help escaping a bad situation, so he brought her here. With some help from Wire, he married the two of us."

Luciana stared hard at Vasha, and I knew she wondered if the trouble Vasha had left behind was similar to what she and Violeta had suffered. The way Vasha was holding herself, and the slight tremor I felt in her small form, was enough to tell me she didn't want to discuss it further. The trauma of her time in Russia was still too fresh in her mind. She'd barely been gone from that horrible life. I hoped she'd heal, eventually, but I knew it wouldn't happen overnight.

"With some luck, we'll be adding to the list of kids around here before too long," I said. Vasha flushed a deep red and I chuckled, then kissed her cheek. She was so damn adorable. "Assuming my wife wants children right now."

She gazed at me and slowly nodded.

"And not because she feels it's her duty," I added.

A slight smile spread across her lips. "I want children with you."

Violeta let out a cry and I jerked my gaze her way. The look on Rocket's face was priceless, a mix of horror and awe.

"My water broke!" Violeta struggled to stand and Rocket helped her. Without another word, he scooped her into his arms and practically ran from the clubhouse.

"You going with them?" I asked.

"Could..." Vasha stopped and bit her lip.

"What is it, *kroshka*?"

"Could we all go?"

Luciana smiled and stood, reaching for Spider's hand. "I think that's an excellent idea. Violeta will want to know her family is there for her. Although, we should stop by Rocket's house and pick up the bag Violeta prepared two weeks ago."

I could feel Vasha withdrawing.

"She means you too," I murmured in her ear. "You're part of their family now. By marriage, you're part of Hades Abyss, just like them. You aren't alone anymore, *zolatka*."

She gave me a hesitant smile and stood. I got up and led the way outside, glaring at my brothers. None had come to introduce themselves, and I was pissed as hell. Not only that the club whores had been inside, but because they'd avoided Vasha when she clearly meant something to me. I hoped Spider ripped them to shreds later. I did notice that Surge and Fox were both absent. Maybe if they'd been present, they could have cleared the place before I arrived with Vasha. Since Spider had called for everyone to meet at the clubhouse, I didn't know where the missing members were.

I helped Vasha into the SUV, then drove to the hospital, stopping along the way to pick up a bouquet of flowers for Violeta and a small stuffed bear for the baby. I knew an infant wouldn't care about such a thing, but when he or she was older, Violeta and Rocket could explain the bear was a gift on the night they were born. Maybe it would mean something to them as they grew older, or maybe it would collect dust and end up in the trash. Either way, I wasn't going empty-handed. While Ryker had technically been the first member of the club to have a kid, he didn't live with us anymore. Spider and Luciana had a daughter, but they'd adopted her. It didn't make Marianna any less loved, or less a part of the Hades Abyss family, she just didn't share blood with Spider and Luciana. We all adored her, though, and I knew Rocket and Violeta's kid would be the same.

If Rocket knew what they were having, he hadn't said a word to anyone. There were bets in the clubhouse as to whether they would have a boy or girl. I'd stayed out of it, but I knew Surge had five hundred riding on the outcome, and some had tossed in as much as one thousand into the pot. Violeta had heard about the bet and just rolled her eyes, telling them they were more immature than her. Even though she was eighteen, she'd had to grow up fast, and in some ways, she really was more mature than some of the men I called brother.

We found Luciana and Spider in the waiting room in the maternity wing. Rocket was nowhere in sight, so I assumed he'd gone with Violeta to hold her hand. I hope she didn't break it. I'd heard horror stories of women in childbirth getting superhuman strength. My sweet Vasha didn't seem capable of breaking bones, but I hoped like hell I'd find out one day. The more I thought about having a family with her, the more determined I became to knock her up as soon as possible. Assuming I hadn't already.

It took hours, but eventually Rocket came out with a huge grin on his face and a small bundle in his arms.

"I'd like you to meet Zoe," he said, pride shining in his eyes.

Luciana ran her fingers over the baby's cheek, then rushed down the hall, most likely to check on her sister. But if Rocket was out here, then I knew Violeta was fine. He'd have never left her side otherwise. Hell, he'd gone on a murder spree to get justice for what she'd suffered not too long ago. Spider hadn't demanded his patch, but he'd hit Rocket where it would hurt -- in his bank account. Once his sins had been atoned for, everything went back to normal. Mostly.

"She's beautiful," Vasha said.

"Maybe we'll have one of our own someday soon," I said, giving her a slight squeeze.

"When you're tired of my wife being back there, just toss her out and lock the door," Spider said. "Otherwise, you might not get rid of her."

Rocket snorted, then turned to carry his daughter back down the hall. Spider shoved his hands in his pockets and rocked back on his heels, a contemplative look on his face. When he hadn't thought anyone was looking, I'd seen the soft way he stared at that little girl, and the way he eyed his wife. It wouldn't surprise me at all if they tried to adopt another kid, maybe when Marianna was a bit older. She had some developmental delays and took up a lot of their time, but they adored her.

Spider eyed Vasha, then gave me a chin nudge to step away for a minute. I led Vasha over to a chair and kissed her cheek before handing her a magazine off a nearby table.

"The Pres needs to discuss something with me. Probably club business. I'll be across the room."

She nodded and sat patiently.

I followed Spider far enough away that no one would hear us, not Vasha and not the nurses at the desk at the front of the hallway. I didn't have any idea what he'd need to tell me right now, but it apparently couldn't wait, and that was never a good sign.

He pulled out his phone, tapped and swiped at the screen, then held it out to me. I saw he had a message from Surge, but the words on the screen chilled me to the bone.

They know where she is.

I tried not to glance at Vasha, not wanting to alert her to a problem. I'd keep her safe, somehow. My gaze lifted to Spider's and he reached over, tapping the screen again until a message from Fox appeared with an image attached. It was a young man, probably not much older than Vasha, and he'd been brutally attacked and killed. On his chest was a pinned note.

She's next.

"That's Anatoly," Spider said. "The man who helped her escape and come to the US. If they found him, then there's a good chance they really can find Vasha."

Bile rose in my throat as I stared at the image. There was no fucking way I would let them get anywhere near Vasha. I'd die to protect her.

"What do we do? " I asked.

"They're coming to the compound for her, from what we can gather. Fox has been working with a few men in the city where Anatoly was found. He was closer than I would like. The Russians might already be in town by now. Fox said the body was at least a day old. If they have access to a private jet, it wouldn't take long to reach us. An hour max."

"I won't let them have her."

He nodded. "I know. But she's not safe here, Slider. After what happened with Violeta, we've taken measures to improve our security, but do you want to risk it?"

"So where do I take her? The chapter in Mississippi can't be much better than here."

Spider wiped a hand down his beard. "They took over an old military facility. It's small, smaller than our compound, but it's also more secure. They have a bunker there with everything you'd need. Food, water, electricity. They even put a TV down there and stocked some other things to keep people entertained if they're confined in the space for very long."

And that's where he wanted me to take her. A bunker, with no natural light. A tomb. What if they did break through and get to us? We'd be sitting ducks in a place like that. Spider had to know that. Was he hoping the Russians wouldn't know about the Mississippi chapter? It wasn't like we could hide there forever. Sooner or later, we'd need to come home. Would the Russians be waiting when we did?

I looked over at Vasha, flipping through the magazine, a smile on her face. This would destroy her. She'd thought she was free. If she knew they were here, that they were coming for her, I didn't know how far she'd retreat into herself. I didn't want to lose her when she was finally opening up to me. It seemed like we were getting somewhere and now we had to deal with her past far sooner than I'd have liked. I'd had every intention of making sure Grigori and the man who'd bought her would never come after her. I just hadn't acted fast enough it seemed.

"All right. I'll take her. We'll need some things from the house, and I'll have to use one of the club vehicles. I don't want her on the back of a bike for that long." Or at all until I knew if she was pregnant. Riding from my house to the front of the compound was one thing. But hitting the road was completely different.

"Take whatever you need. I'll have Cotton and Fangs give you an escort, keep an eye out for trouble. You just focus on your woman and keeping her happy. Don't fuck this up, Slider. Even if you didn't get her in the most conventional way, she's still yours and the two of you could have something really great."

He wasn't telling me anything I didn't know. I'd already decided that Vasha was it for me. Hell, I'd known that before I'd even discovered we were married. Deep down anyway. I might not have been willing to admit it, and had chalked up my feelings to whatever Surge put in my drink, but on a primal level I'd known she was mine the second I saw her in my bed. And I wasn't letting her go. Not now, not ever.

"I'll call Cotton and Fangs, make sure they're ready and waiting. I'll also put everyone on alert. Surge has a picture of Grigori and Vladimir, as well as some of their hired muscle. I'll get those images out to everyone, including you and our brothers in Mississippi so everyone knows who to watch for. It doesn't mean they won't hire others, but at least we aren't completely blind." Spider patted my shoulder. "We'll do what we can to keep her safe. She's one of us now, even if she doesn't have a property cut and isn't inked."

I winced, knowing I needed to handle that shit. I should have ordered the cut the second I knew I was keeping her. The ink, however, probably needed to wait a little longer. After the state I'd found her in when she'd run, I didn't want to add any more stress to her body, and telling Vasha we had to leave because of Grigori was going to be bad enough.

"Let Violeta know we were here?" I nodded to the things we'd brought with us. "Maybe give her and the baby the gifts from us. I don't want to take more time going back there and giving the Russians even more opportunity to snatch Vasha."

"Get her to the bunker. We'll handle things here, and don't be afraid to accept help, Slider. She's your priority, not your damn pride."

I knew he was right. No matter how much I wanted to end Grigori's life with my own hands, it was better to focus on my wife and let the others handle everything else. As long as Vasha was safe, that's all that mattered. In the end, it might be better if I wasn't the one to kill the men coming for her. I didn't want to see fear in her eyes when she looked at me. I'd already proven to her that I was a complete asshole. Didn't need to tarnish my image even more. Vasha wasn't the type to see that sort of display as my way of protecting her. I worried if she knew I'd killed Grigori or the others that she'd simply think of me as a murderer.

Part of me wondered if she could handle this way of life. Sure, she'd been through hell, but if she expected me to walk the straight and narrow, that wasn't going to happen. The club was my life, my family, and I owed them everything. If they needed me, I'd be there, regardless of what it entailed. I knew that Spider was trying to clean things up a little, now that we were starting families and had kids at the compound, but we'd never be completely legit. Guns and drugs were too profitable to turn away from them completely.

Vasha had no idea we were into that shit, and I planned to keep it that way. The less she knew about my dealings with the club, the better. I needed her to feel safe with the men I called family. If she knew we were outlaws, that we killed people, sold guns and drugs, and over the years we'd taken on other not-so-savory jobs, then she might very well ask to leave. And that shit wasn't happening. She was mine, and I wasn't about to let her go.

I made my way to her side and hunkered down in front of her. She lifted her gaze from the magazine, but the slight smile on her lips faded as she looked at me. I didn't know how to tell her we needed to leave, or why. The last thing I wanted to do was stress her out more, or scare her. I knew that saying Grigori had come for her would do both, and she'd likely ask about her friend, the one who was now dead.

"*Kroshka*, we need to take a trip somewhere for a little while."

Her face paled. "They know where I am, don't they?"

I didn't know how to answer that, but I nodded, knowing I couldn't lie to her. Even if I didn't want her to be scared, I also didn't want to keep the truth from her. I needed her vigilant of her surroundings at all times, at least until we reached the bunker. After that, I hoped she'd relax, even if I didn't think I would.

"We're going to go home and pack a bag each, then I'm driving you farther south. The men you met before, when you ran, do you remember them?"

"Yes."

"We're going to their compound. There's a safe place for us there." I reached up and ran my fingers through her hair. "I need you to be brave for me. We'll face this together, and I will do whatever it takes to keep you safe. Believe me?"

"Yes, Slider. I believe you."

I pressed my lips to hers, then stood and took her hand. She rose to her feet and followed me out of the hospital. On the way to the house, I kept an eye on her as well as the surrounding area. Her hands fidgeted in her lap and her feet shifted restlessly. We pulled through the gate and I went straight to the house. I'd barely come to a full stop before she flung open her door and hopped out. I couldn't be mad at her, even though I wished she'd have let me help her. She raced inside, and I followed.

Vasha pulled handfuls of her clothes from the dresser and boxes, then frantically looked around the room. I pulled down two bags from the top of the closet, handing one to her while I packed my own belongings. In the bathroom, I gathered items we would both need and shoved them into a smaller travel bag. It took us no more than fifteen minutes before we were back in the SUV and headed out of town, with Fangs taking point and Cotton right behind us. Two hours into the trip, Vasha was slumped against the window. Even in sleep, her hands twitched and her body shifted.

We drove straight through, making the trip in less than five hours when it should have taken seven. As we neared the compound, a Prospect at the gate held up a hand to stop us. I rolled down the window and waited for the kid to approach, and I did mean kid. He didn't look older than eighteen, if even that. Though he may have had a baby face, his eyes belied the things he'd seen, and the comfortable way he wore the gun at his hip told me enough.

He eyed my cut through the open window and gave me a nod before looking at Fangs and Cotton. "Titan said to expect you. Follow the road to the right and toward the center of the compound. You'll see a few trucks and bikes. That's where you'll need to stop."

"Thanks."

He opened the gate and we pulled through. I followed the directions he'd given and climbed out once I saw the vehicles and Titan. The Pres stood with his arms folded over his chest, a grim expression on his face. I could tell he didn't like this any more than I did. He'd spent time with Vasha, and I could tell the day I'd caught up to them that he was protective of her. I was counting on that right now.

"We've got everything down there you could need. If you'd like any men with you, there are six bedrooms. Most are bunk style, but we moved a queen bed into one of the rooms and pulled out those bunks for now. Thought you and your wife would be more comfortable that way. There's also a five-drawer chest in that room. Reception on your phone won't work, but there's a landline in the common area. Number for my cell and the clubhouse are written down next to it." Titan gave a nod of his head toward what looked like an old barn with machinery inside. "Entrance to the bunker is in there."

I got our bags out of the SUV and handed them off to Kraken and Stone, then lifted Vasha into my arms. She was so exhausted she only mumbled in Russian before quieting once more. I followed them inside the rickety structure. Titan pointed to the hidden entrance and I watched as a pallet of hay bales shifted over to expose a staircase. I carried Vasha down and had to admit I was a bit impressed with the bunker. There was a common area as he'd mentioned that boasted several couches, a large TV and what looked like a Blu-ray player, a cabinet full of movies, a large table with eight chairs, and a fully functional kitchen. Support beams were strategically placed throughout the area. Once I found the room with the larger bed, I laid Vasha down and started putting our things away. There were two bathrooms. One was more private while the other was set up with four stalls for toilets, four sinks, and four fully open shower stalls. No way I was putting Vasha's things in there, so I took the private bath.

I didn't know how long we'd be here, but I hoped that Grigori was stopped soon. This place was more than I'd expected, and I was grateful for their assistance, but it wasn't home.

Chapter Six

Vasha

Waking up in a strange place sent fear spiking through my heart, until I heard the murmur of Slider's voice coming from another room. I glanced around, not seeing any windows or anything really. There was the bed I was lying on and a chest for clothing. I saw our empty bags next to it. Getting out of bed, I made sure my legs would hold me before I went in search of my husband. I knew we had to be at the safe place he'd mentioned, but I was curious about our temporary home.

Leaving the bedroom, I saw a large open area and quickly spotted Slider and three other men at a table. Plates of food were in the center and my stomach rumbled, reminding me I hadn't eaten in far too long. I approached, noting the way they went silent as I drew nearer, even though none looked my way except Slider. He gave me a cautious smile and I realized he was worried about my reaction to this place. I understood why we were here. He was keeping me safe, and I appreciated it, even if I did worry the lack of natural light might make me slightly crazy before too long. Even in the captivity at Grigori's home, I'd still had a window, even if it did have bars across it to prevent me escaping.

"Hungry?" Slider asked, holding out his hand toward me.

I slipped my fingers across his palm and he pulled me down onto his lap. His whiskers scraped my neck as he nuzzled me and I felt my cheeks warm. I recognized Stone, but the others were new to me. One of them smirked a little, even though he hadn't lifted his gaze from the table.

"A little," I said.

Slider reached for an empty plate and filled it with biscuits, eggs, and bacon. There was a gooey white substance that he added to the plate before putting butter on top. I didn't know what it was, but I trusted him. If Slider thought I should eat it, then I would. Or at least I'd try.

As I ate, he pointed to each man at the table. "You already know Stone, but next to him is Lynch. You didn't get a chance to meet Fangs, but he rode here with us. Kraken is taking a nap, but he's here too."

"You have a lot of men above us keeping an eye on things, and making sure you're safe," said Stone. "The four of us have a room a bit down from yours. You and Slider have the private room and a private bath, so you don't have to worry about any of us walking in uninvited."

"We volunteered to stay down here and help protect you," Lynch said. "If you're uncomfortable with anyone here, you just say so and someone else can come down."

I chewed and swallowed, taking in their words and trying to process everything. I didn't understand why they cared what happened to me, or if I felt uneasy. They were men, rough men at that, and it was odd that they had such a tender side. Then again, I'd never known men could be nice until I met Slider. Maybe nice wasn't precisely the word for him, but he was far better to me than anyone else had ever been, even Anatoly. My friend's loyalty had only gone so far, and while he'd helped me escape, there were plenty of times he'd done Grigori's bidding, forcing me to do things or go places I didn't want to.

"Why do you care?" I asked, trying not to sound bitchy. I was genuinely curious.

The men looked at one another before Stone answered.

"Because you're family. We're Hades Abyss even if we're from a different chapter. You're Slider's old lady, which makes you one of us."

My brow furrowed. "Old lady? I'm only eighteen."

Lynch snickered and Slider squeezed my waist. I didn't understand their amusement, but I could feel the slight shaking under me that said Slider was laughing too.

"It's just a term for the woman a biker claims," Stone said. "But if you prefer wife, seeing as how the two of you are married, then that's how we'll refer to you."

Kraken came into the room and claimed a seat at the table, yawning wide enough his jaw cracked. He gave me a slight smile before his gaze flicked to Slider. I felt my husband's grip tighten a little.

I didn't know what I wanted to be honest. As long as I was Slider's, that's all that really mattered. What he called me didn't really matter. The fact he wanted to keep me, wanted a family with me, was all that I cared about. He made me feel safe. No, it was more than that. He made me feel desirable. I didn't feel dirty when he looked at me or touched me. I went up in flames and craved him. Just one look was all it took for me to get wet, not that he'd acted on it since he'd come to find me. I wouldn't break, but he seemed worried. It was touching, and sweet... and incredibly frustrating.

"She's my wife. No reason you can't call her that," Slider said.

Kraken got a strange look on his face before looking away. "Maybe I should see if Wizard could find me a wife like Surge found Vasha for Slider. The sluts at the clubhouse are fun for a while, but eventually every man wants more."

Stone snorted. "Speak for yourself. Nothing wrong with enjoying a different woman every night. It's not like we forced them to offer themselves to us. They're here because they want to be."

Fang's brow furrowed. "I can see the appeal of having the same woman in your bed every night, as long as you can trust her. Not sure I trust anyone enough to claim them."

I shifted on Slider's lap, a little uncomfortable. I knew they said those women came of their own free will, but it seemed so odd to me. Why would anyone want to be with so many men with no offer of something more permanent? While I enjoyed being in Slider's bed, I couldn't imagine letting anyone else touch me the way he did, or kiss me. He was the only man I wanted, and the idea of being with multiple men because it was fun was too foreign of a concept for me. It wasn't that I thought badly of those women, I just... didn't understand. What did they get from it?

"When you're finished eating, I'll show you where our bathroom is. You can clean up if you want. I always like taking a hot shower after a long day on the road," Slider said, pressing a kiss to the side of my head.

A shower did sound nice. I finished eating, then stood and picked up my plate. I carried it to the sink, then returned to the table for the other empty dishes. There was soap and a sponge by the kitchen sink, so I ran some hot water and started washing the breakfast dishes. It was the dead silence at my back that drew my attention. I glanced over my shoulder and nearly

Harley Wylde   Slider/ Ashes Duet

dropped the plate in my hands when I discovered all of them staring at me, and Slider looked a little pissed.

Had I done something wrong? Wasn't I supposed to clean the dishes and clear the table? It's what I'd been taught. I knew things were different in this country, but surely they weren't *that* different. Women still took care of the men and families, didn't they? I turned back to the sink and finished the dishes, then went to the table to clear the leftovers, but Slider reached out and wrapped his fingers around my wrist.

"Vasha, you aren't a maid. You don't have to clean up after us."

"But it's what a wife does. Someone else cooked, so I should clear the table. Is that wrong?"

Kraken rubbed the back of his neck, but Stone, Fangs, and Lynch stood up and walked off. Slider looked both frustrated and amused, even though I didn't know how he pulled it off. The two should have canceled each other out. I had a feeling there would be a steep learning curve as I tried to navigate my new life.

"I did it wrong?" I asked.

"She's like a throwback to the nineteen fifties," Kraken said. "On the one hand, I kind of like it. On the other…"

Slider nodded, seeming to know what the other man meant. I didn't. Was there something wrong with me wanting to take care of them? Even if I hadn't been taught it was my place, I found that I enjoyed doing things like cleaning, dishes, and laundry. There was almost something soothing about it.

"I don't understand," I said.

"Women here are just different," Slider said. "It doesn't mean you're doing anything wrong, *kroshka*. I'm just concerned that you're going off your training and not doing the dishes because it's what you actually want to do. What made you stand up and clear the table?"

I opened and shut my mouth a few times before shrugging a shoulder.

"It needed to be done," I said. "Besides, I like doing things around the house."

Slider shook his head, but there was a smile on his face as he stood up. He reached for me, tugging me away from the table and the remaining dishes. I glanced at the leftovers and wondered if someone would think to put them away. When Slider shoved me into a small bathroom, I noticed that our things were already in here. Had he done all this while I'd slept? It was obvious he'd put our clothing away as well, since the bags had been empty this morning. At least, I thought it was morning. With no windows, it was hard to tell.

"I'll get you something to change into. Go ahead and get in the shower. Towels are in the cabinet under the sink." Slider gave me a nudge toward the shower stall. It wasn't as spacious as the one at his home, but it was still nicer than where I'd bathed in Russia. The water only took a moment to warm up, then I quickly undressed and got under the spray. Slider came back, setting some clothing on the bathroom counter. I watched through the frosted glass as he undressed and my heart started to race. He was joining me?

Slider stepped into the shower and shut the door behind him. The gleam in his eyes told me that maybe he was done waiting. He'd held me at arm's length since he'd found me in that motel. I'd been better for days now, but he'd been too worried about hurting me even though I'd assured him I wouldn't break. I wasn't as fragile as he seemed to think. Just because I was small didn't mean anything. A weak woman wouldn't have survived Grigori. A weak woman wouldn't have run, traveling so very far from home to have a fresh start. He had to know that, didn't he?

He cupped my cheek and pressed his lips to mine before deepening the kiss. His tongue swept into my mouth and I practically melted against him. My nipples hardened and I felt myself growing slick between my legs. That was all it took. Just a kiss. A touch. Knowing that he wanted me made me ache to have him filling me.

"You're so fucking beautiful," he murmured. "If I could go back to that first night, change things… I'd have told you then how you made me feel."

I smiled faintly, knowing he was just being nice. He couldn't have felt anything that soon, right? I certainly had, but I'd been taught that men were different from women.

"How did I make you feel?" I asked as he rubbed his hard cock against me.

"The moment I saw you lying in my bed, I had this need to protect you, to claim you." He kissed me again, harder. "It was like some part of me just knew that you were mine. If I'd only known that you really were mine, then that night could have ended differently."

He slid his hands down the sides of my body to my hips, pulling me tighter against him.

"How?" I asked, my voice sounding breathless even to my ears.

"I'd have fucked you all night. Held you while you slept, and we'd have woken together the next morning. I wouldn't have been an asshole who made you feel unwanted. Maybe if things had been different, if I hadn't chased you off, then you could very well be pregnant right now." He grinned. "I like that idea, you know? The thought of you carrying my kid. I bet you'll be sexy with a baby bump."

"Maybe I already carry your child," I said. It was possible. We hadn't used protection, and while I knew it didn't happen often that a woman got pregnant on the first try, it was still feasible.

He gave me a wicked grin before lifting me and pressing me against the tiled wall. He rubbed his beard against my neck, making my nipples get even harder. Slider groaned as he filled me, his cock stretching me wide. It felt so amazing. I dug my nails into his shoulders and bit my lip to stifle any sounds I might make. There were still four men sharing this space with us and I didn't want them to hear me.

Slider pumped in and out of me as he greedily kissed me, making me feel breathless. He rubbed against me, his body stroking my nipples with every thrust of his cock. It was almost too much. And at the same time, not nearly enough. I wanted more, wanted it all. I craved the pleasure he'd given me before, but I didn't want this moment to end, and I knew as soon as we found our release that it would be over.

"I'm going to fuck you every chance I get," he said, his voice a deep growl. "By the time we go home, you'll be pregnant. I'm not stopping until I've knocked you up. You want that, don't you?"

I nodded nearly delirious with pleasure, not only from what he was doing to me, but his words alone made my heart sing. Yes! I wanted that, wanted a family with him. I hoped we'd have a little girl who could grow up in a better place than I had, a child who would know they were loved.

He reached between our bodies and stroked my clit. Just a few brushes of his fingers and I was coming.

I couldn't stay silent and cried out, begging for more as he took me harder and faster. Slider made me come a second time before I felt the hot spurts of his release filling me. Even after, he was still hard. My eyes went a little wide when he started thrusting again. I'd never known men could do that, be ready again so fast. Grigori had told me… No! There was no place for him when it was just me and Slider. I needed to forget my time in Russia.

"You're so perfect, *kroshka*. You're everything I could ever need or want. I think I owe Surge an entire fridge of beer."

I bit my lip so I wouldn't giggle. Even if Slider hadn't realized I was his that first night, he certainly seemed content with the knowledge now. My heart felt full to bursting. When he pulled free of me, I gasped and went taut. Why had he stopped? Before I could ask, he spun me to face the wall, lifted my hips and sank into me again.

He placed his lips by my ear, giving the lobe a nip. "I can go deeper this way."

I moaned as he slammed into me. Slider took what he wanted, but gave me everything I needed. He gripped my breast with one hand, twisting and tugging on my nipple. I came almost instantly.

"Slider! Yes! More, I need more."

He pounded into me harder. "What did I tell you?"

I whimpered, unable to think coherently enough to figure out what he meant.

"When it's just us, when I'm balls-deep inside you, what do you call me?"

I must not have answered fast enough. He pulled out and delivered three hard swats to my ass cheek. My eyes went wide and I gasped in surprise. Not only that he'd struck me, but that I'd liked it. A lot. Slider spanked me again and I felt my ass start to burn from the strikes of his palm.

"Upton, please," I said. "I need you."

He growled and thrust hard and deep. He took me like a man possessed, driving into me as if his very life depended on it. My husband, my lover, my everything. He was almost savage in his claiming of me, but I enjoyed every moment of it. Never would I have thought I'd like something like this, so rough and raw, but I did. No, I didn't just like it, I loved it. Like when he'd shackled me to his bed. I needed this as much as I needed to breathe.

He made me come again and as my pussy clenched down on his cock, I felt him filling me.

"That's it, *kroshka*. Take it all, every bit of my cum is yours. You want it, don't you?"

I nodded emphatically. Yes! I definitely wanted it, wanted *him*.

He grunted as he stroked into me a few more times, then stilled, buried deep inside. I never wanted this moment to end. As the water cooled, he pulled out of me and then took his time bathing us both. The gentle touch of his hands after the rough way he'd taken me, and the marks he'd surely left on my ass, was almost enough to bring tears to my eyes.

Slider helped me dry off and dress before he did the same. When we stepped out of the bathroom, the TV was playing a movie so loud that my cheeks flushed. They must have turned it up to drown out the sounds of him fucking me in the shower. Slider chuckled as he led me into our room and shut the door, twisting the lock. I stared at it, then him. The feral look in his eyes was all the warning I had. He reached for

Harley Wylde   Slider/ Ashes Duet

me, tossed me into the center of the bed, then followed, pressing his body to mine.

"Didn't you get enough in the shower?" I asked, but I couldn't help the smile that spread across my face. I was happy! Genuinely happy. I'd never thought I'd ever feel like this. In fact… My heart raced a little as I realized I was falling for my husband.

"I don't think I can ever get enough of you, but I thought maybe we'd just lie here for a bit."

He rolled to his side and pulled me into his arms. I snuggled closer and breathed in his scent. If only this moment could last, but good things never happened to me. Anytime I'd ever experienced a moment of pleasure, something had happened to ruin it. Since there were men after me, I had no doubt that something bad was on the horizon. Until then, I'd enjoy my time with Slider. He said he'd protect me, keep me safe, but he didn't know the men he was up against. They were ruthless killers, not at all like my sweet husband. He was so gentle and kind, so good. Those men were evil and would stop at nothing to make me pay for running. It was wrong to let him place himself in danger, but I liked how he made me feel, like I was worth protecting.

"Talk to me, *zolatka*. Something is weighing on you. As your husband, it's my duty to help you carry those burdens. You're not alone anymore."

Maybe not now, but I would be soon. Assuming they didn't just kill me. Having run away, I knew I would no longer be given to Vladimir as his wife. If they didn't execute me, they'd make me a whore. Running hadn't been smart, but it had given me Slider, and that alone made it worth it. I'd suffer anything to have these moments with him.

"They'll come for me," I said. "And they won't stop until I'm dead or back in their possession. You don't know these men, Slider."

He was quiet for a moment and I wondered if he'd finally realized exactly what he was facing. Those men would kill him without a second thought. They wouldn't care that we were married and he was trying to do the honorable thing. They would only see him as weak, and as a roadblock to what they wanted. Me.

"At the risk of you thinking I'm every bit as evil as the men who kept you captive in Russia, there are things you need to know about me, Vasha. I'm not some sweet man who doesn't know how to get his hands dirty. I've done things you wouldn't approve of, things that would frighten you. I tried to tell you before, but I don't think you believed me."

I bit my lip to keep from voicing my thoughts, but there was no way the man who made my body and heart sing could be anything like Grigori or Vladimir. It was impossible. No matter what he said, he was right, I hadn't believed him, never would.

"I've killed people, *kroshka*. The club, Hades Abyss, is known as an outlaw club. I don't think you understand what that means. We do illegal things to make our money, and while we try to ensure those jobs don't hurt innocent people, there's no way to keep that from happening with any certainty." He ran his hand through my hair and sighed heavily. "I'm not the man you think I am. I'm a murderer. I've sold drugs and guns. Done things I shouldn't."

"Do you force yourself on women?" I asked. "Do you kill everyone weaker than you when they disobey, even women and children?"

He went stiff. "Of course not!"

I smiled a little. "You're outraged I would even ask. That's what makes you different, Slider. You're nothing like Grigori or Vladimir. Even if you have hurt people, they likely deserved it. Didn't they?"

"Well, yeah, but... their blood is still on my hands, Vasha. I killed them. Snuffed out their lives without a second thought."

I lifted up so I could look at him. I needed him to see that his words didn't bother me. He might have killed people, but he had a good heart and I knew he'd never harm an innocent. Not on purpose. In a lot of ways, we were still strangers, and yet just looking in his eyes I could see that he was different from the men I'd known. The fact he wanted to give me pleasure, to keep me safe, already put him in another category.

"You're a good, honorable man, Upton. And nothing you can say will ever convince me otherwise. Do you want to know why?"

He just stared at me, but I could tell he was curious why I thought he was so wonderful.

"Because I'm falling in love with you, and I'd never love a monster."

His gaze softened and he tugged me down, kissing me softly.

"I think I fell for you the moment I saw you," he said. "I love you, *zolatka*. And if you need more time to know for certain if you love me, then I'm all right with that. You take whatever time you need. I'll be right here."

"Why?" I asked. "Why do you love me? You don't even know me."

He gave me a crooked smile and tugged on my hair. "Oh, I know you. Despite the brainwashing those men tried, you're still a strong, vibrant woman. It took guts to leave that situation, to come here to a man you didn't know. What if I'd been just as bad as them? But you took that chance because you wanted to feel safe and happy. Not everyone has the courage to go after what they want."

"No one's ever seen me as strong before, except me. I knew I wasn't weak like they told me. I don't always feel strong, though."

Slider kissed me, then hugged me tight. "Everyone has moments they aren't certain they're strong enough to move forward, to go after what they want. It's just human nature, *kroshka*. It doesn't make you weak, or less. All humans have doubts and fears. Even me. Right now, I'm scared of losing you. I will die to keep you safe, but I'm worried it won't be enough, that they'll get to you anyway."

"We'll face them together, then," I said. "If they break through the defenses you've put into place, we'll stand together and stare them in the eyes, let them know they haven't won. Because no matter what they do or say, they can't change how you make me feel, they can't take away the happiness you've given me, Upton. Nothing can ever take that from me."

He rolled me under his body and kissed me hard and deep. I could feel the bulge in his jeans and knew he wanted me again, and I'd gladly let him take me. Maybe sex wasn't the answer to everything, but I loved the way I felt in Slider's arms, loved having him inside me, owning me, making me his in every way possible. The fact it was only him that made me feel that way proved that I was right where I belonged. I'd never wanted a man's hands on me before.

The way I felt when I was with him overwhelmed me, even that first night. I'd been stunned, scared, and felt hopeful at the same time. I'd worried it was too good to be true, that no one could really be as amazing as Slider. Every day that we spent together, I saw more of that side of him -- the tender, caring side -- and I knew I was incredibly lucky.

"Tell me what you need, Vasha."

"Just you," I said.

He shook his head. "That's not what I mean and you know it."

I did. I knew exactly what he meant, but I was scared to ask for what I needed. What if it was wrong? I wasn't supposed to enjoy the spanking he'd given, was I? Women didn't really like being tied up, did they? There were things I didn't know, didn't understand. I'd never had female friends before, or any friends other than Anatoly, and I didn't know how to ask about these things. Slider would tell me whatever he thought I needed to hear.

"Vasha, talk to me."

I smiled a little. He was always doing that, reading me like a book. He could tell when I wanted to say something but was too afraid to voice my desires or fears. Would it always be like this? Was this what being married was supposed to be like? I knew my marriage in Russia would have been vastly different, more of a prison than anything else. I'd have been a possession and nothing more.

"I think some part of me is broken," I admitted. "I… I liked it when you spanked me in the shower. I liked being tied up our first time together. Normal people don't want those things, do they?"

He chuckled, then outright laughed. I squirmed under him, wanting to break free. He was laughing at me! I'd shared my fears and he… he… Everything in me stilled as he gripped my hands and held them over my head. He pinned me to the bed with his body, but it was his eyes that held me spellbound.

Harley Wylde   **Slider/ Ashes Duet**

"What you want, what you need, isn't wrong, *zolatka*. Millions of people enjoy those things, and even more. It doesn't make you broken."

"You've been with women who liked those things?" I asked, both needing and dreading his answer. I didn't like to think of him with other women.

He tipped his head to the side and stared down at me. "No, I've never tied a woman up before you, and I've never had one get hotter and wetter if I smacked her ass." He leaned closer and traced my nose with his. "But I loved doing those things to you, love hearing your cries of pleasure, watching you submit and give yourself to me."

I blinked and tried to clear the fog from my mind. "You want my submission?"

"Only in the bedroom. In here, you're mine to command. Out there," he said, nodding to the door, "I will only give you an order if it's to keep you safe."

I started to squirm under him again, my pussy throbbing with need and my nipples getting so hard they ached. Slider growled and pressed tighter against me. He reached for the headboard, and my eyes went wide when I felt the silken rope tightening around my wrists. I looked up and saw that at some point, he'd attached white rope to the headboard.

"You're going to be a good girl and hold still, aren't you?" he asked.

He shoved my shirt up over my breasts and tugged my bra until I was exposed to his hungry gaze. With a groan, he reached for my pants and began pulling them down until I was bare. Slider pushed my knees up and spread me wide before placing his mouth against my pussy. I whined and twisted as he lapped at me, his tongue flicking against my clit. Nothing had ever felt like this before!

- 106 -

"Going to make you scream, *kroshka*. Make you come so hard you see stars."

I panted as my orgasm started cresting. I could feel it, just out of reach, as he worked my pussy with his lips and tongue. The grip on my thighs tightened and he growled against me. It didn't take long before I felt my release leave me in a gush that I knew had to be soaking the bed. Slider didn't stop, didn't even slow down, just kept working me with his tongue until I was nearly in tears. It felt so amazing, but it was almost too much.

"This pussy is mine," he said. "*You're* mine."

"Yes! Yes, I'm yours. Only yours."

He rose over me, his beard wet from my release. He made quick work of unfastening his belt and pants, then shoved them down. It made my cheeks warm as he wiped his face clean, then sank into me. His cock filled me, made me feel complete. Slider took me hard, the possessive look in his eyes nearly enough to make me come again. It was as if he couldn't get close enough, deep enough. His hand gripped my hip as he pounded into me and I knew I'd wear the marks of his fingers for the next few days, but it only made me burn hotter for him. I wanted that! Wanted him to mark me so everyone would know I was his.

"Harder!" I begged.

He shifted so that he was on his knees, then held me tightly with both hands, lifting my ass as he drove into me. The headboard slammed against the wall with every stroke, but I was beyond caring. A tidal wave of pleasure swept over me.

"Yes! Don't stop!"

I came so hard, but one orgasm rolled into another, until I didn't think I could handle any more. Slider didn't slow, didn't stop. He took complete

Harley Wylde   **Slider/ Ashes Duet**

possession of me, and I loved every moment of it. When he came, it felt like he was filling me to the point of overflowing. He kept us joined, his body heavy as he straightened and lay on top of me. I struggled to breathe for a moment, but I didn't dare ask him to move. This moment was perfect, beyond anything I could have ever dreamed, and I didn't want it to end. His cock twitched inside me and he pumped in and out a few more times before going still.

"I'm getting too old to come this many times so close together," he muttered.

I bit my lip but it didn't stifle my giggle. He leaned up to glare at me, but it just made me laugh harder.

"You're not old!"

"I'm almost thirty. That's quite a bit older than you. The age difference doesn't bother you? One day I'll be going silver and gray while you're still young and sexy."

I reached up and ran my fingers through his hair. "You'll always be sexy. And no, the difference in our age doesn't bother me. Have you seen Vladimir, the man who bought me from Grigori?"

He nodded.

"How could you ever think I would find you lacking? That man was my future, until Surge gave me to you. And you're…" I ran my fingers over his beard and sighed. "You're perfect. I've never seen a man so ruggedly handsome, so strong and brave. I'm lucky to be yours, Upton, and I will never regret being with you."

He kissed me and I could taste myself on his lips. "No, *zolatka*. I'm the lucky one."

"Everyone will be lucky if the two of you will stop fucking!" someone yelled through the door. "This

- 108 -

place isn't exactly soundproofed. You're giving us blue balls out here."

Slider glared at the door, and I felt my cheeks heating again. I'd known they could hear us, but in the moment, I hadn't cared. Now… now was another matter. I hoped that Grigori and Vladimir were handled soon. I didn't want Slider to keep his distance from me, didn't want him self-conscious about claiming me. And I definitely wanted more orgasms!

"Not my fault you can't keep a woman," he yelled back to whoever was outside the door. "You're just jealous."

"Fucking right I am," the man yelled back.

Slider snorted. "Fucking Kraken. I can't wait to see what woman brings him to heel."

That was Kraken? Now I wouldn't be able to look him in the eye, or the others for that matter. They'd all heard us. I tugged at the rope that bound my wrists, but Slider just grinned when he saw me struggling.

"None of that. Keep it up and I'll have to punish you."

My breath froze in my lungs and my heart took off at a gallop. The thought of him spanking me again had me clenching his cock. He growled and withdrew from my body, only to flip me over and pull me onto my knees. His hand cracked against my ass several times, until I was begging him for more.

"Yes! Please!"

Crack! "You like that?"

I nodded so hard my neck hurt.

He fisted my hair and pulled my head back, the slight sting of pain turning me on more. His hand dug into my hip as he positioned me the way he wanted. The way he drove inside had me crying out in pleasure and pain. Slider didn't go slow, wasn't the least bit gentle, but he gave me everything I wanted and needed. It felt like hours that we stayed in the bedroom, only taking short breaks before he'd fuck me again. I was sore in the most delicious way by the time he led me from the bedroom and back into the bathroom. We showered and dressed before joining the others at the table. Someone had cooked hamburgers and fries, and the smell made my mouth water.

None of them would look at me, which made me self-conscious. I hated that I felt like we'd done something wrong. The day I'd spent with Slider in our room had been beautiful, but knowing they'd heard and apparently didn't approve seemed to cheapen it somehow.

"Knock it off," Slider said, growling at them. "You're upsetting her."

Lynch shared a look with Kraken. "Actually, we were just wondering if there were more like her."

I choked on my sip of water. What? I looked at Slider, hoping he knew what they meant. More like me?

"Ask Surge," Slider said. "He found her. I'm sure if you want a Russian bride, he can find you one too."

Lynch sighed and shook his head. "No, it's not the fact she's Russian, although I love hearing her speak. I just want a woman who's open to new things and loves everything I want to give her, in and out of the bedroom. You struck gold with this one. Not sure they made another one like her."

Slider pulled me closer to him and kissed my cheek. "No, they certainly didn't. She's one of a kind."

The rest of the day went much that way. It was pleasant watching movies with them while I cuddled against Slider, then retiring to our room where he

Harley Wylde   **Slider/ Ashes Duet**

made me scream his name several more times. I worried I'd be so sore I couldn't move the next day, but it would be more than worth it. We might be hiding from Grigori and the others, and my life was in danger, but I was going to make the best of the situation. At least I had Slider with me. Things could certainly be worse.

I should have known better than to even think those thoughts. Challenging the powers that be was never a good idea, and I was about to be reminded of that the hard way.

Chapter Seven

Slider

The thick walls of the bunker kept out all sounds from above. Even if someone were to walk directly over the ceiling, we'd never hear them. It was both a blessing and a curse. On the one hand, it meant no one could hear us either. On the other, we didn't know when someone was coming until they'd already arrived. If we had, then those Russian fuckers wouldn't have even made it down the damn stairs. I didn't know how they'd found Vasha, much less the bunker entrance, but they weren't taking her. If any survived, we could question them later.

I didn't know how they'd gotten past the Hades Abyss members aboveground, and I wasn't sure I wanted to know. While not all the members were near the bunker, I didn't doubt that Titan had left at least a few nearby in case they were needed. If everyone up there was dead, then we were pretty much without hope. Either way, I'd go down fighting and do my best to protect my woman. As long as Vasha survived, as long as she remained free from them, that's all that mattered. I'd die a happy man if I knew she was safe.

"Vasha, go to our room and lock the door," I said as I stared down the Russians entering the bunker.

She tightened her grip on my hand a moment before releasing me and running. I heard the door slam and the lock click into place. It let me breathe a little easier. I knew that door wouldn't hold them out for long, but it gave me a chance to focus on ripping them to shreds without worrying over her getting hurt.

"I don't recognize you boys. Grigori can't do his own dirty work?" I asked.

Harley Wylde   Slider/ Ashes Duet

One of them sneered at me. "He is too important to lower himself to the task of killing you."

"Too bad because I won't have a single problem ending his life, or yours for that matter. You signed your death sentence when you decided to come after my wife."

Another of them smiled, but it was a dark grin that promised pain. "You mean Vladimir's whore. She'll be spreading her legs for all of us soon enough. He promised we each get a taste, as often as we want. I can't wait to hear her screams as we tear her apart."

My gut clenched, but I forced myself not to react. I knew that's what they wanted. Letting my emotions rule me right now could be a deadly mistake. Vasha was counting on me to keep her safe, and that meant I needed to focus. Lynch gave me a subtle chin tilt and I knew that he was ready to go. Stone and Fangs also gave a signal, as did Kraken.

We didn't have the numbers I'd have liked, not with six Russians brandishing weapons, but none of us were exactly choir boys. I knew Rocket had faced worse odds when he'd gone on his killing spree to get vengeance for Violeta. He'd been running on pure rage, and while I had plenty of that flowing through my veins, I knew it wasn't going to help me right now.

"Just so we'll know, do you want to be shipped home to Russia when you die, or are you okay with being scattered in shallow graves throughout the state? Because we're fine with either," I said.

The one who seemed to be the leader stepped forward and aimed his gun at my head. Before he could pull the trigger, Kraken got off a shot. Thank fuck for the furniture scattered around and the various rooms that gave my brothers places to hide. Otherwise, we'd all be sitting ducks. The man's body lurched as the bullet slammed into his back. Two more shots were fired and he fell to the floor, his eyes already glazing over. His cohorts didn't seem to understand what they were seeing, almost as if they didn't believe we'd shot one of them, and moved slowly enough we were able to get the upper hand. Or so I'd thought.

It didn't stop the Russians from firing back. I could only hope that I didn't lose any brothers today, but I knew that anytime someone was shooting at us, the odds weren't necessarily in our favor. This life was hard, and often cruel. I knowingly took my life in my hands every time I left the clubhouse on business, but this was different. These fuckers wanted my wife.

Bullets slammed into walls, and I heard men shout from both sides. Lynch and Stone took out two more, but it wasn't enough. As I aimed for another, I heard what sounded like an army descending the stairs. It was apparent they no longer cared about the element of surprise. They had us cornered like rats. I heard Stone shout out in pain and knew he'd been hit. I only hoped it wasn't critical.

Grigori was easy to spot in the center of the group that was coming for us. Six more men flanked him, with a few more bringing up the rear, and I had to wonder if we had enough bullets to take them all down. Even if we did, were there more upstairs? I was thankful that Vasha was hiding and out of sight. The last thing I wanted was for her to be an easy target.

"You have something of mine," Grigori said. "Return Vasha and we'll leave without killing any more of your men."

Any more. Which meant that some of the men aboveground had lost their lives to protect my woman. I wouldn't let their sacrifice be for nothing. I didn't lower my gun and kept my finger over the trigger, just ready to end it all. Even if Grigori's men took me out right after, as long as that fucker was dead, that's what mattered the most. After everything he'd done to Vasha, she deserved the peace his death would bring.

"Vasha isn't yours. She's mine," I said. "My wife. I don't know how you found her, but she's not leaving with you."

He smiled, but it wasn't pleasant.

"Anatoly was most forthcoming before he died. When my men didn't find the little whore with the other Hades Abyss men, a little digging told us where this place was located."

His eyes were dark, a total absence of light. He reminded me of a shark, just waiting for the moment to strike. I wasn't going to give him the opportunity. Instead, I shot the fucker right between the eyes. The look of complete surprise on his face was rather comical. Had he thought I was holding a gun for decoration? Did he think the others who came before him had just died on their own? It was stupid on his part, and his arrogance had worked in my favor.

"Who's next?" I asked.

I'd barely uttered the words before the six Russians opened fire on all of us, with the others getting into better position. There were more coming down into the bunker, and I knew I had to keep myself between them and Vasha. No matter how many fell more took their place. I was starting to worry that Grigori had brought an entire army with him. When Vladimir descended the steps, a fire lit inside me. He was the reason Vasha had undergone those lessons. If he hadn't paid for her, demanded that she be trained a certain way, then she wouldn't have suffered and been degraded. Logically, I knew someone else would have just taken his place and purchased her, but right now he was the only one alive that I could blame.

"Leave him alive," I said before reloading and taking out more Russians.

No matter how many we killed, it seemed they were just replaced with another set of guards. Pain seared me as a bullet grazed me. I swung my gun in that direction, ready to fire back, but another Russian shot off three rounds in my direction, and I felt two of them slam into my body. I didn't falter, didn't go down. I couldn't. Vasha needed me, and I refused to let them anywhere near her. As long as I was breathing, I'd keep her safe.

When the gunfire stopped, only Vladimir was standing. He looked around, seemingly unconcerned, but I noticed the tremor in his hands as he shoved them into his pockets. Yeah, the fucker was scared and he damn well should be. A thought occurred to me. The things he'd done to Vasha had humiliated her. He deserved the same treatment before he breathed his last.

"Hey, Lynch. Is that brothel still near here? The one that flies under the radar."

He nodded. "Yep."

"They still have that special clientele you were telling me about?"

He grinned and I saw blood smeared across his teeth. It seemed he'd been injured as well. "I'll make the call."

My gaze landed on Stone, who was standing, but holding onto his side. Blood had spread across his shirt, but I was hoping it was just a flesh wound. The fact he was standing and coherent was a good sign.

"Stone, tie this fucker up. And make sure we get some money for his sorry ass. I'll put it into an account for Vasha. She can do whatever she likes with it. I'm sure someone will pay decent money to fuck him. Then get checked out by the doc."

While they got busy securing Vladimir's fate, I went to knock on the bedroom door, but I froze when I saw the bullet holes. My heart slammed against my ribs as I busted the lock on the door and shoved it open. Vasha lay across the bed, but she lifted her tear-streaked face and ran for me. I breathed a little easier, seeing that she was all right. Not so much as a scratch on her. I didn't know she'd managed to stay alive and uninjured. The level of the holes in the door would have put them at her chest level, unless she'd hidden on the floor during the gunfire.

"You're okay." I hugged her to me with my good arm. The other had a bullet through my bicep. The second bullet had been a through and through in the shoulder. All things considered, I'd been lucky.

"You're bleeding," she said, her eyes wide as she reached for my shoulder, then stopped. "You need a doctor, Slider."

"Right now, I need to get you out of here, and I need to see the damage up above. I don't know if anyone made it up there."

A sadness entered her eyes as she glanced up at the ceiling. I could almost see her starting to retreat into herself. I had no doubt she'd try to shoulder the blame for this one, but it wasn't on her. It was entirely on Grigori and Vladimir. No one else was to blame. Maybe if we hadn't come here, then the others upstairs would be alive, but I'd have lost Vasha. I had no doubt that being in this bunker had helped keep her alive.

"You're going to see some things you won't like," I cautioned as I led her from the room. Her gasp made my gut clench and I wished I could shield her

Harley Wylde   **Slider/ Ashes Duet**

from the carnage in the room. Blood covered most of the floor and sprayed across the walls.

Stone had Vladimir kneeling, hands cuffed behind his back. The Russian sneered at Vasha, but my sweet wife surprised me. She straightened her shoulders, held her head high, and walked right up to Vladimir. Vasha not only spat in his face, but she rattled off a bunch of Russian that I only caught bits and pieces of, enough to know that she'd cursed him to rot in hell, among other things.

Stone dragged Vladimir up the stairs ahead of us, and I held onto Vasha as I went to check on the others. Titan was bleeding, but alive, as were the other officers. A few members I hadn't known well were dead, and I knew every Hades Abyss member, regardless of their location, would mourn their loss. Philly limped toward us, a bullet through his thigh and another above his hip. He was almost as pale as Vasha and sweat coated his face.

"I worried they'd kill her if they made it downstairs, but we couldn't stop them all. It's our fault they even saw the bunker entrance. One of the men they killed gave it away unintentionally."

I looked around and noticed a lot of dead men in suits and knew they'd come with the Russians we'd taken out downstairs. I gave Philly a nod of appreciation. Even if one of our own had given away her location, my wife was still safe, and that's what mattered. I led Vasha outside. It was daylight and the sun beat down on us. Vasha hid her face against me, and I wasn't sure if it was from the brightness of the day, or because of the bodies on the ground. Despite everything Grigori had done to her, she'd probably not been around many dead men. I hoped she never had to see a sight like this ever again, but I knew with my way of life there was a good chance she'd be in danger again in the future.

I saw two men patching up those who were still breathing and Vasha insisted I go over. It seemed two of the newer members had medical training. After a brief introduction to Smoke and Poison, I let them clean my wounds and stitch me up. Thankfully, the bullets weren't still in my body. Vasha remained at my side the entire time, holding my hand. She was handling everything better than I'd thought she would, which was a little concerning. I could see the tension in her body, and feel the tremor in her hand. But she kept quiet and didn't shed so much as a single tear.

"All done," said Smoke as he cut the thread on the last of my stitches. "Try not to get them wet."

"I'll take care of him," Vasha said.

Smoke winked at her and Poison tipped his head in the direction of their clubhouse. "Head that way. Someone will find you a place to rest. I'll have a Prospect gather your things from down below and deliver them shortly."

Amazingly enough, the SUV didn't have a mark on it. I'd expected bullet holes, scratches, maybe a dent. It was a little eerie that the vehicle was just as pristine as when I'd parked it. I helped Vasha into the passenger's seat before getting behind the wheel. Pulling onto the road that would take us back to the front, I glanced in her direction a few times. Most women would have fallen apart by now. Cried. Screamed. Something. Anything. Not Vasha. She seemed cool and collected. Or she would to someone who didn't know her.

"*Zolatka*, it's okay. You don't have to be brave and strong."

Her gaze met mine and I saw the sheen of tears. "Those men. They lost their lives because of me. If I had never come here, they would be alive and you wouldn't have been shot."

I pulled to the side of the road and put the SUV into park, then turned to face her. She hastily wiped away a tear, as if she were ashamed for crying. I'd never met anyone like her before, and I knew I never would again. Vasha was one of a kind, and she was all mine. Yes, lives had been lost today, but she was alive and would have a happy, safe life if I had any say in the matter.

"They knew what they were doing when they offered us sanctuary. None of those men went into this blindly. Vasha, what happened here wasn't your fault. If you want to blame someone, then lay it at the feet of Grigori and Vladimir. There was no need for them to travel all this way to come get you. I'd imagine there are plenty of women in Russia they could have taken to replace you, but they didn't. I'm glad no one else will suffer at their hands, but even more than that, I'm happy you're here." I reached for her, running my fingers through her hair. "You're mine, *kroshka*. And I'm never letting you go. I love you, Vasha."

"I love you too," she said softly.

"No more, all right? You can't blame yourself for this. I won't let you." I let my fingers graze her chin. "It's my job to take care of you. You're my wife, my everything. I'd have gladly traded my life today for yours if it came down to that."

"No!" Fire flashed in her eyes. "Promise me you'll never do that."

"Can't. I will always put myself between you and danger. That's what love is, Vasha. It means being willing to sacrifice yourself for the person who means the entire world to you."

"I'd never forgive myself if I caused your death."

I leaned closer and brushed my lips against hers, trying not to let her see how much it hurt me. I'd need some drugs soon. Or a bottle of vodka.

"Neither of us is dying anytime soon, Vasha. Let's get to the clubhouse and find out where we're staying for today. I'll probably need to rest tonight before we go home."

She gave a slight nod and settled back into her seat. I knew this wasn't over, that I'd have to convince her again that none of this was her fault. I could see in her eyes that the deaths of those men weighed heavily on her. Then again, she wouldn't be my sweet Vasha if she didn't feel things deeply. She had a big heart, and a gentle soul. I knew I was damn lucky to be able to call her mine.

At the clubhouse, we met with Patriot and he showed us to our lodgings for the night. As an old military property, there were quite a few duplexes and even some larger homes that had probably been occupied by officers at some point. The duplex we would be using for the night was clean, and we'd been assured the other half was empty. The unit was apparently only used for guests. Even though I'd brought Fangs and Cotton with me, they were being housed elsewhere. I was thankful both were still standing, even though Fangs had also been shot.

A Prospect showed a short while later with our belongings and Vasha put them away while I lay in bed. One look at me and she'd asked if we could stay a few days. I could only imagine how rough I looked right now. She'd forced a few painkillers into me, even though I'd wanted to wait until I knew she was settled for the day. It seemed my wife could be stubborn when she needed to be, which only made me smile. After she'd put everything away, she curled against me on the bed, her head on my uninjured shoulder and her hand over my heart.

"We should rest," she said.

I knew she mostly meant I should rest, and I knew she was right. At the same time, I didn't think I could sleep anytime soon. I could have lost her today. We'd been together such a short time, and already she'd slipped through my fingers once and almost been taken today. The thought of having to live without her made my chest ache. Things were still new between us, but sometimes a man just knew when he'd found the woman meant for him, and Vasha was definitely it for me.

I toyed with the small circle in my pocket, then pulled it out. Without a word, I slid the ring onto her finger. I'd bought it while she recovered after she'd run from me. It had never seemed like the right moment to give it to her, but right now, I needed her to know what she meant to me. I could say the words all day, but I knew that words were empty without actions. She deserved the sun, moon, and all the stars. Instead, she'd have to settle for a platinum band with a few small diamonds across the top. It wasn't overly fancy, but it had cost me a chunk of change.

"You got me a ring?" she asked.

"My wife should have a wedding ring. Should have given it to you sooner. Been carrying it around for a while."

"I don't need jewelry, Slider. All I need is you."

I smiled and rubbed my beard against the top of her head. She really was the sweetest woman, and always seemed to know what to say. Well, other than that awkward moment she'd informed me we were married. That had infuriated me, but not for the reasons she'd believed. I was glad that she was back in my arms, that I'd found her and convinced her to stay with me. I'd nearly let her get away, and I knew now that I'd have spent the rest of my life looking for her. Just one taste and she'd gotten under my skin, and wormed her way into my heart shortly after that.

"We'll go home in a day or two. Need to make sure Fangs and Cotton are okay to ride their bikes, and my shoulder might need a good two days before I'm ready to drive all the way home. The other two wounds aren't that bad. Lived through worse."

She snuggled closer. "I don't care as long as we're together. They said we could stay as long as we needed."

I hoped she still felt that way twenty years from now. I knew that I'd never grow tired of her, always want her with me. What I didn't know was whether or not this life would get to be too much for her. It wasn't the first time I'd been shot, and I doubted it would be the last. Could she handle being the wife of someone like me? I took risks, and sometime in the future the price could be my life. The last thing I wanted to do was leave her, but I owed my allegiance to my club. Whatever Spider asked of me, I'd do without hesitation.

"You aren't sleeping," she said, lifting her head to glare at me.

"Sorry, *kroshka*. Too much on my mind I guess, and my adrenaline is still pumping. Might take me a while to unwind."

She rubbed her hand up and down my abdomen, each slide of her palm taking her closer to my belt. I might be banged up, but my cock was working just fine. Her light touch was enough to make me hard as granite. I didn't know what she was up to, but it she wasn't careful, I'd bend her over and fuck her good and proper. It would be worth whatever pain it caused me.

Vasha shifted to her knees, then worked her way between my thighs. I watched her, curious just what she was up to. I had an idea, but surely I was mistaken. She wouldn't really... The clink of my belt was loud in the otherwise quiet room as she unfastened it, then reached for the button and zipper on my jeans. My dick practically jumped out of my pants, eager to greet her. When she wrapped her slender fingers around my shaft, I couldn't contain my groan.

"Don't move," she said, holding my gaze as she leaned down and lapped at the head of my cock.

My hips jerked and it took every bit of control I had to lie still. I'd had my dick sucked plenty of times, but I'd never been this turned on by it. She lapped at the head some more, licking up the pre-cum already beading there, before sliding her lips down my shaft. I didn't think she could take me, but she let go and placed her hand on my hip. Bobbing her head, she worked my cock into her mouth, then I hit the back of her throat and sucked in a breath.

My eyes nearly rolled into the back of my head when she kept going, taking all of me, then swallowing. *Holy shit!* My wife could give porn star worthy blowjobs! She worked me, sucking and licking, wrapping her tongue around my shaft on the downstroke. I knew I wouldn't last much longer. I placed my hand on her head, holding her still as I thrust up into her mouth. It only took another few seconds before I was coming, filling her mouth. Vasha swallowed it all. When she pulled off, her lips were swollen and she licked off the rest of my cum.

So. Fucking. Hot.

"Come here," I said.

She shook her head.

I arched an eyebrow and stared at her. "Vasha."

"No, Upton. I didn't do that so you'd reciprocate. I only hoped it might help you relax enough to fall asleep."

I wanted to argue with her, but she tilted her chin at a stubborn angle and I knew it wasn't a fight I'd easily win. She was trying to take care of me, so I might as well let her. This time. Once the holes in my body were healing, I'd make sure she screamed my name all night long.

"Just come lie next to me." I glanced down at my open pants. "Maybe after I get my boots and jeans off."

She smiled a little as she helped me get more comfortable. I left my underwear on so that maybe I wouldn't be quite so tempted to slip inside my hot wife. Vasha took a hot shower, changed into her pajamas, then joined me in bed. It wasn't long before I felt sleep pulling me under. For the first time I could remember, I felt content. Happy. My woman was safe, and now I could really focus on what I wanted to do... knock her up!

Chapter Eight

Vasha

I love him. I love him. I love him. I wondered if I said it enough, even internally, if it would make me want to kill him just a little less. He'd only remained at the Mississippi chapter for three days before declaring himself well enough to travel. I'd watched him wince and shift around during the drive home, but he'd refused to stop along the way. Even Fangs and Cotton hadn't been able to talk him into it.

We'd been home for nearly a week, and he'd ripped out his stitches the first day home. Instead of having someone put more in, he'd used glue from his toolbox to seal the wounds. Glue! What kind of man was I married to? He was crazy. Absolutely bonkers. Despite the insanity of his actions, I had to admit he was still tempting. Far too tempting. All I had to do was know he was in the same room and I got wet, and then he took full advantage.

I swatted his hand as he tried to slip it under my skirt. I'd tried to dress nice for the party being thrown in Violeta's honor, or rather in honor of baby Zoe. It seemed another club was coming to visit as well, the Dixie Reapers, and I wanted to make a good impression. So far, Slider was only interested in messing up all my hard work. His arm curled around my waist as he hauled me back against him. I could feel the hard ridge of his cock as he ground against my ass.

"Upton, we're going to be late!"

"No one will notice," he said, rubbing his beard against my neck. He knew that made my knees weak! Damn him!

Before I even thought about protesting again, he'd pulled up my skirt, bent me over the armchair and I heard his zipper slide down. He nudged my feet apart and that was the only warning I got before he was balls-deep inside me. I moaned and bit my lip, my eyes sliding shut at how amazing he felt.

"You feel so fucking good." He groaned as he slammed into me again and again. Every thrust had me grabbing tighter to the chair so I didn't topple over. He slid his hand down my back. "My beautiful, sexy wife. So perfect."

I would argue against the perfect part, and the rest for that matter, but I loved that he saw me that way. There were days I wondered what I'd ever done to deserve someone like him. He took such good care of me, and while a lot of women might not like his dominant attitude, I thrived on it. After being bossed around all my life, I should have rebelled, but when Slider gave me an order, especially in the bedroom, it was different. I obeyed because I wanted to, because I loved him.

"Please, Upton."

"Please what?" he asked, his voice a near growl.

"Need to come."

He slipped his hand down my belly and stroked my clit. I cried out as sparks danced across my vision. I came, squeezing his cock so hard. It only seemed to spur him on, and he took me faster and harder. He was never happy with me only having one orgasm and he refused to come until I'd had several. The third time nearly stole the breath from my lungs and I felt the warmth of his cum filling me up.

His breathing was ragged as he leaned over me, his chest pressing to my back. He kissed the top of my head, but didn't move otherwise. I could feel his heart pounding, and could feel mine about to beat right out of my chest. He slid from my body, groaning as he straightened. Slider helped me up and I felt our mingled release running down my leg. I gave him a mock glare, which only made him chuckle, as I hurried to the bedroom to clean up.

A glance in the bathroom mirror made me wince. I was wrinkled beyond redemption, my hair was no longer neat and orderly. He'd made a mess of more than my pussy. Since my outfit, and hairdo, couldn't be salvaged, I stripped off my clothes and started the shower. Now we were *really* going to be late. It bothered me since everyone had been so nice to me. It felt disrespectful. Slider might not care, but I was still new here, still trying to fit in. The last thing I wanted was for people to think I was rude, or that I didn't care about spending time with them.

I quickly washed, but was careful not to wet my hair. When I got out, he was leaning against the counter, but the heated look in his eyes had me holding up a hand.

"No, Upton. Don't even think it."

"Not my fault my woman makes me hard even right after I've come. Maybe we should just stay in."

I gnashed my teeth together. "They're your friends and family. They may not care if you're late, but I'm new here. I don't know everyone that well and I need to make a good impression. I… I want them to like me."

His gaze softened and he came closer. He wrapped my towel around me, then held me against his body. "Vasha, they already like you. The fact you're mine is enough to make you part of the family. You aren't alone, *kroshka*. You never have to be alone ever again."

- 128 -

I nodded and pressed my face to his chest, breathing in his scent.

"Finish whatever you need to do in here. I'll lay some clothes out for you," he said, releasing me and taking a step back. "If I stay in here, I'll just end up taking you again."

He winked as he left the room. I ran a brush through my hair and tried to tame it again. In the end, I had to pull it up and pin it in place. I rubbed scented lotion into my skin before heading into the bedroom. A pretty pink dress lay across the foot of the bed with a pair of silver heels on the floor. I hadn't seen the dress or the shoes before and glanced at Slider. The grin he wore told me that maybe he'd planned to mess me up all along, just so he could give these to me.

"They're beautiful."

"Not as beautiful as you."

My cheeks warmed. I wondered if he would always have the ability to make me blush, or if I'd grow used to his compliments over time. I changed into the new outfit, then slipped my property cut over it. We'd only been home a day when he'd given it to me. I was honored to wear it, loving that it said *Property of Slider* so everyone would know we were together.

He led me out of the house and down to a small SUV he'd purchased the previous day. Even though it was a few years old and he'd bought it used, it still had that new car smell. He'd promised to teach me to drive if I wanted to learn, but the thought of being in control of something so powerful scared me. Maybe one day I'd change my mind, but for now, I'd stick with being a passenger.

At the clubhouse, bikes were double-parked across the front, and more were around the side, as well as a few other vehicles. My hands clenched and unclenched as my stomach flipped and twisted. Slider put his hand at the small of my back and propelled me toward the steps. I looked up at him, but he just smiled down at me, practically shoving me inside the door.

I saw Violeta and Luciana at a table decorated with pink balloons and lavender ribbons. Another woman was with them, one who looked similar enough I knew they had to be related. I saw other women wearing property cuts from the other club, but I was too nervous to go speak to anyone. Slider might think I had nothing to worry about, but I wanted them to like me. I wanted to be included. Never having had friends, except Anatoly, I wasn't sure how to approach them.

Turned out, I didn't have to. Luciana came to me, removed my hand from Slider's, and dragged me over to the table.

"Vasha, you already know Violeta, but you haven't met our sister, Sophia. She's married to Saint from the Dixie Reapers."

As Sophia stood, my eyes went wide as I saw her huge pregnant belly. Whatever was in the water around here, I hoped they would share. I wanted that! I wanted a baby with Slider so much, but I was scared it would never happen. We'd been together not quite three weeks, and I knew it could take time, but... I froze. My lungs felt like they stopped working while my heart rate doubled. Three weeks.

"What's the date?" I asked, almost too scared to believe it might be true.

Luciana unlocked her phone and showed me the screen. Four days late. I pressed a hand to my belly, but what if I was wrong? There were plenty of reasons to skip a period. It didn't necessarily mean that Slider had succeeded in getting me pregnant already. I lifted my gaze to take in the curious looks from Luciana, Violeta, and Sophia.

"Do you think you might be pregnant?" Luciana asked.

"Maybe? It's probably too soon to know for certain. I'm late, but it's happened before."

Violeta smiled. "Were you having hot, crazy sex all the time when you missed before?"

My cheeks burned hotter than ever before. "No. Slider was my first."

A wistful looked crossed all three of their faces, then sadness lurked in their eyes for a moment. Luciana shook it off first. I wondered what it all meant, but I wasn't brave enough to ask. If they ever wanted to share, they'd do it when they were ready. I wasn't one to pry. Slider had mentioned that they would understand what I'd been through, but he hadn't wanted to give me details. Had these women been held captive and groomed for rich husbands? Had they been forced to learn how to please a man they despised?

"Get Isabella," Sophia said.

Luciana gave a curt nod and strode off. When returned a moment later with a striking woman at her side. Her cut said *Property of Torch*. I hadn't met him yet, but since she'd arrived with the other club, I wasn't certain I'd ever get the chance. I didn't know how long they were staying, or they visited all that often.

"Luciana says you might be pregnant," Isabella said. "Since my husband has super sperm and keeps getting me pregnant --"

Sophia gasped. "Again? You're pregnant again?"

Isabella sighed and nodded. "I love my kids, but I may ask Torch to get fixed after this one. He actually tried once, but it failed. Maybe I can convince the doctor to give me a hysterectomy. All I know is I can't handle more than four kids. Anyway, I keep pregnancy tests on hand just in case. I have one left over and it happens to still be in my bag, if you'd like to use it. Still new in the package."

I looked at the women surrounding me and gave Isabella a hesitant nod. "But where..."

"There's a bathroom down the hall," Luciana said. "The Prospects scrubbed the hell out of it earlier so it's clean. For now."

Isabella looped her arm through mine, then picked up a bag from under the table, one I hadn't even noticed, and she led me down the hall to the back of the clubhouse. She pushed open the bathroom door, pulled the box from her purse, and gave it to me.

"I'll stand guard. Just pee on the stick, then wait three minutes. It's digital so it will tell you *Pregnant* or *Not Pregnant*."

I took the package from her and went into the bathroom, shutting and locking the door. I read the instructions, just in case she'd left anything out, then peed on the stick like she'd said. I put the cap back on it, and set it on the edge of the sink. As I waited, I paced, glancing at the stick every now and then. When the display had text on it, I stopped and stared. My heart was hammering, my palms were damp, and I was more scared than I'd ever been. I wanted it to say I was pregnant. So badly. I knew if I wasn't, I'd feel like I'd failed. It was ridiculous, but I couldn't help it.

Walking closer, I stared, not daring to believe what I saw. *Pregnant.* I gave a soft sob and pressed my hand to my mouth. With trembling fingers, I picked up the stick and hurried to the bathroom door. I peered out into the hall at Isabella and nodded. A wide smile broke across her face.

"Congratulations!"

I looked at it again, but it still said *Pregnant*. I hadn't imagined it.

"Better go tell the daddy," she said, giving me a nudge.

I felt like I was floating on air as I went back to the main room and scanned the crowd for Slider. I found him off to the side, talking with Fangs and two men I didn't know. Probably from the other club. I approached, biting my lip to keep from smiling so much. When I reached his side, I waited for him to notice me.

"Everything all right?" Fangs asked. "You look about ready to burst."

Slider focused on me, a frown marring his brow. "You okay, *zolatka*?"

I nodded and held up the stick. He stared, his eyes going wide, then he let out a loud *whoop* before scooping me into his arms and spinning around.

"We're gonna have a baby!" he yelled.

Cheers erupted around us and I clung to him, happier than I'd ever thought possible. The other women in the room came over and introduced themselves, before leading me away from Slider. It was overwhelming, but I listened as they chatted about each of their pregnancies, telling me the horror stories along with the good parts. Was this what it meant to have friends? I had to admit, I liked it. A lot.

"Hey, Ridley, remember that time Farrah tried to light Coyote on fire?" Darian asked, smirking.

"Shut up," Ridley muttered. "You're going to scare her. I admit my daughter is a hellion."

"Just one of them?" Delphine snorted. "Your kids are a menace."

Ridley shrugged, but I noticed she didn't deny it.

"Y'all are going to scare Vasha." Isabella gave them all a glare. "Remember what Torch said before we left?"

"Be on my best behavior," Ridley said with a sigh. "Yeah, yeah. I got it."

"Obviously not," said Isabella.

"How many women are at the Dixie Reapers compound?" I asked. Here it was just me, Luciana, and Violeta. But there were easily ten women present that didn't belong to Hades Abyss.

"There are thirteen old ladies at the Dixie Reapers," Isabella said. "And that number grows every day. Pretty soon, there won't be a single bachelor left. Well, until more Prospects patch in. Some of them are pretty young."

Thirteen? I couldn't even imagine. It must have been nice to have so many other women to confide in, to call your friend or family. I wondered if the other Hades Abyss members would eventually settle down. From what I'd seen during my first trip to the clubhouse, they didn't appear to be in any hurry. Couldn't blame them. It seemed there were plenty of women just begging for their attention and not demanding a commitment from them.

"You get tired of all the testosterone around here, you get Slider to bring you for a visit," Isabella said. "You're welcome in our town anytime."

"Saint and Sophia come up as often as they can," Ridley said. "So it won't always just be you, Luciana, and Violeta."

"I don't want to seem ungrateful. I barely know the others, but I want to. I'm just not..." I bit my lip. "I don't think I'm good at making friends. Never had a chance to have one before. Anatoly was my guard, and while I did consider him a friend, it wasn't the same."

I felt an arm go around my waist, and then Slider's scent teased my nose. His beard scraped my neck as he pressed a kiss there. The ladies gave me a knowing look and wandered off.

"You have made me so fucking happy, Vasha. Love you, *zolatka*."

"Love you too, and I'm every bit as happy, even if I am a little scared. I didn't exactly have a role model for how to be a mom."

He snorted. "Like I have any fucking clue how to be a dad, but you know what? We'll figure it out together. And there is plenty of family here to help us along the way. Spider and Rocket are both naturals when it comes to kids. If we start fucking up too bad, they'll step in and tell us."

I turned to face him, then went up on tiptoe to kiss him. It was just a soft brush of my lips against his, but it was enough for now. I had no doubt that once we were home, he would want to celebrate my news. Even now, I could feel the hard bulge pressing against me.

"Go visit with your new friends," he said. "We're leaving in an hour, then you're all mine for the rest of the night."

I smiled and kissed him again before going off to sit with the other ladies. When Anatoly had snuck me out of Grigori's home and out of Russia, I'd hoped that my life here would be happy. I'd just never dreamed it would be this perfect. Slider was everything I wanted or needed in a man, and I couldn't wait to spend the rest of my life with him.

Epilogue

Slider
Six Months Later

I stared at the screen as the ultrasound tech moved the wand over Vasha's belly. We'd tried before to see our kid, but the little fucker hadn't cooperated. Now though... A smile spread across my face. Yep, no doubt about it. We were having a boy. I only half listened as the tech talked and measured, asking Vasha questions. I was too focused, staring at my son. My throat grew tight with emotion. No way my kid would ever grow up unloved, not the way Vasha and I had. I'd make sure he knew every day how much he was wanted.

"Luka," I said. "We should call him Luka. It's a good Russian name, in honor of his beautiful Russian mother."

She gave me a smile and squeezed my hand. "And I was thinking we'd call him Aten to honor your Egyptian heritage."

I just stared at her. It wasn't like I had any idea what the rest of me was made up of. I'd only known about my mother because of the bit of digging Surge had done years ago. As much as I didn't want to give my birth parents a second thought, I knew that one day our kids would ask about their grandparents. Maybe she had a point.

"Luka Aten?" I suggested.

"I like it," she said. "Luka Aten St. Clair. It has a nice ring to it."

"Well, congratulations, Mom and Dad. I'll print off some pictures of your baby, then they'll schedule your next appointment on your way out. Do you have any questions?" the tech asked.

I'd forgotten she was even there. I shook my head and Vasha did the same. We'd already read every baby book we could find. Neither of us wanted to fuck up our kid. The closer her due date got, the more nervous I became. Rocket had said that when the time came, everything would just click inside me and I'd know exactly what to do and how to act. I wasn't sure I believed him, but I hoped he was right.

I helped Vasha back into her clothes and paid up front while she set her next appointment. When we stepped out onto the sidewalk, I admired the way the sun glinted off her silvery white hair. We'd been together a little over six months, nearly seven, and every day I found her more beautiful than the day before, and loved her even more. It had taken me three months, but I'd finally told Surge thank you for putting her in my bed that first night. Best thing that had ever happened to me.

"Want ice cream?" I asked. It had become our ritual after each appointment.

She shook her head and looked a little green. "I think those days are behind me until this baby arrives. I had a little from the freezer last night and it came right back up."

I rubbed her back and pressed a kiss to her cheek. She'd had a rough go of it. The morning sickness had hit during her second month and hadn't let up even a little. Although, the foods and smells that triggered it seemed to change all the fucking time. Made it hard to buy food, that was for damn sure. Not that I was complaining. I'd do anything for her, even run two towns over at three in the morning because she was craving a particular dish from a diner over there. Whatever it took, I wanted her to be happy, and to know how much I loved her. I could tell her all day every day, but it didn't matter unless I *showed* her.

I helped her into the SUV and drove us back to the compound. I'd left Fox and Cotton painting the nursery. I'd heard the fumes would be bad for Vasha, so they'd started early this morning when we'd left the house. I'd told them to open the nursery window and shut the door to the hall, and I hoped they'd remembered. By the time we got home, my stomach was growling, but my sweet Vasha was asleep with her head resting against the window. As carefully as I could, I pulled her from the vehicle and carried her inside.

She roused outside the nursery and looked at the closed door in confusion.

"You said you wanted the room green since we didn't know if we'd ever discover the gender. Fox and Cotton painted it earlier. The door needs to stay shut probably another day for the smell to die down. I'll let you see it after I get the furniture together."

She snuggled closer. "You're going to be an amazing dad."

Whether or not I was, I didn't have a doubt she'd be an incredible mom. She'd changed her diet, her sleep pattern... anything the books suggested would be better for the baby, she'd taken it all to heart and had done her best to care for our kid before he even got here.

I laid Vasha on the bed, slipped her shoes off her feet, then stretched out next to her. Placing my hand over her belly, I smiled as our kid pushed against me. I didn't know if he hated sharing his mom with me, or if he just wanted to say hi. I couldn't wait to meet him! Although, I hoped he stayed tucked safely inside Vasha until he was good and ready to come out. As sick as she'd been, I sometimes worried she wouldn't carry to term, even though the doctor didn't seem concerned.

"Rest, *zolatka*."

"Thought you'd want to celebrate the fact we're having a boy. Don't all men wish for sons?"

I could hear the exhaustion in her voice. Running my fingers through her hair, I massaged her temples.

"Yes, I'm happy we're having a boy, but I'd have been just as thrilled over a little girl who looks like her mom. I love you, Vasha, and our kid. All that matters is that you're both healthy and happy. We'll have some fun when you're up to it. Right now, just sleep. I'll stay right here."

"Promise?" she murmured, nearly asleep again already.

"Promise, *kroshka*."

I kissed her forehead, the tip of her nose, then her lips. She smiled and burrowed against me. Holding my wife was one of my favorite pastimes, and I knew I'd never grow tired of it. Or of Vasha. Our lives would never be perfect, but I knew they would be amazing, just because we had each other. And now we'd have another person, one we created together, and I couldn't imagine anything better than that.

I watched her sleep, admiring the delicate arch of her brows, the fullness of her lips, and her overall beauty. It wasn't just her looks, though. My Vasha was gorgeous because she had a good heart. Even after all the evil she'd seen, she was still the sweetest, gentlest woman I'd ever known.

And she was mine. For always.

Ashes (Devil's Boneyard MC 7)

Harley Wylde

Nikki -- Being tortured and watching the father of my child die has scarred me. There are deep wounds etched into my soul that no one can possibly understand. They think I loved him, that I'm mourning, but I'm not. The horror of that day lurks in the shadows of my mind, and I can't seem to break free. Not until Ashes drags me to my first ultrasound and I see my son for the first time. I owe it to him to do better, but it's too late. I've lost my job, and I'm losing my apartment. I should have known Ashes would swoop in like a knight on his shining Harley to save the day.

Ashes -- It's my fault that Nikki lost Bane, that their kid will grow up without a dad. My cousin is responsible for what happened to them, and I can't undo that pain. So instead, I take care of Nikki the best I can while trying to maintain some distance between us. I've loved her for years, but I can never tell her. Renegade, the Road Captain for my club and her brother, would kill me if he knew that Nikki plagues my thoughts day and night. I never counted on taking her home with me, or getting caught in the shower with her. But our happily-ever-after wasn't quite in reach. When a series of events nearly tears us apart, I vow that I'll do whatever it takes to get back to her. It never occurred to me that *she'd* be the one to save *me*.

Prologue

Ashes
One Year Ago

The clubhouse was packed, and all my single brothers and the Prospects were cutting up and having a good time, except for the poor jackass at the gate and the two pouring drinks. Still, it was noisy as fuck in here, with pussy available everywhere I looked. Only one problem. None of them were the one woman I wanted and couldn't have.

I'd done my best to make things look like business as usual, but since a certain spitfire had turned eighteen, I'd barely noticed the club whores. They weren't *her*.

Not that I ever had a shot. Her brother would hand my ass to me, if he didn't kill me outright for daring to touch his baby sister. It was better if I just kept things friendly between us -- but not *that* friendly. Only one person knew that I was full of shit and not partaking of the women displaying themselves shamelessly. Jin and I had an understanding. There were certain needs he had, and I helped when he'd pick out a woman each night.

My brothers thought I was the one walking out with the women, and technically I was. I just didn't fuck them. Jin sweet-talked them, then I led them around back out into the darkness. Much like the little blonde he was sending over to me right now. Her big blue eyes lacked the innocence I craved these days. She knew the score and wouldn't mind hopping from one dick to another. The club whores had been fun for a while, but I was getting too damn old for that shit.

"I heard you're going to help me have a good time," she said, her voice raspy like she smoked a pack a day.

"You got it, sweet thing. Let's head outside."

I winked at her, then led her through the door. More than one of my brothers catcalled as we went past, probably thinking I was about to score, but it couldn't be further from the truth. Not that I'd been celibate, but the women in my life had been few and far between since I'd fallen ass over teakettle for the one woman I could never have. In the past two years, I'd only been on dates with about five women. Nothing serious, but I'd hang onto them for a few months, making sure they knew up front there wouldn't be a ring at the end of it, and there was never any sex. I only went hunting for a woman when the loneliness got to be too much to bear. If I'd thought there was ever a chance that Nik would be mine, then it would be different.

When we entered the shadows behind the clubhouse, I drew her to a halt and waited for Jin to catch up. "He tell you what to expect?" I asked.

"Yeah. He's going to fuck me while you pin me down." She smiled widely. "But I'm open to taking on the both of you, if that's what you want."

"Strip," I commanded.

She quickly complied, just tossing her clothes and shoes to the side. I waved a hand at the ground and she immediately fell to her knees, reaching for my pants. Brushing her off, I stepped away and shook my head. I wasn't here for that. No way I was letting this one near my dick. Who knew what she might be carrying? If Jin wanted to take the risk, that was on him.

"Lie down on your back. Jin will be here in a moment."

She licked her lips in what was probably supposed to be a seductive way, but she was too drunk to pull it off. "You going to get me ready?"

"Something like that."

She giggled and stretched out on her back on the grass. I knelt at her head and pulled her arms up by my thighs, holding her wrists tightly. The woman arched her back, thrusting her breasts up. If she thought she was tempting me, she was wrong.

I heard footsteps, then saw Jin coming toward us. He paused and admired the view. I was glad he liked it since she wasn't doing a damn thing for me.

"Bend your knees and spread your legs," I said. "Let him see what he's getting."

Her breath caught and she did as I said, a flush climbing up her chest and neck. Wasn't sure if it was the alcohol or she was that turned on. Jin started moving toward us again, unfastening his belt and pants. He dropped to his knees between her legs, then pulled a condom from his pocket.

"I'm on the pill," she said, her eyes wide.

Oh, yeah. Definitely not putting my cock near this one. I knew her game, and I was sure Jin did too. Wouldn't be the first time some slut tried to trap one of us. Hell, a few years back, some whore had decided to poke holes in the condoms sitting in the community bowl at the clubhouse. Scratch had about gone through the roof over that one. Cleaned house, but the bitches who came around were all the same. After one thing only -- ol' lady status.

Jin gave a humorless laugh. "Yeah, like I'm getting trapped by some club slut. You want my dick, I'm wrapping it first."

Her eyes narrowed as Jin put on the condom, then without giving her any warning, he gripped her ass and thrust deep. Her body jolted with every slam of his hips while she whimpered and moaned. The slut was fucking acting, but I knew Jin didn't care. Her getting off wasn't his priority. As long as he came, he didn't care about anything else.

"Tighter," she said. "Hold me tighter."

I shifted so I could put both her wrists in one hand, then gripped her throat with my other. She sighed and bit her lip. Jin fucked her harder, grunting as he came. When he pulled out, he removed the condom and tied it off before wrapping it in the foil package and shoving it into his pocket. I knew he wouldn't chance leaving it where she could get to it.

"Your turn," she said, smiling up at me.

"No, thanks. Not my type."

I released her and stood up. Jin gave me a nod and I left, but not before I heard him command her to turn over, then the sound of his belt hitting her flesh. He definitely had a type, and they all kept coming back for more. Tonight's choice was new, but I had no doubt I'd see her again. She seemed like the kind of woman to get off on being used.

When I rounded the clubhouse, I ran into some hang-around who apparently thought he was someone. I paused in the shadows and listened as he mouthed off to a club whore.

"Yeah, I'll be patching in before you know it. These guys need my skills," the punk said.

The woman ran her hand up and down his chest. "And what kind of skills are those?"

"Ran my own meth lab for a while, until the heat got to be too much. I'm the best around these parts when it comes to cutting drugs and selling shit." He looked down her barely there top. "These assholes don't know shit about the business."

Oh, really? Not that we were into meth, but we had the pot sales locked down pretty tight. And we never sold to kids. There were some gangbangers around town who did that shit, and we got it off the streets as fast as we could. I had to wonder if this little asshole was one of the ones killing people with his fucked-up drugs. About six months back, there had been an epidemic of drug overdoses. Mostly meth.

"You're smarter than them, huh?" she asked.

"Oh, yeah. Won't be long before I'm running this place. That old man will be stepping down or I'll force him down."

Now *that* I'd fucking pay to see. Cinder would flatten this dickhead without breaking a sweat. Enough was enough.

"So you can run things better?" I asked, stepping into the dim light off the porch. "Want to put your money where your mouth is?"

He looked me up and down. "You're not an officer. Just a patched member."

"Which is way above your pay grade since you aren't even a Prospect. I suggest you leave and don't come back."

He barked out a laugh. "And who's going to make me?"

I didn't bother with words anymore. I wasn't sure this idiot could understand what anyone said anyway. Hauling back my fist, I let it fly and nailed him right across the jaw. His head whipped to the side and he staggered back a step, but I wasn't done. I whaled on him, blow after blow to his ribs, stomach, face. Someone needed to make an example so other little fucks like this one didn't come around.

He dropped to the ground and I kicked him in the gut, then spat on him. "You are nothing. You've always been nothing, and you'll remain nothing. No one would miss you if I ended your life right here and now."

"You fucked up," he said, then spat out blood at my feet. "I'll end your sorry ass. You and all the others."

"Finish it." Havoc's voice reached me from the darkness. He hadn't been inside, but apparently had walked up in time to figure out what the hell was going on. "Now, Ashes. End this shit."

I hauled the little shit stain up and hammered his temple until my hand throbbed. When he still wouldn't fucking die, I snapped his neck and let him drop to the ground. Breathing hard, I glanced in the direction of Havoc's voice and the Sergeant-at-Arms moved closer, coming into the light. He nudged the dickhead on the ground, then snapped his fingers. Two Prospects hurried over and hauled the body away. I didn't care where they took it.

"You hear anyone else mouthing off like that, handle it. If you can't take care of it, then let me know and I'll step in. The last thing we need is a bunch of troublemakers trying to patch in."

I gave him a nod and got on my bike, going straight home. This end of the compound was quiet, and dark. I went up the steps and flicked on the lights as I went inside. A cold beer sounded good and I grabbed one from the fridge, snatched a hand towel from the laundry room, then went into the living room and turned on the TV.

Adrenaline was coursing through me, and I needed sex as much as I needed air. The club sluts weren't going to get the job done, though, and no way in hell would Renegade let me anywhere near his sister. So my hand had been getting the job done for a while now.

It sucked that my life had come to this, but meaningless sex just didn't do it for me anymore. Hell, I couldn't even get hard for the whores at the clubhouse. Those days were behind me. Keeping it from my brothers was going to get harder and harder though. For two years I'd walked that fine line, but a day would come when I couldn't conceal my true feelings. They'd know something was up, but no fucking way could I ever let Renegade know I was a goner for his baby sister.

Flipping to one of the porn stations I streamed, I selected a movie and unfastened my pants. I downed half my beer before picking up the lube and slicking my palm. As the woman on the screen deep-throated the man, I started stroking. It wasn't long before my eyes were closed, only focused on the sounds and picturing sweet little Nikki on her knees, sucking me off.

I tightened my grip, giving a slight twist on the downstroke. Faster. Harder. Everything in me grew taut as my balls drew up, then I was coming. I grunted as spurts of cum jetted over my hand, wishing like fuck I could do more than daydream about the only woman I'd ever wanted long-term.

Using the towel to clean myself off, I made sure I got everything off my hands, then tossed the towel to the side and picked up my beer again. I finished watching the movie, then called it a night after a quick shower.

Pathetic. That's what I was… a pathetic excuse of a man, much less a biker.

If anyone ever found out I hadn't fucked a woman in years, I'd never hear the end of it. I let them suck me off, sometimes. And I made sure they were satisfied, but my dick hadn't been inside anyone since I'd fallen for Nik. I'd fooled around with my dates, but it never went all the way. My brothers wouldn't understand. Especially since I couldn't have the one I wanted. No way her brother would ever let her be with someone like me.

Chapter One

Ashes
Six Months Later

I hated seeing Nikki like this. What should have been a joyous time for her only made her sadder. Losing Bane, especially in such a brutal way, had done a number on her. It had been half a year since his death, and still she was barely living. None of us had a clue the two had been so close. Even her brother, Renegade, had been kept in the dark. I'd made it my responsibility to keep an eye on her. If it weren't for my addict cousin, Bane would still be alive, and Nikki wouldn't be facing motherhood alone.

Her belly swelled with her kid, hers and Bane's, and I thought she was pretty damn adorable. Even when she hadn't showered in a few days, there was just something about Nikki that made you look twice. She wasn't stunning, or gorgeous like the women in Hollywood, but the girl-next-door look was really doing it for me. Not that I would touch her. I had no right. Besides, she was still mourning the loss of Bane.

"Hey, Nik, your calendar says you have a doctor's appointment today. Shouldn't you be getting ready?" I asked as I leaned against the entryway to the living room.

She'd curled on the couch, still in her pajamas, and was staring vacantly at the TV. I knew she wasn't watching it because a movie that looked damn close to soft porn was playing, and that wasn't her thing. At least, it hadn't been since I'd started coming over here every week.

"Nik." Moving farther into the room, I hunkered in front of her, slowly reaching for her hand. I gave it a slight squeeze, pulling her attention to me. "There you are, pretty girl. Come on. You need to shower and dress for your appointment. I'll give you a ride."

"Appointment?"

I nodded. "Doctor. Have to check on the kiddo and make sure they're all right."

Her eyes turned glassy with unshed tears. "I'm supposed to find out the sex today. I get to see my baby and I..."

I reached up and wiped away the tear that slipped down her cheek. "I know, sweetheart. I know. I'm so damn sorry Bane can't be here for this, but you don't have to go alone."

I'd like to think Bane would have been with her every step of the way, but I honestly didn't know. He'd enjoyed the club pussy as much as anyone else. The fact he'd been with Nikki, and she was the sister of our Road Captain, made me think he'd been more serious this time. If he hadn't died and he'd fucked around on Nik, then Renegade would have gelded him.

She gave me a slight nod and I helped her stand. Not trusting her to actually take a shower and not just crawl back in the bed, I led her down the hall to her room. I'd picked up a bit the last time I was here, but the place already looked like a cyclone had hit. From what I knew of Nikki, she'd been something of a neat freak before losing Bane. The men who took her had beat her pretty bad, but even worse, they'd made her watch as they tortured and killed Bane, a Prospect no one had realized she was seeing.

I went into her bathroom and turned on the shower, set out a clean towel for her, then stepped out. Nikki shuffled past me, more zombie than human at the moment. I left her to it and started picking up the mess in her room and stripping the bed. When I turned to shove everything in the hamper near her closet, I sighed and stared at her. She was still standing in the bathroom, vacantly looking at the shower.

She needed help, but she refused to go talk to a shrink, and Renegade insisted she'd be fine and to leave her be. I couldn't, though. Either my brother wasn't aware of just how bad Nik had gotten, or he was choosing to ignore it. I understood he was preoccupied with his new woman and daughter, and the kid they had on the way, but that didn't change the fact his sister needed him. I could go to the Pres and ask him to speak to Renegade, but I didn't want to do that. Nikki needed someone, and I was happy to help. I considered it penance for my fucked-up cousin being responsible for what happened to Nikki and Bane.

"Nikki, I need you to take a shower and get ready for your appointment," I reminded her again.

When she still didn't move, I knew I'd have to take things further than I should. I reached up and eased the elastic from her hair, letting it tumble down her back. Bracing myself for however she might react, I reached for the hem of her shirt and slowly started to lift it, hoping like hell she'd snap out of it and shove me away, then undress herself. Her bare breasts came into view, and I slammed my eyes shut, and cursed the fact I was getting hard. It was all kinds of fucked up. I managed to get her shirt off, then shoved her pajama pants down her legs. Settling my hands on her hips, I noticed she hadn't been wearing panties. It was tempting to let my hands wander over that smooth skin, but I held back.

I brushed past her and tested the shower water, warming it a little more, before I reached back and took her hand. I tried really fucking hard not to look anywhere but her face as I stuck her under the shower spray. She sucked in a breath, her eyes going wide, and

I could tell the moment she was coming back to the present and getting out of her head.

"Ashes?" she asked.

"Yeah, Nik. Just... shower, okay? I'll put some clothes out for you, then wait in the living room."

My gaze dropped to her breasts, and I knew it made me an asshole, but I couldn't seem to stop myself from going even lower. The swell of her belly made my fingers twitch as I fought the urge to reach out and place my hand there. Nikki seemed to read my mind and reached out, taking my hand in hers, then pressed my palm to her belly. I stared a moment before looking up to see her watching me.

"It's okay if you want to feel the baby," she said. "You've been here every week helping take care of us. It's almost more your kid than Bane's."

I shook my head. "No, Nik. The baby is yours and Bane's, and everyone knows it. The kid will know it too. We'll all tell him or her about their dad, and how he died trying to save you. He'll be a hero in his kid's eyes."

Her lower lip trembled. "I'm scared, Ashes."

Ah, hell. I could handle about anything, except tears. I slipped off my cut and laid it on the counter, then toed off my boots. I stepped into the shower and gathered Nikki in my arms, not caring that I was getting soaked. She cried and clutched at my shirt. It was all kinds of fucked up that she was naked, and my dick was more than aware of the fact. If Renegade saw me right now, he'd kick my ass.

"Everything's going to be fine, Nik. You don't have to do any of this on your own. The club is behind you one hundred percent. You know that, right? It's not just Renegade. We're all here for you."

- 152 -

She sniffled and looked up at me. "No, not everyone. Just you. My brother hardly comes by, and I never see the others unless I go to the compound."

I bit my tongue before I said something I shouldn't. I'd thought long and hard about her situation. The fact she lived alone and didn't have anyone to check on her, other than the club, meant that she'd be safer at the compound. If anything happened, it would take too long to reach her. Hell, that was if anyone even knew she needed help. I wanted her to move behind the gates, but it wasn't my place to say anything. She wasn't mine.

The pain in her eyes twisted my insides. I wanted more than anything to see her smile again, to see the happy, carefree Nikki I'd come to know over the years. Renegade kept her from the club as much as possible, and for good reason, but this Nikki wasn't the same woman I'd been watching for so long. If I hadn't been preoccupied back then, I might have noticed she was spending time with Bane. Truthfully, I'd tried damn hard *not* to notice her. I'd known Renegade wouldn't want her with a brother.

"Nik, you have a lot of people who care about you."

"Do you?" she asked.

Hell yes! Not that I was going to tell her that. She might only be a decade younger than me -- okay, a bit more than that -- but as far as her big brother was concerned, that was too big an age gap. I found that fucking hilarious considering he was older than me and his woman was Nikki's age. I knew he was just being protective of his little sister, and I couldn't blame him. Nik was pretty fucking awesome, even though her world had been ripped apart. The fact she was still standing, hadn't given in to her grief, proved that she was stronger than she realized.

"You know I do," I said, deciding to leave it at that.

She glanced at my chest and the corner of her mouth turned up in a slight smile. "You got in here still dressed."

"Wasn't exactly going to strip naked first."

She sighed and nodded, taking a step back. "I'll finish my shower and get dressed. I promise I won't take long."

I got out and waited for her to close the frosted-glass door before I stripped to my boxers. While she finished her shower and got ready, I threw my things in her dryer, including the boxers. The laundry room door was mostly shut and would give me time to cover myself if she came this way. I leaned against the machine and folded my arms, staring at the wall and trying to sort the crap in my head. Nikki was in a rough spot and the last thing she needed was a horny guy taking advantage. It's why I wasn't here every day, even though I'd feel better if someone checked on her the days I wasn't around.

Fact was that Nikki turned me on more than any other woman. It had been that way since she'd turned eighteen and I'd noticed she wasn't a kid anymore. Didn't matter. She wasn't for me. The last thing Renegade wanted was for Nikki to live in our world, and I didn't blame him. Not even a little. She'd already been roughed up after dating Bane for a short time. She could face much worse if she were permanently attached to one of us. It would put a bigger target on her. Being Renegade's sister was bad enough, but if she wore a property patch too? Fuck.

No, it was better to be her friend and keep my dick in my pants. I glanced down at my cock, which was so damn hard it hurt. Even now I wanted her. I shut the laundry room door the rest of the way and snatched a towel out of the hamper in the corner. I gripped my cock and gave it a stroke. I knew Nik's apartment as well as my own home and reached up into the cabinet where she stored her extra shit. Grabbing a bottle of lotion, I slicked my palm before stroking my dick again.

It was wrong, to stand here jerking off to the sight of her in the shower, but it was the only hope I had of fitting back in my jeans at least somewhat comfortably. I closed my eyes, focusing on the feel of her bare breasts pressed against me, how full they were. Grinding my teeth together, I tried to remain silent, but as I tugged harder, I couldn't stifle my groan. My body shuddered as I came. I caught my cum with the towel, then wiped off my cock and hands. Looking around the laundry room, I tried to figure out what the fuck I should do with the towel.

Since I'd been the one doing her laundry lately, I just shoved it between the washer and the wall, making a mental note to grab it the next time I was here and do a load of towels. The last thing I needed was Nikki finding that and freaking the hell out. She'd either think some perv had broken into her home and jacked off on her towel, or she'd know it was me, which might be worse. If she said anything to Renegade, I'd get my ass stomped.

By the time I heard her moving around in the main part of the apartment, my clothes were mostly dry, so I dressed and went to get my boots and cut from her bathroom. She'd placed my cut at the foot of her bed and my boots were on the floor nearby. I just stood there a moment, looking at my cut lying on her rumpled bed. It almost looked like it belonged there, which was stupid. No fucking way I belonged in Nik's life as anything other than her friend.

I pulled it on and put on my boots before heading out the door, with Nikki right behind me. She locked up her place, then I took her keys and unlocked her little SUV. She'd had a small car before, but when her pregnancy became known, a few of us had pitched in to help buy her something a little roomier. Well, mostly I had, but I hadn't told her that. As far as she was concerned, it was a gift from her brother and a few club members.

It wasn't the first time I'd taken her to an appointment, so I knew the way. I pulled into a parking space right out front of the clinic and helped Nikki out of the SUV. She walked inside and went straight to the counter while I found two empty seats next to each other.

"What do you mean I owe money?" I heard Nikki ask.

As far as I knew, she had insurance. I stood and went to check on her, hoping to keep her stress level down. Nik was dealing with enough already. I placed my hand at her lower back and stared down at the woman behind the counter. She blinked up at me, a blush suffusing her cheeks. The way she smiled and batted her eyes had me wanting to snarl. She didn't know if Nik and I could be a thing, and she was going to flirt? I hated that shit.

"What's the problem?" I asked.

"Ms. Adams owes money from her previous two visits. Until her account balance is paid, we can't see her today," the woman said in a sickly sweet voice.

"How much?" I asked.

I felt Nikki tense. I slid my hand from her back to her hip and gave it a squeeze. No way in hell I was letting her walk out of here without seeing the doctor just because she had a balance. The woman looked from me to Nik and back again.

"Well, we aren't really supposed to disclose a patient's details."

I contained my growl of annoyance as I looked down at Nik. "How much, sweetheart? And don't lie."

Nikki pressed her lips together, but eventually the fight went out of her. It was nice to see that spark, if even for just a moment. She went on tiptoe and whispered the amount in my ear. I pressed a kiss to her temple and pulled out my wallet. Giving the bitch behind the counter my credit card, I watched as she ran it for the full balance, then I signed the slip.

I took Nik's hand and led her over to the seats I'd found for us. When she sat, she seemed to almost curl in on herself. I didn't let go of her hand, and rubbed my thumb across her fingers. It wasn't the time or place, but I wanted to know why her insurance hadn't been paying for her visits. I'd been leaving her mail in the kitchen, but now I wondered if she'd been paying her bills. Had the insurance lapsed?

"Have you thought of any names?" I asked.

She licked her lips and focused on me. "I always liked Oliver for a boy or Lacey for a girl."

I smiled at her. "I like those names. You'll know soon enough which one to call the baby."

Nik pressed a hand to her belly. I could tell that she wanted to be excited, but felt guilty about it. Bane wasn't here, and nothing would bring him back, but she seemed to think that meant she had to suffer forever. No one would think less of her if she moved on. They'd only been on a few dates, if even that, when he'd been killed. I knew some of the guys had gotten serious about someone that fast, but I didn't think Bane and Nikki had been there yet. She was loyal to a fault, though, and I knew she hated that she'd survived and he hadn't. We'd talked about it some, when she wasn't practically catatonic. She didn't outright say she'd felt anything for him, but I could tell she did carry a large amount of guilt, and seemed traumatized by the way he'd died.

Even more proof that she wasn't cut out to be an ol' lady. She wasn't tough enough, but God did I love her. I liked how soft and sweet she was. It would take someone like her to temper my hard edges, but my world would swallow her up and spit her out.

"Nikki Adams," a nurse called out from a side door.

Nikki stood, then tugged on my hand. My heart thumped hard. She wanted me back there? I'd never gone back before. In fact, I usually ran a few errands while she was here, but she'd seemed off today so I'd stayed. I was glad I had, or she might not have been seen at all.

"Just lie down on the table. The tech will be in momentarily," the nurse said as she showed us into a room. "You can just lift your shirt for this one, as long as you can tug your pants down a bit."

Nik nodded and I helped her onto the padded table. She stretched out and put her head on the little paper-covered pillow. I noticed her hands were trembling and I stood next to her, running my fingers up and down her arm before brushing her hair back from her face. "It's going to be fine, Nik. You'll see. Aren't you excited about seeing the baby?"

"Are you?" she asked.

I couldn't help but smile. "Yeah, I am."

The technician bustled into the room, grinning. "All right, Mom and Dad. Let's see if the little one will cooperate."

My chest grew tight and I waited for Nik to correct her, but she never did. I looked at her rounded belly and placed my hand there while the tech got everything ready. The kid in there might not be mine, but that didn't matter. Bane had been a friend, and almost a brother, and I'd adored Nik for a while now. Didn't mean I'd be raising the kid with her, though, not even if it was what I wanted.

Was it? I hadn't thought about it before, hadn't let my mind go there, but now I couldn't stop thinking about it. Being with Nik every day, holding her at night, feeling the baby kick as she slept against me. Yeah, I'd fucking love that, but it wouldn't happen. Not my kid, not my life. Not my old lady. But shit, if she were, I'd die a happy man. As far as my brothers were concerned, I was still happy with club pussy. I'd made sure to walk out with a girl almost every night I was at the clubhouse, but no one knew that's all I did. Well, technically.

There was one person at the clubhouse who knew I was head over heels for a woman, and it wouldn't take much for him to figure out it was Nik. A Prospect. Jin was willing to keep my secret. In exchange, I led the club girls outside and into the shadows, then held them down while Jin made them scream in pleasure. They got off on it and everyone went home happy. Everyone but me. My dick only got hard for Nikki these days, which sucked big-ass donkey balls because I wouldn't be getting any from her. Rosie-Palm was the only one getting me off, and if I kept jerking my dick two or three times a day, I'd get carpal tunnel.

The tech brushed my hand aside, bringing me back to the present. She lifted Nik's shirt up to the bottom of her breasts, which I noticed were braless still. Fuck. Me. Then she tugged Nik's pants down until I could almost see her pussy. I shifted, willing my dick to stay down, but it was already at half-mast. The tech squeezed KY Jelly on Nik's stomach, then used a little wand thing to smear it around.

"Aw. There's the little one," the tech said, pointing to the screen.

"Can you see if it's a girl?" I asked.

"Little stinker is turned wrong," the tech said. "Hang on. Let's see if we can get them to turn a little."

She used her other hand to press on Nik's stomach and slowly the baby began to move. She'd pause here and there to tap some keys and the picture on the screen would freeze a moment. The suspense was getting to me, but eventually I saw what I knew had to be a penis. Or the kid had three legs.

"Congrats, Mom and Dad! You're having a baby boy!"

I saw the tears in Nik's eyes and leaned down to brush my lips across her forehead. "Little Oliver. He's beautiful, Nik. You did good."

She nodded and sniffled, staring at the screen with wide eyes. Something told me this was exactly what she'd needed. Now that she'd seen the baby, could call them by name, maybe she could get back on track. Whatever she needed, I'd see that she had it. Anything. No matter the cost, I'd do what I had to.

"I'll just print off a few pictures for you, then you're good to go. You can schedule your next appointment at the front on your way out," the tech said.

Once I had the pictures in hand, and the tech had wiped the lube off Nik's stomach, I helped her right her clothes and stand up. I kept staring at the images on the way to the front desk and only half-listened as she set up her next visit.

"I'm sorry, Ms. Adams, but we can't set another appointment without a payment method on file."

This bitch! I was getting tired of her shit. I pulled out my wallet again and practically threw my damn card at her. It was taking everything I had not to reach across the damn desk and knock the shit out of her. I'd never believed in hurting a woman, but this one was tempting me to break that code.

"So put the fucking thing on file. What's your damn problem?" Nik's hand went to my arm and she gripped me tight. "Something wrong with her coming here?"

The bitch shook her head, going pale as she added my card information to the system. Then she handed it back and I put it away before dragging Nikki from there. I was seconds from stomping that bitch into a mudhole. Fucking cunt! I never thought of women like that, always tried to respect them, even the club sluts, but this one... I couldn't believe the way she'd treated Nik.

"Ashes," she said softly.

"I'm sorry, Nik. I shouldn't have acted like that."

"Why did you?"

"Because it pissed me the fuck off that she was treating you that way. Why didn't your insurance pay? And why the hell didn't you say something?"

She worried at her lower lip and glanced away. "Because the policy lapsed. I haven't been going to work and I lost my job."

I ran a hand through my hair. "Nik, what's going on? I know you miss Bane, and I'm sorry as fuck we didn't get there in time to save him, to keep you from getting hurt, but this is nuts. You have a kid to think about. How are you going to keep your apartment?"

She blew out a breath and looked up at me. "I'm not. I didn't know how to tell Renegade, or anyone else."

What. The. Fuck. "Start talking, Nik. Now, dammit."

"I'm being evicted. I drained my savings to keep the utilities on and food in the fridge, when you weren't buying my groceries that is, but I didn't have enough for everything. I haven't paid rent in two months."

"When do you have to be out?"

"In three days."

Jesus fucking Christ. This woman was going to be the death of me.

"We have to tell your brother."

"No!" She shook her head so hard I worried she'd snap her neck. "He has enough on his plate."

"Dammit, Nik! I'm not going to let you be homeless. I'm an asshole, but I'm not *that* big an asshole." I knew I was going to regret this. "Come stay with me."

She blinked at me, but didn't say no. It was a start. I got her into the car and knew I had less than three days to convince her, and get all her shit packed up and moved. But it wasn't just her. She had to think about baby Oliver. One way or another, I'd get her to the compound. I only hoped all hell didn't break loose when Renegade found out his baby sister was in my house.

I was a dead man.

Chapter Two

Nikki

I'd packed my things and Ashes had shoved them into the back of my SUV. At least, the essentials. A truck would have to pick up my furniture and other belongings, not that I had any idea where I'd put any of it. As of right now, I was homeless. Ashes had insisted I follow him to the compound, or more specifically his house. I should have known when the Prospect at the gate's jaw dropped that he'd go blabbing to my brother. It hadn't taken Renegade long at all to show up.

"Why the fuck is my sister in your house?" he demanded, shoving Ashes against the living room wall.

"Someone needs to look out for her. You obviously aren't," Ashes said, his jaw tight and his eyes narrowed.

"What does that mean?" my brother asked, his voice a near growl.

I bit my lip and stared hard at Ashes, willing him to keep my secret. I'd known it would be in vain. He might be helping me, but he had a bond with Renegade that surpassed whatever friendship we might have. Although I often wondered if he was only helping me out of guilt. He'd apologized several times for his cousin's part in what happened, but I didn't blame Ashes in the least.

"She's homeless, you ass," Ashes said.

Renegade backed up and turned to face me. "What? Why didn't you tell me you needed help?"

Ashes cast a glare his way and opened his mouth, but I held up a hand. I knew he was about to defend me, but it wasn't necessary. Renegade might be a bit overwhelming at times, but I knew how to handle him. My big brother meant well, but he'd been a bit preoccupied lately, and I understood. Darby and Fawn -- and their unborn child -- were his entire world at the moment, and that was exactly as it should be. I didn't fault him for it in the least. "You've have a lot on your plate," I said. "I'm a grown woman, Renegade. I don't need you swooping in to save me all the time."

He folded his arms over his chest and looked down his nose at me. I already knew what he was thinking. The fact I was homeless proved I wasn't doing so great in the adulting department, but losing Bane, watching those men beat him to death, had taken a toll on me. We hadn't been close, our relationship having barely even started, but the brutality of it all still haunted me. Add in pregnancy hormones and I was a big, hot mess.

"It's fine. Really. Ashes is going to let me crash here for a little while…"

I couldn't even finish my sentence before my big brother was shaking his head. "No, you aren't going to stay here. Do you really think I'd let you stay with a womanizing asshole like this one? Fuck no! If you don't want to stay at my place, then I'll help you get settled somewhere else."

Ashes looked away, but not before I saw the flash of anger and hurt in his eyes. He'd been so sweet to me, so thoughtful, and my brother was treating him poorly. I didn't like it, but saying something would just make things worse. Renegade saw a different side of Ashes than I had. The man was single, so what did it matter if he was a bit of a man-whore? It wasn't like the other guys at the club were any better. I knew my dear brother had been cut from that same cloth until

Harley Wylde   Slider/ Ashes Duet

he'd met Darby. Even Bane… No, I didn't want to think about Bane. Not right now.

"I didn't want to be any trouble," I said.

"Nikki, you're my sister. If you need help, say something. I thought you were doing fine."

I pressed my lips together. I hadn't been fine since he'd found me tied to that chair. Telling him that wouldn't go over well. My brother had been in his own world and had barely given me a second thought. The few times I'd seen him, I'd held it together until he'd left. It wasn't like he stuck around for long. Ashes had seen me at my worst the last few months. He was the only one who knew that I'd been falling apart. "Ashes has been checking on me," I said.

Renegade cast another glare toward the man who had made sure I stayed alive, and I didn't like it. Moving closer to my brother, I hauled back my arm and punched him in the abdomen. He didn't even flinch, but he did growl at me. "What the fuck, Nikki?"

"That man has made sure I eat, make it to my appointments, and he's even cleaned my damn apartment. You have no right to look at him like that."

My brother's face flushed and I knew he was about to erupt. I just didn't understand why. Ashes had been so wonderful. It wasn't like the man was interested in me *that* way. He just felt guilty. Who would ever want a broken woman like me? Some part of me had shattered that day. I hadn't loved Bane. We'd barely known one another, except in the intimate sense. My heart wasn't broken. It was more the trauma of watching him die, and knowing that I carried his son. A baby boy who would never know his daddy.

"You have a choice, Nikki," my brother said. "You can either come with me and I'll figure something out, or you can stay here. But if you remain

- 165 -

Harley Wylde   **Slider/ Ashes Duet**

in Ashes' house, you'd better make damn certain this is where you want to be."

My brow furrowed as I looked up at him. "What's that mean?"

"It means his ass better claim you if you're going to live here."

My mouth dropped open. I couldn't believe he'd just said that. There was no way I would ever put Ashes in that position, not after all he'd done for me. The fact my brother could even say such a thing made me angry. Who died and made him God? He might be part of the Devil's Boneyard MC, even claim an officer's position, but still... he wasn't the boss of *me*. I shouldn't have to answer to him.

"You know, you left me in foster care after our parents and brother died. If you didn't get a say then over where I slept, you don't get one now."

He rocked back on his heels and paled a little. "Damn, Nikki. That was harsh."

Ashes moved closer, slowly reaching for me. I felt his fingers brush my hip before he slid his arm around my waist. I trembled and pressed against him. It felt like my heart was crashing against my chest, and it was getting hard to breathe. Everything started to spin a little.

"When did you eat last?" he asked.

I shrugged a shoulder, honestly not knowing. Probably whenever he'd fed me last. I knew I needed to do better, for the sake of the baby at least. Food just hadn't been all that appealing lately. Things were different, though. I'd seen little Oliver. He wasn't just some random baby kicking me. Watching him on the screen had changed things. I knew I couldn't keep wallowing. There was a kid depending on me, and I

- 166 -

needed to make sure he had a place to live and got the nutrients he needed as long as he was in my belly.

Renegade eyed us. "You've really been taking care of my sister all this time?"

"Yeah, I have," Ashes said. "You had your hands full and I was happy to help her. She doesn't always remember to eat, or when her appointments are. I've been making sure she has food in the kitchen and eats something while I'm there."

Renegade blew out a breath and ran a hand through his hair. "Shit. I don't like this. Not one fucking bit."

I didn't want to stress him out, not after everything he'd been through. I just needed him to understand that it wasn't his decision where I stayed. Maybe I was on club property, but I was still my own person, the ruler over my own fate. "You're my brother and I love you, but you don't get a say in my life. You have a pregnant woman and a kid at home who need you more than I do. Go home to them." The room spun a little and Ashes swept me up into his arms. I clung to him, not having much choice to do anything else. "I'll be fine here."

He paced a moment before coming to a stop a mere foot away. Hands on his hips, he looked like he was about to argue, but he simply nodded. "All right," he said. "But the Pres needs to approve it, and Ashes damn well knows it."

"I'll handle it," Ashes said.

"See that you do." My brother gave me one last look before walking out and slamming the front door behind him.

I sighed and pressed my cheek against Ashes. "Well, that went about as well as I'd expected it to. At least he left without tearing shit up."

Ashes snorted. "Yeah, like my face."

Maybe it was wrong, but I giggled. He probably should be worried about something like that. My brother had always hit first and asked questions later. Not with women, but men were fair game. I didn't delude myself into thinking my brother was Prince Charming, but I did know he'd never abuse a woman or kid. It just wasn't who he was, and I could tell Ashes was the same.

No one had ever been as sweet to me. Part of me just wished that he was doing it for a reason other than guilt. It hardly seemed fair that the first time a decent guy paid me attention it was because his cousin was responsible for getting me beat to hell and killing my baby daddy. Maybe one day a man would look at me and want to keep me. I'd read enough fairy tales growing up that I wanted my own prince, my happily-ever-after. Didn't matter to me if he wore leather and rode a Harley or if he dressed in suits and worked a nine-to-five job. All I cared about was how he treated me and if he loved me. My brother cared, I knew he did, but he hardly ever said the words. I craved someone's love, but I started to worry I'd never have it, especially with a baby on the way. Yeah, my kid would hopefully love me, but it wasn't the same thing.

"Think you can sit at the kitchen table?" he asked.

"I'm pregnant, not broken," I said then winced because in a way I was broken. Just not in the sense that I couldn't sit up on my own. "I'm sorry if me being here is going to cause you problems. If the club has an issue with it, I can find somewhere else to go."

"Let me worry about that."

He carried me into the kitchen and eased me down onto a wooden chair. It was the first time I'd been to Ashes' house and I couldn't help but be a little curious. The living room hadn't been what I'd expected. Oh, the leather couches and not a single personal touch just screamed bachelor, but the walls had been a soft, tranquil green. I'd expected nearly every room to be what I called builder's beige, that wretched neutral tone contractors used because it was so cheap.

The kitchen walls were a blue gray and the cabinets were white. His table even matched, being white with a light pine-colored butcher block top, and all four chairs were also white. A towel was tossed next to the stove and I could tell from the checkered pattern he'd likely just grabbed it and tossed it into his shopping cart. It didn't look even remotely like something Ashes would choose. Although, to be honest, I was amazed he even *had* kitchen towels. It was my experience that most single guys didn't unless they were a little more in touch with their feminine side.

"My brother isn't really going to make you claim me, is he?" I asked.

Ashes tensed, but his back was to me and I couldn't see his expression. I knew he didn't think of me like that, but it hurt my pride a little. Would being with me be so horrible? Maybe he just didn't want a kid who didn't belong to him. Couldn't blame him. I had no doubt that finding a decent guy would be a challenge. I didn't think I was ready for a relationship at the moment, at least not with just anyone. If I thought I had even a chance with Ashes, then I'd jump in with both feet.

"Your brother is the Road Captain, but no… he can't make me claim you."

I chewed on my lower lip. "He can't, but someone here can, right? Like Cinder or Scratch?"

He didn't answer, which told me plenty.

Losing my apartment, and seeing my baby for the first time, had been a wake-up call. No matter what happened now, I needed to focus on little Oliver, and make sure I stayed healthy and provided a safe home for him. If Ashes would just give me a few days, then I'd figure something out. There had to be a job somewhere in town I could get to at least give me enough money for another place to stay. Or maybe I could convince Cinder and Scratch to let me have a small home here at the compound, at least until after Oliver arrived. Ashes had been right. I was safer here, where I had people to help if I needed it.

Even though it was far from morning, Ashes made eggs with biscuits and bacon. He placed a plate in front of me and I picked up the pepper shaker from the center of the table, adding a bit to the eggs. Then I pulled my biscuits open, broke up the bacon, and made bacon sandwiches out of them. He gave me a slight smile as he sat across from me, his plate nearly overflowing with food. I didn't know where he put it since I didn't see an ounce of fat on him. Lucky bastard. I so much as looked at food and gained weight. "Thank you."

"You need to eat more," he said before shoving a bite of egg into his mouth.

"Not what I meant, but I appreciate the food too. You've been watching over me for months and I don't want you to think I'm ungrateful. It's been hard, but seeing Oliver... I think I'm ready to move forward. I need to focus on my baby and get my life back on track."

Ashes gave me a nod.

"I can help unload the car after we finish eating." My cheeks flushed since I'd just assumed he was going to do it. Maybe he'd planned for me to all along? But no, not with the way he'd handled me so carefully the last few months.

"I don't have the guest room set up just yet. I'll get it done before tonight, though. If you want to rest until then, you can use my bed. Sheets are clean. Just changed them this morning before I headed over to your place."

I pushed my eggs around. I didn't want him to think he had to stay glued to me. Just because I was in his house, it didn't mean I intended for him to be my shadow. As a single guy, and one in the MC at that, I knew he had his choice of women and probably had a different one every night. Would having me in his house make him feel like he couldn't party with the guys like he typically did?

I was starting to second-guess coming with him. I'd known my brother wouldn't handle it well, and I had no idea what the others would think. Even worse, I didn't know what Ashes was thinking or feeling. He was probably just being nice and giving me a place to crash for a bit, but what would he expect in return? With me being six months pregnant, I seriously doubted he'd want sex from me. Maybe I could clean a little, even though from what I'd seen, his home was spotless.

"Nik, you're thinking too hard. What's wrong?" he asked.

"Maybe me being here isn't such a great idea," I said.

"Is this about the bedroom? Because I can have it set up in the next hour or two." He watched me carefully. "Or is this about what your brother said?

Harley Wylde   **Slider/ Ashes Duet**

Don't worry about it, okay? He's just pissed that he didn't realize you needed help."

"It's not just that. What am I supposed to do here, Ashes?"

He set his fork down and pushed his chair back. I watched as he came around the table and hunkered down next to me, taking my hand in his rougher one. Was it wrong his touch made me shiver? It made me wonder what his hands would feel like touching the rest of me.

"The only thing I want you to do is rest, get plenty to eat, and take care of yourself and Oliver. Needing help doesn't make you weak, Nikki. It just makes you human. I don't mind being the one to give you shelter, to lend a hand."

My lips twisted in a grimace. "Because you feel guilty."

He nodded before holding my gaze. "It started out that way, partially. Honestly, I've always admired you. I think you're a sweet, beautiful woman and getting to be your knight in shining armor isn't exactly a tough gig to handle. Spending time with you is payment enough if that's what's worrying you."

"You almost make it sound like you'd date me." I gave a humorless laugh, but it died quickly at the look in his eyes. He wouldn't, would he? Was that what he'd meant when he said he'd admired me? Had Ashes wanted to date me at some point and my big brother had warned him away? It seemed like the type of thing Renegade would do. He hadn't wanted me near the club, only inviting me over in emergencies or for the rare special occasion.

"Any guy would be lucky to have you, Nikki. Your brother will never permit a biker to claim you. What he said earlier, he was bluffing, hoping to get me

- 172 -

Harley Wylde   **Slider/ Ashes Duet**

to send you away, or make you leave with him on your own. If he'd known about Bane, the two of you would have never been in that warehouse. He'd have lost his shit at the mere thought of some Prospect daring to touch you. When you're ready to stand on your own two feet again, then you'll find the right guy. I just hope he's worthy of you."

Chapter Three

Ashes

After a mostly sleepless night, the last thing I wanted to hear was my damn phone going off. I cracked open an eye and groaned at the too bright light. I slammed my hand down on the nightstand, then felt around until I could grab the phone. My blurry vision couldn't make out the caller name on the display, and at the risk of pissing off the wrong person, I muted the call and rolled back over. My fucking bed smelled like Nikki, which was my own damn fault. I'd been late putting the spare room together so she'd crashed in my bed for a nap. Now her scent covered my pillows and blankets. I could have changed them, but I guess I was a masochistic fucker because I couldn't bring myself to do it.

The phone went off again and this time I knew I needed to answer. I swiped the screen and held it to my ear.

"Yeah."

"I call, you better damn well answer," Havoc said.

"Sorry. Tired as fuck." Pissing off the club's Sergeant-at-Arms wasn't the best way to start the morning. I had no doubt Havoc could pound my ass into the ground without breaking a sweat. And if he didn't, his psycho wife might very well try it.

"We have Church in an hour. Drink a pot of coffee, down an energy drink. Do whatever you need to be clear-headed and present on time."

Fucking hell. I couldn't think of anything going on that would warrant that kind of threat. It sounded like Cinder was likely on the warpath, even though I didn't know why. Maybe someone looked at Meg

Harley Wylde   Slider/ Ashes Duet

wrong and he was out for blood. Things had been fairly quiet lately. Sure, the women who ended up getting claimed always brought some trouble with them, but since that shit went down six months ago and we lost Bane, it had been a smooth ride. Maybe too tranquil, now that I thought about it. "I'll be there."

Havoc hung up on me and I sighed, closing my eyes again. It was going to be a long fucking day. I didn't regret bringing Nikki here. Having her in my house, knowing she was safe and wouldn't end up on the streets, made any discomfort worth it. I only hoped I didn't walk around with a hard-on all the fucking time, much like the one tenting the sheets even now.

If I was going to be in Church on time, better get my ass into the shower. It was going to take that and a fuck ton of coffee to get me going. Although, I should probably take care of my little problem first. Or rather, my big eleven-inch one. Yeah, I'd measured, and any guy who said he hadn't was a fucking liar or knew he had a tiny dick. I threw off the covers and padded naked into the bathroom. After starting the shower, I took a second to brush my teeth and stared into the mirror. My beard had grown in, longer than I liked. Some of my brothers had some bushy beards that the ladies seemed to love, but I could take it or leave it. I'd need a new razor before I shaved it all the way off, though. I ran my hand over it, then pulled the trimmers from the drawer and took the length down until it was tight along my jaw.

I gathered the hair from the sink and tossed it into the trash, then pulled out a towel before getting in the shower. My dick wasn't as hard as before, but it hadn't completely deflated either. I washed my hair and what was left of my beard, then rinsed. Bracing a hand against the wall, I bent over and let the hot water pound my neck and shoulders. I turned my head one way then another, hearing a loud *crack* both times.

I'd been tense since Renegade had burst into my home, pissed off that his sister was here. Even though I'd told Nikki I wasn't worried, I'd lied. Having Cinder or Scratch demand that I claim her wouldn't be a problem for me, but I didn't want to force that on her. Nikki was still healing, trying to figure things out, and she didn't need more shit thrown at her. I knew Havoc had decided Jordan was his and that was that, but I didn't work that way. I could admit the thought of tying Nikki to my bed and convincing her to stay was tempting, but I wasn't that much of an asshole. Not with her anyway.

Maybe I could have figured out another solution, but part of me had just really wanted her in my house. I'd felt that way for years even though I'd tried to bury it. Not deep enough apparently. In my gut, I knew that Nikki was mine. If things were different, if she weren't Renegade's little sister, then perhaps at some point she'd have come to realize she was meant to be here with me. But wishing for things to be different wouldn't change anything.

The way she'd looked in my bed, her hair fanned across the pillows, was something I wouldn't easily forget. It had been so fucking tempting to crawl in beside her, draw her close to my chest, and just hold her while we slept. The swell of her belly shouldn't have looked so fucking cute, but it did. Knowing her son was in there, growing inside her, made me feel things I wasn't ready to analyze. I'd never thought of myself as a family sort of guy, until I'd found out Nik was pregnant. Even if the baby wasn't mine, it didn't keep me from wondering what it would be like.

"Ashes."

I closed my eyes tighter. Now I was even hearing her damn voice. Would she always plague my thoughts?

"Ashes."

My eyes opened and I glanced through the glass door. Shit. I wasn't imagining her voice. She was here, and the way she looked at me... My cock began to stir again, getting hard, and I quickly shifted to hide myself from her. She didn't need me lusting after her. I would anyway, but it didn't mean she had to know about it.

"Did you need something, Nikki?" I asked, wincing inwardly when my voice came out deeper and rougher than usual. She had me tied in fucking knots and she wasn't even trying.

I heard a faint rustle and figured she was leaving, having seen way more of me than she likely had wanted. Turning back to look at what I figured would be an empty bathroom, shock held me immobile as a very naked Nikki entered the shower, her gaze unsure and hesitant. Christ! Was she trying to kill me?

"Nik..."

"If... If you don't want me here, I'll go." She folded her arms over her breasts, her cheeks flushing as she glanced away.

Not want her here? What the hell was going on? Did she think it was a requirement that she give me her body in order to stay with me?

"Talk to me," I said. "What are you thinking, Nik?"

Her gaze was fastened on the shower floor. At first, I didn't think she'd answer. When she finally did, it about took me to my fucking knees.

"I know that I'll probably end up alone, at least until Oliver is grown and out on his own. No one will

Harley Wylde   **Slider/ Ashes Duet**

want to take on both me and a kid, especially as big an asshole as my brother seems to be, determined to save me even if I don't want or need him to. If you don't want me, I'll understand."

I reached for her, my hands gripping her gently and giving her just enough of a shake that she looked up at me. The vulnerability in her eyes was heartbreaking. Did she really believe no one would want her? The fact she didn't see what a treasure she was, a gift that any guy would be lucky to claim... it fucking floored me.

"Not want you?" I snorted. "Nik, have you never noticed I'm in a constant state of arousal around you? All I have to do is think of you and I get hard."

"You're not just saying that because you think the club might force you to claim me?" She stared at me. Hard. "I'm pregnant, Ashes. Like, really pregnant. Pretty soon I'll be the size of a whale. Then I'll have a kid to take care for the next eighteen years, one that isn't yours."

I hesitated only a moment before I took her hand and lowered it to my cock. Interest flared in her eyes as she slid her soft fingers along my shaft. She dropped her gaze as she stroked me a few times. The look of wonder on her face was nearly my undoing.

"That's what happens whenever I'm around you," I said. "Can't control it no matter how much I try. I've wanted you for a long time, Nikki."

"Me?" she asked.

"I noticed you shortly after you turned eighteen. Knew I didn't have a shot at being with someone like you, even if Renegade wasn't standing in the way. I don't blame him for wanting a different life for you. You know things can get rough around here. Putting a target on you or Oliver is the last thing I'd ever want to do. Being here, at the compound, is one thing… being claimed by me? That's different and you know it."

Her grip didn't loosen, but her hand stilled. She stared up at me, a flicker of emotion in her eyes that I couldn't quite discern. Before I could process what was happening, she pushed up on her toes and pressed her lips to mine. It only took a moment before I reacted. Tugging her closer, I took control of the kiss. I'd dreamed of this so many damn times, what she'd taste like, feel like. Nothing compared to the reality of having Nikki in my arms.

I backed her to the tiled wall, crowding her with my body. There was a slight hitch in her breath, and then she seemed to melt against me. Nik lifted her leg and wrapped it around my thigh, opening herself to me. She deserved romance, a slow seduction. She wasn't some club whore and I shouldn't take her against the damn shower wall like one. Then she rubbed herself against me and I knew I wouldn't be able to hold back.

"Nik, we should wait." I wasn't sure if I was trying to convince her or me. As she rubbed against me again, all I could do was groan and fight the urge to bury myself deep.

"I don't need flowery words or a date first, Ashes. I want you."

"Archer. Call me Archer," I said, something inside me tightening at the thought of hearing my name after so long, especially on her lips.

"Archer?" she asked.

"Archer McCray." I smiled a little. "It's the name on my birth certificate. No one's used it in a long-ass time."

Nik reached up and cupped my cheek. "I know what it means that you shared that with me. Archer, I..."

I kissed her again, silencing whatever she was going to say. Gripping her just below her ass cheeks, I lifted, then lowered her right onto my cock. A groan was pulled from me as her tight, hot pussy sucked me in, taking every damn inch as if she were fucking made just for me. Not many women had been able to handle me over the years, but my sweet little Nikki only whimpered and wiggled, needing more.

"That's it, baby," I murmured. My cock flexed inside her before I raised and lowered her again. "Fuck, Nikki! You feel so damn good."

"You feel amazing, Archer." Her nails bit into my shoulders. "It's never..."

I kissed her, not wanting to hear about the men in her past. All that mattered was right now, for this moment, she was mine. Holding her tight, I thrust into her. Part of me wanted to hold back, but the soft sounds she made, the way she clung to me, made it difficult. When her pussy clenched down on me, what little control I had, snapped. I drove into her, hard, fast strokes. I'd always wanted to make love to Nikki, but this was different... this was... claiming. I wanted her to know she was mine and *only* mine.

I shifted the angle as I slammed into her again and again. Nikki gasped then cried out my name, her cream coating me. I pressed my forehead to hers, our gazes locked, as I came, filling her up. My heart raced and as the haze of passion began to dissipate, everything in me went still. Shit. Fuck. Dammit!

"Nik, I... I didn't use anything."

She giggled a little. "I don't think I can get any more knocked up than I already am."

I looked down at the swell of her stomach, my heart pounding. "But…" I swallowed hard. I'd never been bare inside a woman before. She'd felt incredible, but I didn't think it was just because I hadn't used a condom. "I'm clean. I haven't even been with anyone in a while. Got tested after the last time."

She sobered, and reached up to run her fingers along my jaw. "I'm clean too. I wasn't even thinking about that. I trust you, Archer. I know you wouldn't do anything to hurt me."

I felt like I couldn't breathe for a moment. She might trust me to keep her safe, but I hadn't even been thinking. I'd just wanted her, needed her, so I'd taken her. What if I hadn't been tested yet? What if I'd given her something? I could have hurt not only her but Oliver. A woman had never made me lose control like that before. It scared the shit out of me.

She kissed me, her lips soft as they brushed mine.

"Why, Nikki?" I asked as I pulled away, but she locked her leg around my thigh and wouldn't let me slide free from her body. "Why did you get in the shower with me?"

"Does it matter?"

"Yeah. It kind of does. If you think it's a requirement for giving you a place to stay… it's not."

Hurt flashed in her eyes before she looked away. "I just wanted you, okay? Isn't that enough?"

I reached for her chin, turning her face back toward mine. The emotion in her eyes nearly gutted me. Whatever was going through her mind, it was obvious my question had wounded her deeply, and that was the last thing I'd wanted. I'd do anything for Nikki. Walk through fire, take a bullet… I'd give my life for her.

"Just seems a little too good to be true, Nikki. You've never glanced my way with any sort of interest. I've wanted you for so damn long, but I don't think you came in here for the right reasons. I just want to understand. If this is a one-time thing, then tell me now because I don't think I can let you go. Now that I've had you, tasted you, it will kill me to watch you walk away."

Nikki pressed her face into the crook of my neck and wrapped her arms around me tight. "I don't want to leave."

"Then you won't."

"Damn right she won't!" a voice boomed. Nikki gasped and I made sure her body was hidden from view before I turned my head to glare through the glass.

"What the fuck, Scratch? You just barge into bathrooms now?"

"Congratulations, Ashes. You now have an ol' lady, and no, I'm not fucking asking. No vote needed. You just screwed Renegade's baby sister. You either claim her, or I'll let him gut you. Everyone in this fucking club knows she's off-limits."

Except Bane. He didn't give a shit. Probably better to keep that thought to myself.

"I won't force her to be with me," I said. "She's been through enough, Scratch. Don't do this to her."

"I didn't," he said. "You did. Get the fuck dressed and get to Church."

With that, he turned and walked out. I was almost scared to look at Nikki, worried what I'd see in her eyes. The last thing I expected was the soft smile curving her lips.

"Archer… you're a dumbass."

I blinked and stared. "What?"

"Dumb. Ass. I came in here to seduce you because I've wanted you for a while too. Now shut up, kiss me, then go take care of business. The sooner you go, the faster you can come home."

"You're not mad?"

She shook her head.

I kissed her like she'd demanded, washed quickly, then dressed and went to Church. All the while, I couldn't get the thought of her sweet smile off my mind, or the way she'd responded to my touch. I only hoped shit didn't hit the fan when Renegade found out Nikki was mine now. No fucking way he'd meant it when he said I'd have to claim her if she stayed here.

* * *

"Ashes has something he'd like to tell everyone, don't you?" Scratch asked after everyone had taken a seat.

Well, fuck. Just throw me in the fire. Thanks, VP. I wondered about my chances of leaving this room without a busted lip or some bruises.

"So, it seems I have an ol' lady." I rubbed the back of my neck. "Nikki is mine."

Renegade growled from across the table. "You fucking asshole! You touched her, didn't you? You damn well know I didn't mean for you to actually claim her."

Oh, I'd done more than just touch her, but I didn't think he wanted the details. Even now I could taste her on my lips. All I wanted was to get Church over with and head back home, and maybe pick up where we left off. Now that I'd had her, my craving for her seemed to have doubled. Possibly tripled.

"I didn't take advantage of her, if that's what you're thinking." And I was a little pissed that anyone at this table could ever assume I'd do that to Nikki, or any woman. Then again, I'd let them think I was a man-whore like most of them the last few years, not wanting my secret to get out. "She wanted me as much as I wanted her. Hell, she started it!"

That, apparently, was the wrong thing to say.

Renegade's chair crashed to the floor as he came over the table toward me. I shoved my chair back and stood right as his body flew into mine, knocking me into the wall. My head cracked and pain exploded through my skull, but before I could react, Renegade was coming at me with his fists. I did my best to protect myself, but I tried not to beat on the guy. He was only trying to defend his sister, and I could respect that.

He did a number on my ribs and as I fell to the floor, he slammed his fists into my back a few times. I coughed and blood dripped onto the floor. Out of the corner of my eye, I saw him draw back his foot, but before he could connect, someone dragged him away. I staggered to my feet and swayed a moment, the room spinning from the blows to the head. Maybe it had been stupid to not fight back, but he'd told me to keep my hands off his sister, had already expressed his displeasure over her being in my house, and I'd crossed even that line and taken things further.

It was the only freebie he was getting. If he came after me again, I'd fight back.

"Renegade needs some time to cool off," Havoc said. "We got word about a possible deal on the other end of town. Our contact is supposed to meet us at a warehouse over on Clearwater Road. I think you should go and see what's up."

Harley Wylde   **Slider/ Ashes Duet**

"Alone? Do we know anything about this guy?" I asked, my jaw cracking with the effort. Normally, I wouldn't question the Sergeant-at-Arms, but right now, I wasn't sure anyone at the table had my back. As far as they were concerned, I'd taken things too far with Nikki, but I'd loved her for years. Maybe if they knew I hadn't touched a woman in all that time, but I'd have to give up my man card if I made that confession. They didn't know I hadn't fucked the club whores I'd led outside.

"Yes, alone. Why? Do you need someone to hold your hand?"

I flipped him off and walked out of Church. Better to get this shit over with so I could go home, although fucking Nikki would hurt a bit after the beating Renegade gave me. Granted, I'd let him, but that didn't change the fact my head and ribs hurt like fucking hell. If this shit went sideways, I was going to be pissed. If they wanted to make me pay for making Nikki mine, then so be it.

Every bump in the road made me wince, but soon I was pulling up to the warehouse. The fact it looked deserted had my nape prickling. Something wasn't right about this. Just how much did Havoc know about this guy? For that matter, he hadn't told me a name or given me a description. It wasn't the usual way things were handled, but I'd apparently fucked up and they all wanted me to pay. How the fuck would I know if the right man showed up?

I killed the engine and got off the Harley. I needed to go inside and yet, I hesitated. My fingers twitched and my stomach knotted. Everything inside me screamed to go the other way. Instead, I forced one foot in front of the other until I stepped into the darkened interior of the warehouse. The scent of urine and mildew burned my nose as I progressed farther inside.

I didn't hear so much as the skitter of rodents. That eerie feeling was building. The wrongness of the situation grew with every step I took. Where was the guy I was supposed to meet? Or anyone else for that matter? Had Havoc sent me on a wild goose chase? I was nearly convinced that no one was going to show when I heard the creak of a door, but it wasn't the one I'd entered.

Pulling the gun from the back of my pants, I gripped it tight and scanned the interior. Everything was silent again. Still, someone was there. Had to be, unless vermin had learned to open doors. Or maybe a bum. It wasn't unheard of for places like this to house the homeless when they needed a place to crash.

I prowled the interior, hoping to either run into the man I was meeting, or determine there was no one here so I could fucking leave. There was a pile of flattened boxes in the corner that looked like a makeshift bed. Another corner had stacks of newspaper that was most definitely someone's toilet. My nose wrinkled in distaste as I quickly moved away from the offensive stench. My boots clanged as I went up the metal stairs to the second floor. Maybe the door I'd heard was up here.

I'd covered every damn inch of the place and didn't see or hear anyone. Heading back down the stairs, I decided it was time to go. Whoever was supposed to be here had evidently flaked out. Before I could reach the doors, there was a deep voice that called out.

"You the Devil I'm meeting?" said a voice from... somewhere. There was just enough of an echo that I couldn't locate the man speaking.

"Yeah, I'm the Devil sent to meet you."

"Good."

His voice came from right behind me, but before I could turn, something smashed into the back of my head. I groaned and dropped to my knees, my gun falling from my hand and sliding across the floor. Whoever had hit me, bashed me over the head again and again. Something wet dripped down my forehead. Blood. Fucking hell! Was the asshole trying to kill me?

I swung out, trying to connect with him, but my fist glanced off his thigh. All he did was fucking laugh, then he nailed me in the ribs. He came at me again, and I tried to fight him off. I connected with his face, making him snarl and stagger a step back. I didn't see the next two blows that landed against my temple. My vision started to fade, and I felt my heart slowing. I worried that this might be the end, that I'd never get home to Nikki.

I struggled to stay awake, to keep breathing. She needed me. What would happen to her and little Oliver if I never went home? Would the club still protect her? Would she miss me?

My mind whirred with what-ifs as darkness closed in and I passed out.

Chapter Four

Nikki

I couldn't stop smiling. The way Ashes had taken me against the shower wall, the obvious concern that I'd regret it... he really was the sweetest man. Sometimes it was hard to believe he was a badass biker. I knew all the guys might have a hard outer shell but a gooey center when it came to women they cared about, but I'd never thought he'd be one of them. Yeah, I'd let Bane take me to bed on our first date, but I'd known even then it wouldn't go anywhere. My brother had made sure the bikers stayed clear of me. Defying his authority and sleeping with Bane had been fun, and I'd possibly have gone out with him a few times, but after just an hour or two I'd known it wasn't the forever kind of thing. I'd never told anyone that.

After Ashes had left for Church, I'd taken my time showering until the last drop of hot water had been used, then I dried off and dressed. I explored his home, then checked out the fridge and pantry to get some ideas for breakfast. I hated that he'd had to leave without eating anything. We'd both overslept this morning. Then again, I'd been doing a lot of sleeping the last three months. I'd woken when I heard his phone ring, but when Ashes hadn't come out of his room, I'd decided to get nosy.

Seeing him in the shower... My cheeks warmed and I clenched my thighs at the memory. His body was a work of art, all sleek muscles and ink. Most of his tattoos couldn't be seen unless he was shirtless, and I wondered about the meaning behind each one. I'd also worried that someone as fit as him would take one look at my naked body and be disgusted, but the way he'd tried so hard not to look when he'd put me into the shower at my apartment, I'd hoped that maybe he was interested.

Damn my brother for making Ashes stay away all this time! We could have had years together! Maybe I wouldn't have been with the mistake I'd dated for so long. Chad. Even now I wanted to sneer just thinking of him. If Ashes had shown an interest, I'd have gladly dumped the douchebag asshole sooner. It pissed me off that Renegade was always meddling in my life. I knew he meant well, but I didn't need a babysitter. I was a grown-ass woman and I could take care of myself. Being with Ashes would have never been a mistake, at least I didn't think so. Maybe the man he was back then was different from the guy who had been taking care of me. Or maybe not. I'd never know since my big brother had taken that from me.

As the time ticked by and I hadn't heard from Ashes, I started to worry that Renegade had found out what happened and beat the hell out of him. I wouldn't put it past him. I knew that I wasn't supposed to go to the clubhouse without an invitation, but that was before Ashes had claimed me. Things were different now, weren't they? Scratch had demanded that Ashes make me his, so I had a right to go look for him. At least, that's what I'd tell anyone who asked. I could play stupid for a few days at any rate.

I slipped on some shoes and then left the house. I followed the meandering road through the compound, taking my time so I wouldn't overdo it. After sitting on the couch day after day, I didn't know what my body was capable of handling, especially while I was six months pregnant. I could have taken my SUV, but exercise was good for me. By the time I reached the clubhouse, I saw only a handful of bikes out front. One of them looked similar to what Ashes usually rode, but

Harley Wylde   **Slider/ Ashes Duet**

I couldn't be certain it was his. I didn't know the difference between the bikes, but the colors and size seemed right.

Taking a breath to steel my nerves, I went into the clubhouse and came to a halt when I saw Havoc, Magnus, and Phantom were seated around a table. There was a Prospect behind the bar, and I could hear voices farther back down the hall. Magnus lifted his eyebrows when he saw me and Havoc shot a scowl my way.

"What the hell are you doing here, Nikki?" he demanded. "Haven't you caused enough trouble?"

I stumbled back a step, not expecting the Sergeant-at-Arms to be so harsh with me. The few times we'd talked before, he'd always been nice. I didn't know how to respond and just stood, frozen in place. Phantom stood and came toward me, his expression unreadable, which made unease prickle down my spine. Were they not told that I was with Ashes now? Or were they pissed about not getting a vote? Would they have voted against us being together?

"Nikki, you shouldn't be here. You need to go home," Phantom said.

"I was looking for Ashes. He didn't come back and I haven't heard from him. I thought..."

Phantom didn't say anything at first. I could see the indecision in his eyes.

"Your brother didn't take it well when Scratch informed us that Ashes was claiming you. Renegade had thought the idea of being stuck with the same woman all the time would make Ashes back off."

My brother really didn't want me here. My stomach churned. Even though I hadn't experienced much morning sickness, the acidic burn at the back of my throat was all the warning I needed. I bolted for the hall and the bathroom I knew was in that direction, not stopping until I'd slammed the door open and fallen to the ground in front of the toilet. Booted steps came running and I heard someone skid to a stop in the doorway as I threw up again and again.

By the time I was finished, I was shaking and felt weak. Tears leaked from the corners of my eyes and I felt snot dripping from my nose. A handful of toilet paper appeared in my line of sight and I cleaned myself up. Standing on shaky legs, I took a shallow breath and then another. I swayed and hands gripped me, keeping me upright.

"Jesus, Havoc. She's pregnant. Did you have to be such an ass?" Magnus asked.

"I wasn't trying to upset her, but she needs to know she caused trouble. Renegade was fucking pissed and went after Ashes like he was possessed or some shit," Havoc said.

I whined and looked up at Magnus. "Ashes…"

"He's fine," Magnus assured me. "Cinder sent him out on a run. He'll be gone most of today."

Havoc muttered something that sounded like *bullshit*.

"Did my brother hurt him?" I asked.

"He beat on him a little, but Ashes was standing and able to ride when he left here," Magnus said. "Might be bruised and tender for a day or two, but he's fine, Nikki."

"I'll take you home in one of the trucks," Phantom said from somewhere behind Havoc. "You should rest."

I didn't want to rest! I wanted Ashes back. Part of me knew I was being irrational. He was part of this club and would be gone on various jobs. It was something I'd have to adjust to if I was going to be with him. Maybe if I had seen him before he left, or heard from him, then my stomach wouldn't be churning quite so much. I followed Phantom outside and got into one of the club trucks. At the house, he started to get out, but I waved him off. The last thing I wanted was to come across as weak and pathetic, even if I had just thrown up in front of him. "I'll be fine."

Phantom nodded. "You have the clubhouse number. Call if you need anything before Ashes gets back. I'm sure he'll be here by dinner."

I went into the house and the first stop was the bathroom to brush my teeth. Despite the nausea, I was a little hungry so I made a snack and decided to watch a movie. I needed the distraction so I wouldn't think about Ashes and my brother going after him. How could Renegade have done that?

My brother was the last person I wanted to see, so I was thankful he didn't come try and talk to me. I didn't want to hear anything he had to say. He was treating me like a child. It was my life, and I should have a say in who I dated... or... I stared at the wall. Ashes had claimed me. I was his ol' lady, which meant more than just dating. It hadn't really sunk in until this moment. The Devil's Boneyard men didn't claim a woman and let her go. It was a lifelong commitment. Even a tighter bond than marriage.

The new reality of my life was starting to settle in my mind. I wouldn't be raising Oliver alone. Ashes would be by my side all the time and not just a few days a week. And... my cheeks burned as I thought about how incredible sex was between us. I wasn't the most experienced when it came to that sort of thing, but Bane hadn't been my first either. No one had ever made me feel the way Ashes did. Even though it had been intense and fast, I'd come harder than I ever had before. For that matter, only Bane had ever made me come at all. Well, aside from my own hand or a vibrator.

My stomach rumbled and I had a sudden craving for peanut butter cookies. From what I'd seen of Ashes' kitchen, there wasn't a cookie in sight, but it didn't mean I couldn't make some. I got up and rummaged through the cabinets and pantry, hoping he'd have all the ingredients I needed. Other than crunchy peanut butter and eggs, Ashes didn't have the other stuff the recipe called for. I was dressed and I *did* have my car here. My bank account was pretty much empty, but maybe I had just enough room on my credit card to buy the few groceries that were missing for my culinary plans.

I grabbed my purse and keys then went out to my SUV, only to find a Prospect leaning against it. I froze, not sure if I should go back in or just tell him to move. I hadn't really spoken to Jin before, even though I was aware of who he was. He'd worked the gate a few times when I'd come to visit Renegade.

"Going somewhere?" he asked.

"I need some things from the store."

He nodded and looked down at his boots. "And you're going to buy those things with what money? Your brother said you're so broke you lost your apartment and that's why you're really here."

My heart felt like someone had just stuck a knife through it. That's what my brother thought of me? That I'd let Ashes claim me just to have a place to stay, or money to spend? Did he really think I was that mercenary or shallow? My purse hung limply from my fingers and my keys dropped to the ground. Tears burned my eyes and made my throat tight as I turned to go back inside. Why would he tell someone that?

"I'll just..." I pressed my lips together as I reached for the door, but a hand on my shoulder stopped me.

"Hey, I didn't mean to upset you."

"It's fine. I just didn't realize my brother thought so little of me."

Jin sighed and turned me to face him. "Look, I know Ashes pretty damn well. I've known for a while there was some woman he was hung up on, and since I heard he claimed you, I'm guessing it's been you all along. Don't let your brother fuck with your head. He'll come around."

I nodded and wiped at my cheeks.

"If you want to go to the store, I'll take you. But we're stopping at the clubhouse first to get some cash. I don't think Ashes would want you spending your money on food. He'll see that as his job."

"Fine. I just wanted to bake some cookies and I don't have everything I need."

Jin smiled. "Cookies are always a good reason to go shopping."

I snorted, then laughed. If he truly felt that way, he'd make some woman very happy whenever he settled down. Jin led me over to the SUV and helped me into the passenger's seat before he took the keys and got behind the wheel. He stopped for the cash like he'd said, then hit the road into town, not stopping until he reached the nearest grocery store. I'd thought maybe he'd stay in the car, or at least trail behind me. Not Jin. He took control of the shopping cart and walked beside me, reaching the items on the top shelf and even throwing in some extra stuff like fresh fruit.

"Do you know what you're making for dinner?" he asked.

"No, but Ashes had some ground beef in the fridge and a bag of frozen chicken breasts in the freezer."

He arched a brow and looked at me, clearly not impressed with the selection. Yeah, I wasn't too thrilled with either option. But at the same time, I didn't want to spend money if it wasn't necessary. I didn't know if Ashes would have to pay the club back for whatever I used right now, and since I didn't know about his finances, I wasn't about to spend a lot of money without talking to him about it first.

Jin seemed to sense my hesitation and led me over to the butcher. I chewed my lower lip as I looked at the pre-seasoned meat, the fresh seafood, and steaks so thick that I just knew they'd be good and juicy. When I didn't make a selection after a few minutes, Jin gave me a nudge. I ended up getting two chicken breasts rubbed with a lemon pepper seasoning, a large salmon filet, and two of the steaks.

After picking up some side dishes, the ingredients for the cookies as well as for two pies and a cake, I let Jin load the cart up with grape juice, apple juice, and sweet tea. It seemed all Ashes had was tap water, milk, beer, and coffee. The doctor had already limited my caffeine intake so I'd stopped drinking coffee most days. By the time we checked out up front, I was a bit worried over the total. Jin didn't seem concerned and peeled off a few hundreds to pay. It didn't escape my notice the cute clerk was checking him out.

I turned to hide my smirk. Sure, we could have been a couple, but we weren't so I didn't see the harm in her eyeing him like a piece of candy. Now if Ashes had been with me, then I might have given her a piece of my mind. After he got his change, I led the way back to the SUV in the parking lot. Jin loaded the groceries while I waited in the car.

The last thing I anticipated when we got back to the compound was for him to not only unload the car, but help put everything away. I eyed him, wondering who had taught him to be so considerate. Or domesticated for that matter. Most of the bikers I'd met were a rough sort who only remembered their manners after the fact, or just didn't care to begin with. Even my brother was the same way. I knew our mom had taught him the proper way to act around women, but Renegade had seemed to think women were there for the taking, and should be bent to his will. Until he'd met Darby.

"Thank you," I said.

"I'll be outside if you need anything else, Nikki. Phantom asked that I stick close until Ashes gets back."

I gave him a nod and as he walked out of the kitchen, I began gathering the ingredients for the peanut butter cookies. Working in the kitchen kept my mind and my hands occupied. I'd made two batches before I heard the front door open and the scuff of boots. Smiling, I turned to greet who I hoped was Ashes, but the smile quickly fell from my face.

Ashes had returned, but... not in the same condition he'd left. Blood trickled from a wound on his forehead, more covered his knuckles, and he staggered as if he were barely upright. I rushed toward him, wrapping an arm around his waist and staring up in eyes that looked back with confusion.

"Ashes, what happened?" I asked.

The confusion quickly turned to anger and he shoved me away from him. His gaze dropped to my belly before he snorted and turned toward the fridge.

"You can leave. Go back to the clubhouse."

My jaw dropped. "Wh-what? What do you mean go to the clubhouse?"

"I don't want a whore in my house."

It felt like ice had been dumped over me, chilling me all the way through. I stumbled back and stared at him in horror. Why would he say such a thing to me? Did he blame me for whatever happened? Did he think it was my fault that Renegade had attacked him? "Ashes, please… what did I do wrong?"

His mouth twisted as he glared at my stomach again. "From the looks of things, you must do something pretty damn well to have gotten knocked up. Don't try to pretend that brat is mine. Get the fuck out!"

I gasped and nearly fell in my haste to run from the house. Havoc, Cobra, and Ripper pulled up on their bikes as I tumbled from the house and landed on my knees in the grass. Ripper rushed over and helped me up. I didn't see Jin and figured he must have left when he saw Ashes come back.

"Nikki, what's wrong?"

"Ashes. He… he…" I pinched my lips together in an effort to hold back the tears. "He called me a whore and told me to get out of his house."

Havoc cursed and went stomping inside. I could hear shouting, but not the actual words. There was a loud crash, then another. I stared, wide-eyed, and then ran back into the house. It didn't matter that Ashes had gutted me with his words. He'd been injured, and I didn't want Havoc to hurt him further.

The Sergeant-at-Arms had Ashes pinned to the floor, but the man who I'd thought to be so sweet and caring was snarling and cussing at Havoc, threatening to kill him and anyone else who fucked with him. I'd never seen so much anger coming from him before and it frightened me. What had Ashes been through today?

"Ashes." I tried to kneel next to him, but Ripper held me back. Tears slipped down my cheeks as I pulled away and dropped down beside him. "Archer. Please stop fighting."

He froze at the sound of his real name. I knew it was wrong to use it in front of his brothers, but I was desperate to reach him, reach the man I knew was in there somewhere. Maybe whatever had caused the head wound did more damage than break the skin. I only knew the man pinned to the floor wasn't the same one who'd claimed me earlier. Whatever had happened, it had changed him.

"I don't want you to get hurt. Please. Archer, you have to remember."

I could feel the tension in the room. Ashes panted and glared at me, his hate-filled eyes making me tremble.

"Remember?" Havoc asked. "What the fuck is going on?"

I took a shaky breath and reached out to run my fingers over the scruff on his jaw. It was Ashes, and yet it wasn't. The man in front of me looked like him, but wasn't acting like the man I'd come to know. Something was wrong. Really damn wrong.

"You don't know who I am, do you?"

"No," he said, his tone biting. "Just some whore in my house."

"Fucking hell," Cobra muttered. "Hey, ass hat! That's your woman you're calling a whore."

Ashes blinked a few times, studying me. "Mine?"

I nodded. "I'm yours. Try to remember. Do you remember this morning? Before Church was called?"

His brow furrowed and pain crossed his features. "All I remember is waking up in a warehouse. I was bleeding. I don't even know how I came to this place. Just got on the bike outside and rode here. No one stopped me when I came through the gate. I… I kind of remember this place, remember being part of a club, but everything is hazy."

"Do you remember who you are?" I asked, dread filling me.

"No." He frowned. "I don't think so. Saw the name Ashes on my cut. The Devil's Boneyard MC sounded familiar. For that matter, I know what the hell a cut is, and most people don't. Some things are there, but mostly everything else is gone." His gaze held mine. "I remember the name Archer."

"He needs a doctor," I said, looking at Havoc. "Can you get off him, please?"

"Shit." Ripper and Cobra both knelt next to me. "We'll find out what the fuck happened to you and we'll take care of it. Why don't you let Nikki help you get cleaned up? We'll have the doc here soon to check you out."

Havoc slowly stood and backed up, his body tense as if prepared for Ashes to attack again. Ashes stood slowly, a hint of vulnerability in his eyes under the hostility. I took his hand and led him from the room, down the hall, and into the bedroom. Pushing the door shut, I wondered if he'd prefer that I leave. While he looked around, I went into the bathroom and started the shower. My heart was pounding. I didn't know what would happen if Ashes never remembered me. What if he didn't want me anymore?

I heard the shuffle of his steps as he came up behind me. I saw his hands hover over my sides before he gently settled them on my hips.

"I'm sorry I don't remember you," he said. "And I'm sorry I reacted the way I did before. Some part of me just knew this was my house, but..."

"You didn't remember that I was living here, that we were together."

"Right," he said softly.

"I'll get you some clean clothes while you shower. I can just leave them on the bed."

I turned to face him and his gaze searched mine before dropping to my belly. He placed his hand there right about the time Oliver rolled and kicked. Ashes jolted then smiled.

"His name is Oliver," I said.

"A boy?" Ashes looked at me again. "We're having a boy?"

I hesitated only a moment, then nodded. The man was going through enough without me complicating things and explaining about Bane. With some luck, he'd wake up tomorrow and remember everything. I hoped this was only a minor setback and whatever had happened to him wouldn't have lasting consequences.

"The water's getting cold. You should wash off. Do you want jeans and a T-shirt laid out, or some sweats? I don't know where you're injured other than your head and knuckles."

"Sweats might be better."

Before I had a chance to leave, he removed his cut and pulled his shirt over his head. I couldn't hold back my gasp. He was covered in heavy bruising across his chest and down one side of his ribs. Tears sprang to my eyes as I gently traced the wounds. Who had done this to him? If my brother had caused any of this, I was going to kill him.

"Archer."

He placed his hand over mine, holding my palm against his chest. "I'm fine."

No, he damn well wasn't "fine," but I knew better than to argue. I'd just be wasting my breath.

He toed off his boots and removed his socks, jeans, and underwear. There were a few cuts on his thighs and more bruises. When he turned to get into the shower, I whimpered. It looked as if he'd been beaten with a bat. Ashes got under the water and slicked his hair back, leaving the door open. He didn't even glance my way, just held out his hand.

"What?" I asked.

"Get in with me," he said.

"You... I... You don't remember me, but you want me to shower with you?"

He glanced at me. "You're my woman, right? My ol' lady?"

I hesitated a moment, but what he said was true. I was his, even if it had only been for a day. Not even a full day.

"Yes."

"Then get your ass in this shower, woman."

I took my time undressing, noticing the way his gaze heated with every inch of skin I exposed. By the time I was naked, he was pulling me under the spray with him. His hands settled at my waist, or where I'd once had a waist. He stared at me, as if searching for even a wisp of a memory that included me.

"How could I forget you?" he asked.

"Let's get you cleaned up so the doctor can look at you." I reached up and brushed my fingers over the wound on his head.

Harley Wylde   **Slider/ Ashes Duet**

"Everything will be fine, Nik."

My eyes widened. "What did you call me?"

"Nik. That's your name, right? Nikki?"

"Y-yeah, but you're the only one who really ever calls me Nik."

He leaned down and lightly brushed his lips against mine. "Maybe my memory is coming back already."

He devoured my lips and I couldn't resist him. Clinging to his shoulders, I held on as he claimed me all over again. I only hoped he remembered it, and me, this time. And I hoped like hell that he hadn't injured himself further by taking me so roughly. I'd loved every second of it, but from the bruising on his body, I knew he had to be hurting.

Chapter Five

Ashes

Two months and I still had huge gaps in my memory. The rest of me had healed just fine. Thankfully, nothing had been broken, except my brain. Every now and then I thought I remembered Nikki. A flash of her at a party or with another man. Several of her with her brother. But not a damn one that reminded me how we'd ended up together. I could have asked, but I kept hoping it would all come back to me. There was a tug in my chest whenever she was near, and I found myself falling for her all over again. She was the sweetest woman, and I knew I was damn lucky to have her.

Her belly had gotten bigger and she looked like she might pop at any moment, even though both she and her doctor assured me it wasn't time yet. I found myself pressing a hand to her baby bump every chance I got, loving the feel of little Oliver pushing back. Our son. I smiled, wondering if he'd look like his mom or like me.

Nikki had tried to put some distance between us, attempted to sleep in the guest room those first few nights, but I'd refused to let her. If she said she was mine, then I wanted her with me. I'd taken her against the shower wall not long after learning that she wasn't some club whore like I'd accused when I'd first come home. Maybe it was wrong. All right, so it had definitely been wrong, but I'd hoped it would spark a memory. Being inside her had felt incredible, and really damn familiar. Any time I reached for her, she'd always come willingly. I'd been gentle, or tried to be.

Until this morning, when I'd accidentally hurt her.

Which was why we were now at her doctor's office, and she sat on the padded table wearing one of those gowns. There'd been a bit of blood, and it had scared the shit out of me. I'd immediately helped her dress and brought her in, insisting they make room for her in the schedule.

I grasped her hand, needing the comfort of her touch as I worried about her and our baby. If I'd done anything to hurt Oliver, or Nikki, I'd never forgive myself. It was bad enough I couldn't be around her brother without an argument starting. I didn't even understand why he was so pissed at me. We were brothers, part of the same club, and family. I could only imagine how furious he'd be if he knew I hurt Nikki today.

The doctor came in, smiling broadly. "Good afternoon, Nikki. I see you're a few days early for your appointment. The nurse said you'd bled a little today."

Nikki nodded. "We, um…"

My woman blushed so hard her entire face turned red.

"We were having sex," I said. "But she cried out in pain and I noticed she was bleeding. I made her come straight here."

"We're going to check on baby Oliver first, then I'll need to check you and see if there's still some bleeding or if you're dilated." The doctor patted Nik's knee. "Just let me get the portable machine brought in."

The woman turned to go and Nikki cried out. I stared, jaw dropping, at the water dripping off the table. Holy shit!

"Or we can deliver a baby," the doctor said.

Harley Wylde   Slider/ Ashes Duet

"What? No!" Nikki started breathing hard and I could see the wildness in her eyes. She was in a full-on panic. "It's too soon!"

There was something in the doctor's eyes that said she agreed, but by the way her jaw firmed, I knew whatever she said next would be to help keep Nikki calm. Maybe it was too early, but I didn't know exactly what that meant.

"Your baby is developed enough that Oliver will be fine, Nikki. He's only three weeks early. There may be some health risks down the road, but delivering at this stage is much safer than if he'd arrived two or three weeks ago."

I'd been reading the baby books, and even though I still didn't know much of anything about babies or the birthing process, I could tell the doctor was trying to ease Nik's fears. She was right about the health issues, though. I also knew that keeping Nikki calm was necessary. If her blood pressure and heartrate spiked, it could stress the baby. I'd read that just the other day as I tried to prepare for the arrival of our son. I smoothed my hand over her hair and leaned down to press a kiss to her cheek.

"Easy, sweetheart. You've got this."

"I'm going to call over to the hospital and get a room ready for you," the doctor said. "Think you can walk to the hall and I'll have a wheelchair brought around?"

Nikki nodded, her grip on my hand tightening.

"So, Dad, keep her calm and we'll be saying hi to little Oliver soon enough."

The next three hours passed so damn slowly I thought I'd lose my mind. I stayed with Nikki in the delivery room. Sweat soaked her hair as she screamed, cussed, and pushed for all her worth. The way she

- 205 -

squeezed my hand, I thought she might break all my fingers, but I didn't care. If I could ease her pain, I would. Little Oliver just didn't want to cooperate. His head would start to come out, then the doctor said he'd just retreat back inside Nikki. They were close to getting forceps when he finally shot out of her into the doctor's waiting hands.

I smiled down at Nikki, so damn proud of her. Until the murmurs of the staff in the room caught my attention. Along with the silence.

"What's wrong?" I asked.

The doctor gave me a sad look as the nurses rushed Oliver from the room. What the fuck was going on? I looked at Nikki and saw tears slipping down her cheeks. The doctor pressed on her stomach and said something about delivering the placenta, then they were cleaning her up. Nikki was moved to another bed and placed into a room in the maternity ward, but we still hadn't seen Oliver.

"Where's my son?" I asked the next nurse who stopped in.

She gave me a smile, but she had that same spooked look I'd seen right before Oliver had been taken away. Something was wrong, but I didn't know what. And I knew Nik needed answers too.

"They'll bring him to you soon."

"What happened? Why wasn't he crying? Don't babies cry when they're born?"

"The doctor will answer your questions soon enough. Please, try not to worry. Do you need anything?"

I shook my head and held Nikki's hand. I could feel the tension rolling off her. My gut was churning over the fear of losing Oliver before we ever really had him. I'd spent the last two months talking to the kid, and now I might never get to meet him.

"Archer, what if… what if…"

I leaned down and pressed my lips to hers. "Hush. He'll be fine. We'll get to hold him soon."

She nodded, but I could tell she didn't believe me. Hell, I didn't believe me either.

Another hour went by and finally, a small clear bed was wheeled into the room. A blue bundle lay inside, and my heart swelled with so much love for the tiny boy inside. Nikki pushed herself higher up in bed and I released her hand to go to Oliver. My hands shook as I picked him up. He yawned and smacked his lips, then turned his head toward me.

"He's hungry," the nurse said. "Better give him to his mom."

I nodded and carried him to Nikki. She dropped the front of her gown and reached for Oliver. Seeing her nurse our son was probably the most beautiful thing I'd ever witnessed. I reached out to stroke his cheek as he suckled.

"Baby Oliver was six pounds seven ounces," said the nurse. "And he's nineteen inches long."

"He's perfect," Nikki said, her voice choked from unshed tears.

"Yeah, he is," I agreed. "And he looks just like his mom."

"I'll leave the three of you to bond. There are diapers and wipes provided by the hospital, as well as some other goodies you get to take home with you. Just buzz the nurse's station if you need anything. The doctor will be around shortly to check on you."

Oliver greedily sucked at Nikki's breast before she switched him to the other side with a grimace. He was in a gown the hospital had for every baby born

Harley Wylde   **Slider/ Ashes Duet**

here, and I didn't like it. He had clothes at home, things we'd picked just for him. It bothered me that his bag was back at my house, along with Nikki's. I pulled my phone from my pocket and shot off a text to Dixon.

Get the two bags just inside my front entry. Bring them to the hospital. Oliver is here!

I got a thumbs-up emoji as a response, but I had no doubt he'd tell everyone our son had been born. It wouldn't be long before the club would stop by, hopefully not all at once. If Renegade made an appearance, and I knew it was likely, he'd better damn well behave and not start shit.

I sat on the edge of the bed watching my woman and kid, my heart feeling full. They were beautiful, and *mine*. When Oliver was done eating, and Nik had covered up again, I settled on the bed and pulled her against me, our son in her arms. I might not remember my life, or this woman, but I doubted I'd ever been happier than I was right now. I hoped that Oliver would be the first of several kids for us.

The doctor stopped by and explained Oliver hadn't been breathing at first, but they'd managed to clear his airway, given him some oxygen, and he was now able to breathe on his own. It had been a scare for everyone, but not as serious as they'd first feared since he was born too soon. I knew I'd be watching him like a hawk, probably from now until the day I died.

The door opened a short while later and Dixon came in, a smile on his face as he saw little Oliver. He set the two bags down at the foot of the bed and came closer. Slowly, he reached for Oliver, stroking a finger down my son's cheek.

"He's cute," Dixon said.

"How long before the others show up?" I asked.

- 208 -

Harley Wylde   Slider/Ashes Duet

"Scratch, Cinder, and their women are downstairs right now. I'm sure the others will be along soon enough."

Nikki yawned and nuzzled closer to me, her eyes heavy.

"Sleep, baby. You need to rest," I said.

She murmured something and fell almost immediately asleep. I smiled, admiring my beautiful family.

"You did good, man," Dixon said. "Listen. Renegade is on his way here. I can't promise he won't be an ass, but he wants to come see his nephew."

I held back a growl, but just barely. I didn't know what the fuck his problem was, but the bastard hated me. "If he upsets Nikki, I'll personally remove him from the room."

Dixon nodded. "Look, the guy's my friend, but when it comes to Nikki he can be a little... overprotective. And I think the fact that she was in such dire straits and he didn't know..."

Wait. What the fuck did that mean?

"Dire straits?" I asked.

Dixon's expression shut down.

"Dix, start talking. Now."

"Shit," he muttered. "Look, Nikki was living in an apartment across town. You found out she was being evicted and brought her home with you. Renegade lost his shit, and that's why he's such an ass to you. Because you got his little sister out of trouble, saved her, when it should have been him."

I looked at Nikki and Oliver. Something was off. If Nikki was mine, and Oliver was mine, why hadn't they been living with me. How long had she been in the apartment? No, the right questions was how long had she been living in my house? Had I not wanted her

- 209 -

for some reason? I tried to remember, but it just made pain spike through my brain. The headaches were fewer now, but still hit hard when I tried to force the memories to come back.

"I know you have questions," Dixon said. "But I think I've said more than enough."

Or maybe he hadn't said quite enough.

I didn't get a chance to question him more before the room door opened again. This time the Pres and VP came in with their women.

"We aren't staying long. Left the kids with Jordan and Havoc," Scratch said. "Those two will have them trained as assassins within the hour. I kind of like that my kids are sweet. Too much time with that hellion of theirs and my sons might change from angels to the Antichrist."

I coughed to cover a laugh, but I knew he wasn't wrong. I'd only been around Lanie a few times since I came home without my memories, but that kid would scare Lucifer.

Clarity smacked his arm. "Be nice. You know you love that little girl. She's going to be fierce just like her parents."

"God help us," Cinder said.

"Your son is beautiful." Meg smiled at Oliver. "Makes me want another one."

Cinder tugged her against his side. "Fuck, woman. I'm too old to chase after another kid."

Clarity looked sad for a moment. "At least you have the option of having another one. Poor Jordan and Havoc."

What did that mean? I had a feeling it was something else I'd forgotten. Clarity seemed to notice the confusion on my face and decided to elaborate.

Harley Wylde   **Slider/ Ashes Duet**

"Jordan had a miscarriage with their second child. Because of complications during her recovery, the doctor suggested they not try for more kids so Havoc got snipped," Clarity said.

"That sucks. I don't remember that happening." Then again, I didn't remember anything before waking up in that warehouse. Everything before that was just a blank canvas. Nothing. Empty space.

The door slammed open and Renegade stormed inside, a dark look on his face. My body tensed as I prepared for whatever fight he might start this time. He looked at Nikki and Oliver, his gaze softening a moment, before turning back to granite when he faced me again. Why did he hate me being with Nikki? I adored her, and I could tell she was happy with me. I supposed I could understand to a point, but Nikki and Oliver were mine. Why was that so hard for him?

"You shouldn't be in here," he said. "They're not your fucking family."

Cinder cursed and tried to shove Renegade from the room.

"What the fuck does that mean?" I demanded. "She's mine, and so is Oliver."

Renegade sneered at me. "You may have claimed her, but that kid isn't yours."

My heart nearly stopped, and everything went still as I processed his words.

"Would you shut the fuck up?" Scratch demanded. "If you're going to start shit, you need to leave. We talked about this."

Oliver wasn't mine? I looked down at Nikki and the baby. Was that the secret I'd seen lurking in her eyes several times? I'd decided I was imagining things. Had I known before losing my memory? Or had Nikki cheated on me? She didn't seem like the type. I

- 211 -

scanned the baby's face, looking for any sign that he might be mine. He felt like mine.

Renegade was forced from the room and Scratch placed a hand on my shoulder. "Son, I'm only going to say this once. That kid has never known a dad other than you. You've been with Nikki from the moment she knew she was pregnant, took her to her appointments, made sure she ate, took care of her the best you could. Doesn't matter if that kid carries your DNA or not, he's yours and he will always be yours. Unless you decide to walk away. But that's not the Ashes we know. The man we know isn't a quitter and doesn't back down."

His woman took his hand and moved closer to his side, looking at Oliver then me. "Scratch isn't Caleb's biological father, but he's the only one that boy has ever known. And Caleb adores his daddy. When you look at Oliver, what do you see?" she asked.

"My son," I said.

"Then that's all you need to know," Cinder said. "Whether your memory comes back or not, that boy will always be yours. You'll be the one he watches, the one he learns from, the one he calls daddy."

I nodded, my throat tight with emotion. I still needed to know... "And Nikki?" I asked, almost not recognizing my voice. "Did she..."

"She didn't cheat on you," Meg said. "You've known her a long time, but you didn't start seeing each other until after she discovered she was pregnant. Although I suspect that you've had feelings for her longer than that."

The weight on my chest eased at that knowledge. It would have torn me apart to think of her sleeping with someone else after she was mine. Hell, I didn't like the thought of her being with another man even when she hadn't been mine. I didn't remember anyone but her. Still, I knew she hadn't been my first. I'd been to the clubhouse enough times when the club girls were there to know that I'd been with at least a few of them, or at least they made it sound like I had been. I had no memory of them at all. I just hoped that I hadn't cheated on my woman. I'd have to kick my own ass then.

"Whether your memory ever returns or not, those two are your family. It's clear to anyone who sees you and Nikki together that you love her, and she's over the moon for you," Cinder said. "Don't let her asshole brother make you feel like it's all a lie. I'll handle Renegade, and find out what's crawled up his ass."

"We'll ask the others to give the three of you some time," Cinder said, his gaze going to Nikki and Oliver.

I looked down and saw Nik was awake, and chewing her lower lip, worry clouding her eyes. Smoothing her hair back from her face, I leaned down and pressed a kiss to her forehead. Renegade's outburst had made me doubt her for a moment, doubt what we had, but they were right. She was mine. Oliver was mine. And that's all that mattered.

The others left and I took Nikki's hand, giving it a squeeze. "You missed your brother," I said.

"What did he do?"

"Said that Oliver isn't mine."

Her face drained of all color. The hand still gripped in mine trembled. I could tell she was scared now that I knew the truth, but I didn't understand why. It was obvious that I'd made her mine. She even had a property cut to prove it, even if I hadn't seen her wear it. It was understandable since it probably didn't fit very well while she was pregnant, but now that Oliver was here, she'd get to wear my name on her back, show the world she belonged to me.

"Scratch and Clarity said something before they left. Whether Oliver is mine by blood or not, he's still my son. I love him, Nikki, just like I love you. Whether or not we share the same DNA doesn't matter."

Her breath hitched and her eyes filled with tears. "You love me?"

Shit. Had I never told her that? Maybe I was an asshole just like her brother. I didn't like the idea of that, but why I hadn't I told her sooner? The others were right. I loved her, even if I didn't remember being with her before the incident at the warehouse. "Yeah, sweetheart. I love you. Both of you."

I hugged her to me, making sure we didn't squish Oliver. I didn't know what the future would bring for us, but I did know that I saw Nikki by my side through it all. Maybe my memory would return one day, or maybe it wouldn't. Sometimes I got flashes of what I think happened to me. I just hadn't been able to piece it all together yet.

When those memories did return, I knew one thing. I wanted vengeance. Whoever had done this to me had stolen my life. Thankfully, Nikki was helping me remember things here and there, but we hadn't been together forever, and she wouldn't know club business. I hated having this large void in my head. Placing my trust in people I didn't remember had been hard.

"You're not mad I didn't tell you?" she asked.

"No. I wish you would have, but it doesn't matter. I'm sure the way I treated you when I first came home scared you. Just like I'm slowly learning to trust everyone at the compound again, you didn't

Harley Wylde   **Slider/ Ashes Duet**

know if you could trust me anymore either. You had Oliver to think about, and I'd been an ass to you right off."

She smiled a little. "Yeah, but you quickly made it up to me."

"That I did." I smiled, remembering how I'd asked her to join me in the shower, taken her against the wall not caring if anyone remained in the house who might hear. Once I'd known she was mine, that had been enough.

Whatever happened, whether my memories came back or not, I wasn't going to let it hamper my life with Nikki and Oliver. They were my entire world, and I owed it to them to keep moving forward. We'd make new memories, just like we'd been doing the past two months, and I'd cherish each and every one.

I just needed to find a way to make peace with her brother. I knew it bothered Nikki when Renegade came after me. Why the idiot couldn't see what he was doing to his sister left me confused. It was obvious he cared about her, so why hurt her the way he had been? It wasn't something that would get resolved right now, but soon… We needed to sit down and talk. For now, I was going to enjoy the time I had with my woman and son. And I wouldn't let anything ruin it.

Chapter Six

Ashes

The gray light of early morning streamed through the windows and I blinked in confusion, trying to figure out what woke me. I felt small hands pulling at my underwear and I glanced down the length of my body to find Nikki kneeling between my thighs. She was biting her lip and staring at my hard cock, clearly not aware I'd woken. What the hell was she doing? The doctor had warned us she shouldn't have sex for at least six weeks, not until after her appointment, and it had only been three weeks since Oliver had been born.

"Nik, what are you up to?" I asked, my voice still husky with sleep.

I loved my son, but damn… that boy woke up every two hours wanting to eat. Nikki and I were both exhausted, her more so than me. Even when I got up to get our son, it wasn't like I could feed him, so I'd still have to wake her. There were dark smudges under her eyes, but she was still the most beautiful woman I'd ever seen.

She flashed me a smile, then leaned down and licked the length of my cock, making me hiss in a breath as my hips bucked. Jesus! She was trying to fucking kill me. I reached down, intent on pulling her away. As much as I loved having her mouth on me, it wasn't necessary. I might have once been the kind of guy to get off and not care about the woman, but with Nikki things were different. Before I could stop her, she'd taken at least half my dick into her mouth and used her hand to stroke the rest.

"Damn. Baby, that feels so fucking good."

She hummed, making my balls draw up, as she sucked me harder. The little flicks of her tongue just under the head had me fisting the sheets as I fought for control. It would be so easy to wrap her hair around my hand and shove my cock down her throat, but I didn't want to hurt Nik for anything, and I knew I wasn't exactly small.

She shifted and changed her angle, and holy Christ! I damn near came right then and there. I heard Oliver start to whimper through the baby monitor and knew he'd be screaming for his meal in a moment. Nikki just doubled her efforts to get me off.

"Nik. Baby. Oliver is…"

She did this purr type thing as she swallowed more of my dick and I swear I nearly blacked out from the pleasure. Where the fuck had she learned to do that? I was so close to coming when she pulled away, giving me one last lick.

Wait. That was it? She was going to work me up, then leave?

Oliver started to quiet again and Nikki gave me a smile before reaching over me for the drawer next to the bed. Now what was she up to? When she withdrew a bottle of lube, I pushed myself upright. No. No fucking way. The doctor had been very damn clear that she couldn't have sex yet.

"Nikki, you know we can't. You heard the doctor."

"Yes." She snapped open the lube and started working it down my cock. "I did hear her. I also asked her about other ways we could play."

"Nik… I'm not going to do anything that might hurt you or delay your recovery. Baby, I know you're still tender, and --" My brain short-circuited when she straddled my legs, then leaned over, trapping my cock between her breasts. As she rocked, stroking me, I stared at the erotic sight and wondered where this naughty version of Nikki had come from, and how long she'd stick around. Holy fuck!

"This might work better if I lie down and let you fuck me. Well, you know, like this and not..." Her cheeks flushed.

I tapped her and she got up. I quickly reversed our positions, getting even harder when she pressed her breasts together and I thrust between them. Her nipples were red and sore from feeding Oliver, but she didn't act like she was in pain. If there'd been a hint of discomfort on her face, I'd have stopped no matter how turned-on I was, and I had to wonder if she was hiding her discomfort from me. There was a sparkle in her eyes that said she'd missed the intimacy between us as much as I had. Then the minx flicked her tongue out, licking the head of my cock on the next stroke.

"Jesus, Nik. You're killing me."

"Fuck me, Archer. Come all over me."

My balls drew up at her words and I thrust harder and faster. It only took seconds before I was coming. Ropes of cum spurted across her chest, up her throat, and even splashed onto her face. I couldn't catch my breath as I stared down at her. I'd have imagined a lot of women would have been freaked out about having cum all over their faces, but not Nikki. She just looked pleased with herself.

"That was so fucking hot," I said. "Come on, beautiful. I'll start the shower for you."

I got off the bed and helped her up, then led her to the bathroom. While the shower warmed, I studied her. Fatigue clung to her, but she never uttered a word of complaint about Oliver or the things she did around the house. Hell, she could have slept a little longer and instead had found a way to get me off, even though I still couldn't touch her for another few weeks.

"I didn't hurt you, did I?"

She shook her head. "No. I mean, my boobs are sore, but not because of what we just did."

I felt bad that she'd just done that for me, even though she hurt. Somehow, I'd make it up to her. It hadn't been necessary. It was sweet, and hot as fuck, but she needed to take care of herself and not worry about me so much. Despite what men said about needing sex on a regular basis, my hand and I would have gotten along just fine until she was fully healed. After she'd rested a bit, I'd have a talk with her.

I tested the water again, then nudged her under the spray. As much as I'd have loved to get in with her, I knew she also needed some alone time. While Nikki washed, I used the sink to rinse off, then went into the bedroom to pull on a pair of sweats before checking on Oliver. He was lying on his back, staring up at the mobile over his crib. Awake but not screaming.

"Good morning, Oliver."

His legs started kicking when he heard my voice and his head jerked one way, then another as he tried to find me. I moved into his line of sight and reached for him, cradling him against my chest. The scent of a dirty diaper wafted from him. I was amazed he'd been so quiet if he needed to be changed. I loved my son, but he was always vocal when he needed a new diaper. Or food. A cuddle… Really if he was awake, then he could find something to fuss about.

I eased him onto the padded top of the changing table, grabbed a fresh diaper and the wipes, then set about cleaning him up and put him in a fresh outfit. He sucked on his fist and I knew he was hungry, but Nikki hadn't appeared yet. I hated to drag her from the shower before she'd had a chance to relax and enjoy it, but the little man wouldn't be satisfied with his hand for long.

I snorted to myself. He wasn't the only one. Not that I would dare have sex with Nikki before she was healed. I wouldn't have even thought to touch her this morning if she hadn't instigated things. Still, it bothered me she felt she'd needed to do that when she could have used the time to rest. We'd definitely have a discussion later. Right now, our son needed to eat.

"Hey, Nik," I called as I walked into our room.

She stepped out of the bathroom with a towel wrapped around her head and another around her body. "I figured he would be getting hungry, so I tried to hurry."

Nikki had proven to be an amazing mother, but I didn't like the way she always put herself last. I'd have to find a way to make her relax, even if it was just for a little while, or take a much-needed nap. Something. Anything. When she wasn't taking care of Oliver, she was cleaning, cooking, or finding something else that needed her attention and couldn't wait. She was wearing herself out, even if she didn't realize it.

She slipped on her robe, tying the sash before coming closer.

I handed Oliver to her, then followed her to the kitchen. She sat at the table and started to nurse our son while I pulled out everything I'd need to make scrambled eggs, toast, and bacon. I wasn't a gourmet chef by any means, but at least she'd have a filling meal and not have to cook. The books and articles I'd been reading said she needed a lot of protein, so I added some shredded cheese to the eggs before I plated them. Nikki hated grease, so I patted the bacon with some napkins to soak up as much as I could.

When I set her plate in front of her, she gave me a tired but appreciative smile.

"Thanks for cooking, Ashes."

"I'm happy to do it, Nik. I've told you to slow down and not do so much around here. When I'm home, I'm perfectly capable of helping with the cleaning or cooking. I can't exactly feed Oliver so there's not much I can do to help with that, except get him for you and make sure he has a fresh diaper."

I sat down across from her and she reached out. I laced our fingers together, giving her hand a squeeze. "You're doing an amazing job, Nik. And I'm not just saying that. You're a wonderful mom and Oliver is lucky to have you."

She smiled at our son before looking back up at me. "No, I think we're lucky to have you."

I ate my food quickly while she finished feeding our kid, that way I could hold him so she could eat. I'd thought about asking if we could switch him to a bottle so she wouldn't have to do so much, but the pediatrician had harped on the benefits of breast milk, so I'd kept quiet. Seeing Nik with our son, I had a healthy dose of respect for all the moms in the world. No matter how tired, hungry, or sore she was, she just kept going and taking care of everyone.

"You're one hell of a woman, you know that?" I asked.

Her cheeks flushed and she ducked her chin, looking at Oliver.

"I mean it, Nik. You do so much for us and never take time for yourself. That needs to change. You're not in this alone. I'm perfectly capable of cleaning the kitchen or washing the clothes. You don't have to do it all on your own."

She sighed and her gaze met mine. "I know. I just… I'm not the only one going through a lot, Ashes. You're still adjusting to everything after your accident, and I don't want you to do too much. I know you try to hide it from me, but I can tell when you have a headache, and I've noticed they're happening more frequently."

She wasn't wrong. I *had* tried to hide it from her, and they were definitely happening more often. I'd convinced myself it was a lack of sleep, but I had to wonder if something else was going on. There were times when flashes of what I assumed were the past would hit me, one after another, until my brain felt like it might explode. I kept hoping that one day I'd wake up and be back to normal. Then other times, I worried that if that happened maybe I wouldn't be as happy as I was right this moment. What if everyone hadn't been completely honest with me? Not remembering might not be the worst thing ever.

"I just didn't want you to worry. The flashes of memory are coming faster and more frequently, but not enough of a glimpse for me to piece anything together."

Her lips tipped up in a smile. "That's a good thing, though. It means that maybe your memory will come back soon."

Was it, though? A good thing? Because I wasn't entirely sure of that. I knew that everyone wanted me to remember, but there were times I thought maybe I was happier this way. Yes, it sucked to have nothing but blank space where my life should be, but I was building a new one with Nikki and Oliver, one that I really loved. I wasn't ashamed to admit that I was scared of that changing once the memories came back.

I reached for Oliver, setting him against my shoulder and rubbing his back. He belched loud enough that it made me laugh. It always amazed me that someone so small could be so loud, or stinky for that matter. The kid was adorable regardless of the nasty diapers or having to get up at all hours of the night. Having him and Nik in my life made everything better.

While she ate her breakfast, I stood with Oliver and carried him down the hall to his room. Past experience had taught me that he'd be ready to be changed about now. I made quick work of putting a fresh diaper on him, and as he yawned widely, I decided to see if he'd lie in his crib. Sometimes he would doze off, and others he'd scream the house down because he wanted to be held. And Nikki usually gave into him.

All right. So I caved too. What could I say? My son had me wrapped around his little finger.

Oliver settled in his crib, smacked his lips, and started to fall asleep. I knew if I didn't convince Nik to come lie down with me, she'd start cleaning. When I got to the kitchen, she was already placing the dirty dishes and pans in the sink.

"Oh, no, you don't!" I reached out, snagged the belt of her robe, and tugged her back. "No dishes. No cleaning. Our son is going to sleep, so we're going to go rest while we can. You know damn well he'll be up again in another two hours."

She sighed and leaned back against me. "I know. You're right, but... there's always just so much to do."

"And it will get done, Nik. It doesn't have to be done *right now*."

She didn't put up much of a fight as I led her back to our bedroom. I stripped her robe from her, pulled a nightgown over her head, then made sure she got into bed. I climbed in next to her, then wrapped her in my arms so she wouldn't try to sneak out of the bedroom. I'd already threatened twice before to tie her to the bed if she didn't rest. I was starting to think I might actually have to do it. "Sleep, sweetheart. Oliver is fine. The house can wait."

She sighed and snuggled into me. "Fine. Tyrant."

I smiled and pressed a kiss to the top of her head. There were times it was hard for me to believe I barely knew Nikki. I'd tried to throw her out of my house that first day, but once I'd found out she was mine, everything had changed. I'd spent as much time with her as possible, learned what she liked and hated, and just enjoyed her company. I didn't know the men I called brothers all that well, but I'd honestly been avoiding them for the most part.

Scratch and Cinder made sure I was present for Church or any mandatory functions, and I did know everyone to some extent. I'd grown fairly close to one of the Prospects, Dixon. He was my go-to person when I needed something, but the others had a tendency to stare, as if they were waiting for my memory to magically come back. It made me feel awkward when I was around them. The jobs I'd been sent on weren't much better. I knew that I was supposed to trust these men, but I didn't have the memories to back that up, and they all felt like strangers.

A soft snore slipped out of Nikki's lips and I hoped that Oliver would rest for a while. He was wearing his mom out. Maybe I needed to talk to some of the others, the ones with kids, and see how they managed to balance everything. I hated that Nik was running herself into the ground, and I felt like I wasn't taking up enough of the slack. Not that she gave me much of a chance to help. No sooner would I notice something needed to be done than Nikki was there, taking care of it. If I tried to make her sit down, she brushed me off and said she would in a minute, except that minute never came.

Maybe I needed to hire some help for her? Would she slow down if I hired a housekeeper to come in at least once a week to take a little bit of the burden off her? She certainly didn't seem to want me to help with anything. It bothered me. A lot. She was here with me, and let me claim Oliver as my son, and yet… most of the time it was almost as if she thought she had to do it all on her own, like I wouldn't want to help take care of them. Had I been that big of an asshole before I lost my memory? Was there something I'd done or said in the past that made her feel she had to do it all alone?

I needed answers, but I wasn't certain I was ready for them.

Grabbing my phone off the nightstand, I swiped to unlock it. I hesitated only a moment before I messaged Scratch.

Was I an asshole to Nikki before I lost my memory? Say something that made her think she had to do everything herself?

It only took a moment to get a response from him.

Not that I'm aware. Did she say something?

I snorted. No. But the way she acted sometimes I had to wonder if she'd tell me even if I had been a dick to her. *No. Just this feeling I had… might be nothing.*

The phone rang and I answered quickly before it could wake up Nikki.

"Why would you think you were an ass to her?" Scratch asked.

"She's always trying to do everything on her own. If I get up to clean something, she stops me and does it herself. I can't exactly feed Oliver, but I try to help where I can. She just doesn't seem to want my help."

Scratch was quiet, and I looked at the phone to make sure the call hadn't dropped.

"Maybe this isn't about you," Scratch said. "You won't remember, but there was a time when Nikki was in a serious relationship with someone. He treated her like trash. Maybe part of what she's fighting against is the emotional abuse that ass heaped on her."

Could that be it?

"You could always ask her," Scratch suggested. "If she tries to run off, make her sit and listen to you."

"Am I supposed to tie her to a chair? Because that's about the only way I could force her to sit still."

"Do what you have to, Ashes. If you think she's taking on too much, then she probably is. Maybe she feels like a failure as a mom if she can't handle it all on her own. Who the fuck knows what's going through her head? You certainly never will if you don't get her to open up."

He had a point. "You're right. I'll talk to her. Right now, I've convinced her to take a nap."

"Good. If you need anything, you let us know. You have family, Ashes. The two of you aren't in this alone."

The call disconnected and I set my phone aside. Instead of resting with Nikki, I decided to do something else. If the house was already clean, and the laundry already done, then she wouldn't have a choice but to sit and relax after Oliver was fed. Rolling out of bed, I went to the kitchen and started on the dishes, then wiped down the counters and table, mopped the floor, and worked on the laundry.

Oliver slept for nearly three hours, which meant Nikki had a nice long nap. By the time both of them woke, the house was damn near spotless and the laundry was washed and folded. If she wouldn't let me help her, then I'd just have to tackle a few things here and there when she slept. I refused to let her do everything herself. If she kept this up, she'd drop from exhaustion before long.

Nikki stared at everything with wide eyes as she cuddled Oliver to her. "You cleaned?"

"Yep. Now you have no choice but to relax today. I'll take care of lunch and dinner. The only thing you need to worry about is our son and getting in at least one more nap today."

Her eyes turned glassy with tears. My heart wrenched in my chest and I knelt next to her chair. "Hey, none of that. You're doing a great job, Nikki. I mean that. But Oliver is my son too, and helping take care of him -- taking care of *you* -- is something I want to do. I need you to stop shutting me out and taking on every task around here."

"I love you," she said softly.

"Love you too, beautiful." I hesitated only a moment. "I'm not him, you know? Whatever asshole made you feel like anything you did wasn't enough. That's not me. And if it was me before, it's not now."

Did that even make sense?

She reached out to cup my cheek. "It wasn't you. It wasn't even Oliver's sperm donor."

I glanced at our kid. "You never talk about him."

"Bane was a short fling. We only had one night together, and we both knew it wasn't a lasting kind of thing. It was fun, and I was on the rebound having just dumped my ex. Chad is the one who treated me like garbage."

"You didn't love Bane?" I asked. For some reason, I'd never dared to ask. And yet, I'd wanted to know. So damn much. Then I'd feel guilty for being jealous of a dead man.

"No. I never loved Bane. Seeing him die, the brutal way they attacked him, it's haunted me for a long time. And maybe I felt a little like it was partially my fault. If I hadn't gone out with him, against Renegade's wishes at that, then maybe he'd still be alive. It's hard to say."

I smiled a little. "So it's not just me that your brother hates."

"He doesn't hate you. He just doesn't want anyone in the club to date me. Or claim me. Or breathe in my direction for too long. He's worried that this way of life will get me killed, especially after what happened with Bane."

"You were there," I said. "When Bane died."

She nodded.

A flash of her depressed, sitting on a couch and staring at nothing, entered my mind. I'd seen her that way, moping after Bane died.

"You saved me, Ashes," she said. "You checked on me every week, several days a week, made sure I ate. You took care of me when no one else would. I wasn't mourning Bane as a boyfriend, so much as the loss of a man who had died too young. No one else noticed how much that day impacted me, except for you."

"And I fell in love with you," I said. It wasn't something I remembered, but something I felt. I just *knew* that I'd loved Nikki.

She hesitated. "Yes, I think you did."

And the fact she wasn't sure meant I'd never told her. For that matter, the way she said it, made me wonder if she was just telling me what she thought I wanted or needed to hear. Why would I claim her and never say those words to her? It was just another piece of the puzzle that I wasn't sure I wanted to put back together. Maybe some things were better left in the past... even if it meant I never regained my memories.

Chapter Seven

Nikki
Halloween Night

Little Oliver had no idea what was going on. I'd stuffed him into a Pooh Bear costume, which I'd found to be quite adorable with his chubby little cheeks. At two months old, he'd filled out a lot. It was hard to believe he'd been born early. The club lovingly referred to him as our little chunk, and they weren't wrong. Oliver had packed on the weight just in the last three weeks alone. It gave me hope that everything would be fine.

Ashes stopped in the nursery doorway, leaning against the frame, hands in his pockets. The man was so damn sexy it sometimes hurt to look at him. Even though I'd had time to heal, he hadn't touched me yet. He didn't realize it, but we were breaking that dry spell tonight once Oliver went to sleep. But first, we had a club Halloween party to attend. A family event now that there were more kids at the compound.

Oliver wouldn't be able to partake in any of the fun stuff Meg and Clarity had planned for the children, but I had still wanted to dress him up. I planned to take a lot of pictures tonight. Even if he was only two months, it was still his first Halloween. Next year, he'd have more fun, but this one was special.

"You ready?" Ashes asked.

"Yeah. I just need to grab his diaper bag and make sure there's plenty of diapers and wipes in there. And an extra pacifier."

"I'll get it. The car is warmed up if you want to carry him out. I'll be there in a minute."

I stopped to kiss his cheek on my way past him, breathing in his scent. Even if he didn't remember who he was before, he still sounded and smelled like the Ashes I'd always known. There were times I forgot that he'd lost his memories. The way he watched me, though, that hadn't changed. It was the same heat I'd seen the day he brought me here. Even now, it felt like he was undressing me with his eyes as I slid past him.

I carried Oliver outside and buckled him into his seat before getting in the car. The heat was running because a cold snap had come through today. In Florida, it wasn't often the weather turned cool, but some northern storm had pushed cooler winds down our way and instead of the eighty degrees we'd been having, it was only sixty tonight. I was sure people up north where the temps were in the teens were laughing their asses off at the sight of us Floridians all bundled up like the ice age had hit.

The clubhouse had orange lights strung across the front and cobwebs hanging off the gutters. I knew once the family event was over, it would be business as usual for the single guys, and I was grateful we got to use it first. I definitely wouldn't be putting Oliver down on the floor, not even if I'd brought his play mat. No telling what was down there, even if it did get mopped regularly. I didn't trust it.

Ashes got Oliver and the baby bag, then placed his hand at my waist as we walked inside. Clarity and Scratch were at the table in the corner with their boys, Caleb and Noah. Little Caleb was dressed as a knight and Noah was wearing a dragon costume. They were adorable! I saw my brother and Darby with Fawn and little Gentry. Fawn was a princess, complete with tiara, and Gentry was dressed as a lion. My heart ached at the sight of them. I wanted things to be the way they'd once been, but I didn't know if we'd ever get there.

- 231 -

Harley Wylde   **Slider/ Ashes Duet**

The past month alone, Ashes had opened up more with the club. I'd watched as he'd kept his distance for the longest time. It had broken my heart. While he still wasn't as close as he'd been with everyone before, it was nice to see him interact with everyone and relax. My brother just wasn't one of the men who made that happen. He and Ashes still butted heads every time they were in the same room together.

The door opened behind us and I turned to smile at Cinder, Meg, and their son, Tanner, who wore a scarecrow outfit. The thought of the Pres's son wearing something so sweet made me giggle, but I knew that tough old man would do anything for his family. A few single guys mingled near a table with food and punch, and I hoped like hell they hadn't spiked it. That was the last thing I needed while I was breastfeeding.

"Come on, it looks like Scratch is pulling some tables together. We'll go sit with him and Cinder."

I nodded and grabbed his hand, following his lead. He set Oliver's carrier on a chair between him and Scratch, then pulled me down onto his lap. I leaned against him, feeling safe and loved, but then Ashes always made me feel that way. Sometimes I saw the man he'd always been, but there were times he lost his temper in a way that frightened me. I knew it was because of his lost memories and the way he felt, not remembering anything of his life, and the headaches were getting increasingly worse. I couldn't fault him for it, and he never hurt me or Oliver. The moment he even realized what he was doing, he'd leave the house and go ride for hours. I hated it for him and wished there was something I could do, but the stubborn man refused to see a doctor.

Ashes kissed my cheek, then rubbed his beard against me, making me want him even more. I loved it when he did that. He always kept it soft so he wouldn't scratch my skin. I'd learned that the stuff he used on it was what I smelled every time he was near. It had a musky oak type of scent that I just loved. Then there were the times I'd wake up and find him clean-shaven. I just never knew which Ashes I'd find from day to day.

Renegade and Darby came over, but my brother looked uncertain as he gazed at me. I wasn't sure what to expect of him this time and waited to see what he'd say. If he ruined my night, I might very well have to kick his ass. Or at least I'd try.

"Okay if we sit?" he asked.

"Depends," I said. "Are you going to be an ass?"

He winced and Darby elbowed him. Cinder had already spoken to him, and while he'd been slightly less hostile toward Ashes, he'd still been something of a dick. My big brother might not have wanted me to be part of the club, but I was and there was no turning back. He just needed to accept it.

"I'm sorry. I shouldn't have taken out my anger and frustration on Ashes, or attacked your relationship the way I did. I wanted a better life for you, one that wasn't filled with danger, and I lashed out. Didn't help that I hadn't realized you were in trouble and someone else stepped in to help you."

"Those are excuses, and poor ones at that," I said. "You beat on Ashes! Then because of you, he got sent off on that stupid run and lost his memory. As if that isn't enough, you dare to come to the hospital, then tell him that Oliver isn't his. What the hell?"

Ashes tightened his hold on me. I wasn't sure if he was thankful for the support or just wanted me to shut up. I was likely embarrassing him in front of his brothers, but I was tired of Renegade's shit. Yeah, he was a big bad biker around here, but he'd always just be my brother. Family was supposed to support one another. He seemed to have missed that memo along the way and I was tired of the way he was treating Ashes.

Renegade swung his gaze to the man holding me. "I'm sorry I've been a dick. It's obvious my sister cares about you and I shouldn't have tried to run you off. I just didn't want this life for her."

"I can understand that," Ashes said. I could feel the hesitation in him and wondered what he was holding back. "Are you really the reason I was sent out that day?"

I was surprised he hadn't already asked more about what happened. Or maybe he was worried what he'd discover. I knew that Ashes wanted his memories back, and yet there were times I wondered if maybe he was better off not remembering certain parts of his past. What would it be like to have a clean slate? A fresh start with no guilt of any past wrongdoings?

"Yeah, I am," Renegade said. I could see in his eyes that he regretted that decision.

"What's done is done," Scratch said. "Nothing we say or do will change what happened. But I may have a bit of good news for you. Havoc tracked down the men Ashes was supposed to meet that day. They were paid off and we were set up. I figured as much when they went to ground right after it happened."

"That's good news?" Ashes asked.

Scratch shrugged. "At least we have something to go on. If we can piece together what happened that day, then maybe it will help bring your memory back."

"Not that I don't love the fact you're discussing club business in front of us women," Clarity said, "but

Harley Wylde   Slider/ Ashes Duet

we *are* here to celebrate Halloween with the kids. Maybe we should get started on the fun stuff?"

Scratch kissed her cheek and nodded. "All right. You and Meg get everything going."

"I can help," I offered. "As long as Ashes doesn't mind watching Oliver?"

My man patted my hip and nudged me off his lap. I knew he adored our baby and normally didn't mind helping with him. But I also knew he had an image to uphold, and even if the brothers present were all fathers, I didn't know how he would react. He gave me a wink and a nudge of his chin letting me know it was fine to leave. I joined Meg and Clarity by the table draped with crepe paper covered in pumpkins and ghosts. Someone, likely a Prospect, had even put up some balloons.

"How are things really going?" Meg asked.

"Good. He sometimes loses his temper when he can't remember something, or rather when he gets bombarded by what he calls flashes that don't make sense to him, but he never takes his anger out on me or Oliver."

Clarity and Meg shared a look.

"What?" I asked.

"The Ashes we know, from before the incident, would never lose his temper around a woman or kid, much less his own. Are you sure everything is okay? You aren't scared being there with him?" Meg asked.

"We're fine. Really." I wasn't sure if I was trying to convince them or me. "He leaves when he realizes he's let his anger take over."

Clarity rubbed her hands together. "Then let's get things started. I had the Prospects lay out the food and drinks, all non-alcoholic. If the guys want beer, I'm sure they'll just grab them from behind the bar. I just didn't want any of the older kids to pick one up out of curiosity."

I heard the door open but ignored it. The way Meg's eyes went wide as she stared over my shoulder made my shoulders tense. Then the cloying scent of way too much cheap perfume assailed my nose right before Oliver started to cry. Don't ask me how I knew it was my son and not my nephew, but I just did. I could tell his cry from any other baby's. I didn't know if that was a maternal thing or just a gift I had. Turning to see why my son was so upset, my eyes narrowed as I stared at some trashy woman shoving her cleavage in Ashes' face.

My hands clenched at my sides, and I growled as I started across the room. The way she pawed at him was enough to make me grind my teeth. It was only the way he was trying to shove her away that tempered my rage even a little. I'd never felt anger over another woman coming on to my boyfriend in the past, but Ashes was mine and I would damn well fight for him if I had to.

"Get your hands off him," I said.

She turned her face toward me, her lips painted a dark red. It was a stark contrast from her bleached hair with dark roots, layers of black mascara and eyeliner, all set in a ghostly pale face. The makeup couldn't hide the lines around her lips telling me she either was or had been a smoker. She also looked quite a bit older than me. Unless partying at the club had just prematurely aged her. I knew a lot of drugs and alcohol could do that.

She eyed me up and down before facing Ashes again, dismissing me like I was nothing. *Oh no, she fucking didn't!* I marched around the table, reached out and grabbed a handful of overprocessed hair, and pulled the bitch away from Ashes. She teetered on her heels before landing on her ass. When she tried to stand, I shoved my foot in the center of her chest and knocked her back down.

"Just stay down there. You don't talk to him, you don't touch him, and you sure the fuck don't offer yourself up like a whore to him."

She sneered at me. "I can do whatever I want. You don't make the rules."

I felt a presence at my back, the type that only Scratch and Cinder could pull off. One of them placed a hand on my shoulder.

"She may not make them, but we do. She's also his ol' lady, so you'll show her some fucking respect. You were told not to show up here this early, and whoever let you in is going to be dealt with. I have no doubt you got him all worked up, but it's no excuse. It's family time, and you have no place here right now." Cinder moved forward, and I knew it was Scratch holding on to me, probably worried I'd lose my shit on the bitch. "You can come back in three hours."

"Feel free to crawl back. I'm sure you'll spend the night on your knees anyway," I said.

Scratch squeezed my shoulder, but I felt the vibration of his silent laughter.

Ashes stood, our son in his arms and stared down at the woman on the floor. Then he turned his back on her to face me, a dismissal if ever I saw one. Tipping my chin up, I met his gaze. All I saw was warmth and concern. I pressed a kiss to his lips, letting him know I wasn't upset with him. Just with the slut who had dared to go after him. There was no way he'd have asked for her attention. He'd looked decidedly uncomfortable when I'd walked up to the table.

"We good?" he asked.

Harley Wylde   **Slider/ Ashes Duet**

"Yeah. Just need to take out the trash."

I stepped around him and Cinder, grabbed the woman by the hair again and started dragging her ass out of the clubhouse as she shrieked and squawked. I could hear the other ladies clapping as I slammed the door shut, the woman still lying on the porch, her face twisted and flushed a bright red. Maybe she'd think twice before going after a man who was claimed, and everyone by now knew that Ashes wasn't single anymore. It seemed some of the club sluts didn't care.

"Feel better?" Cinder asked.

I paused, trying to determine if he looked pissed. I was still trying to learn my way now that I wasn't just the sister of a Devil but claimed by one too.

"Maybe."

He cracked a smile before sobering again. "Good. Now let's show these kids a good time."

I went to Ashes and kissed him and Oliver. Ashes leaned down, his lips brushing my ear. "That was so fucking hot. I can't wait to get you home and put Oliver to bed."

My nipples went instantly hard and my panties grew damp. I was starting to worry he'd never touch me again! If I'd known all I had to do was beat some whore's ass, I'd have done it a week ago. He nuzzled my neck, then kissed my cheek.

I could feel my cheeks burning when I joined Meg and Clarity again. We set up a pin the tail on the werewolf game, a bean bag toss with a board shaped like Frankenstein, and someone had filled a large bowl with water and apples on a table away from everything else. Havoc pumped some kid-friendly spooky music and songs through the speakers and I smiled as Allegra and Caleb started bouncing and dancing. It didn't take long for the other kids to join in, except for the babies.

I noticed Jordan kept eyeing Oliver with longing. I took him from Ashes and walked over to her, then held out the baby. "You can hold him," I said.

Her lower lip trembled, and it was the only time I ever remembered Jordan showing a vulnerable side. I heard she'd lost her shit when Havoc went missing, but I'd never seen her look close to crying before. Losing her baby, and knowing she'd never have another, must have been tearing her apart. I couldn't even imagine if Oliver hadn't survived.

"You know, if you want to keep him sometime, you can. Not that I think you're a glorified babysitter, but... I'm just saying, if you get baby fever and need a fix, I'm sure Oliver would be happy to visit with you."

She held my son close and hugged me tight with her other arm. "Thank you," she whispered.

"I know we aren't exactly friends, Jordan, but have you thought of maybe adopting? It's not the same as giving birth to your own, but I'm sure there are babies out there who need a home."

A shadow fell over me and I tipped my head back to look up at Havoc. He had an arched eyebrow as he stared at me before settling his gaze on his woman. "She's right. Might be something we should look into."

Jordan nodded and kissed Oliver's forehead. "Okay."

I left them and went to find Ashes. He'd claimed a table with Scratch, Renegade, and Jackal, each with a beer in their hands. It seemed Clarity had been right. The guys had wanted alcohol so they'd gotten bottles from behind the bar. The table still didn't have a drop of alcohol where the kids could reach it. Instead of intruding on their time, I went back to Clarity and

Harley Wylde   **Slider/ Ashes Duet**

Meg, but Josie had joined them since I'd walked off earlier.

Darby was talking to Jordan, and I saw Havoc head in the direction of the other guys. A Prospect was standing behind the bar, but was busy doing something on his phone. I felt so out of place. I never had before, but at other gatherings I'd just been Renegade's sister. Now I was Ashes' ol' lady. These people were my family, yet most of the time I felt like I was on the outside looking in. It wasn't that they didn't include me in stuff, but I just felt… like I didn't belong. Maybe it was because I knew the real reason Ashes had claimed me, and it didn't have anything to do with him loving me. He hadn't confessed his feelings until after his injury, and while I'd loved hearing those words, I worried that once his memories came back he wouldn't feel that way about me. Might even be angry that I hadn't corrected him. It ate at me all the time.

"What's wrong?" Josie asked.

"Nothing." I gave her a weak smile. "I'm fine."

Josie's look clearly said she didn't believe me. I wasn't ready to confess my fears to anyone. Part of me felt guilty. It was wrong to hope he never got his memories back. I kept telling myself he'd be better off, not remembering any bad stuff from his past, but deep down I knew I was just scared of his reaction to me and how we came to be together. I'd told him quite a bit already, even if I hadn't told him everything.

The kids played their games, ate cupcakes, and ran wild for over two hours. By the time the party was winding down, I was more than ready to go home. Jordan had held Oliver until he'd gotten fussy and needed to eat. Cinder had let me use his office to feed the baby since I hadn't been that comfortable breastfeeding in front of my brother. Now Oliver was

Harley Wylde   Slider/ Ashes Duet

asleep in his carrier. Ashes gently rocked it every few seconds while he talked to Scratch, but I'd tuned them out. Some of the women hated not knowing what was going on the club, but I honestly didn't want to know, unless it was going to take Ashes from me.

The Prospects were going to clean up the mess and get things ready for the single guys to start their night of drinking and women. As all the families headed out, Ashes put his arm around me and lifted Oliver's carrier from the chair. The heated look in his eyes still made my stomach flutter. No matter how much I worried how he'd react when he remembered everything, I still craved his touch. I'd fallen for him, even as I'd told myself not to get attached.

"Ready to go home?" he asked.

"Yeah. I need to get Oliver changed and into bed."

Ashes kissed my cheek, then stood with the carrier in his hand. He helped me up and led me out to the car. Once Oliver was secure and I'd buckled my own seat belt, Ashes put the car into gear and drove through the compound toward our house. I hurried inside to get out some pajamas for Oliver and a clean diaper. Ashes brought him inside and laid him on the changing table. While I got our son ready for bed, I heard Ashes moving around in the bedroom. The sound of water running made me pause and stare at the wall, trying to figure out what he was doing, but I shrugged it off and put Oliver to bed.

I pulled his bedroom door all the way shut, knowing that we'd hear him on the baby monitor if he got fussy, and I went to find Ashes. My jaw dropped when I entered the bedroom. The lights were off, but he'd lit about a half dozen candles around the room

- 241 -

and I saw the soft glow of more candlelight in the adjoining bathroom.

"Get naked and get in here," Ashes called.

I stripped off my clothes and shoes, then padded into the bathroom. He was laid back in the tub and held his hand out to me. I stepped over the side and let him pull me down in front of him, his legs bracketing my body. Leaning against his chest, I sighed as the hot water seemed to just drain the stress from me. I didn't know how he knew I needed this, but it was heaven. "You're pretty amazing," I murmured.

"There were times tonight you looked freaked out. I didn't know if someone had said something to you, or if you had a lot on your mind."

I shrugged a shoulder and skimmed my hand across the water.

"Nik, why do I sometimes feel like you're keeping something from me?"

Every muscle in my body went tight at his words. My heart started to race and I wondered if my happy little family was about to unravel. Would he force me to tell him? Would he be angry?

"You know I love you, right?" he asked. "Nothing you say or do will change that. I don't know what life was like between us before, but I've learned what an amazing, compassionate, sweet woman you are. And tonight I learned you're a badass when someone flirts with your man."

I didn't feel like a badass. Yeah, I'd gotten jealous and felt territorial, but... I wasn't like Jordan. I couldn't kick someone's ass, even though she'd tried to teach me some self-defense. After Bane and I had been taken, she'd been worried what would happen if I were in that situation again. I'd been beaten badly, but I knew things would have been so much worse if my brother hadn't shown up that day. It had nearly cost him his life too.

"What would you do if you found out that our relationship was a lie?" I asked softly.

"A lie? How is our relationship a lie?"

I licked my lips and braced myself for whatever he might say or do when I confessed the truth. "You only claimed me because you were ordered to. Oliver's dad was a Prospect. Bane. I know I've mentioned him before, but I never told you everything. Just bits and pieces. He and I were taken and beaten. Bane didn't make it, but I did, and I found out a little while later that I was pregnant. Your cousin was behind it, me and Bane getting taken. The only reason you spent so much time with me during my pregnancy was because of your guilt, even though I'd told you time and again it wasn't your fault. I didn't lie when I said you took care of me after Bane died. You did. It just wasn't because you loved me."

He rubbed a hand up and down my thigh.

"When I lost my apartment, you brought me here. Renegade lost his shit and pitched a fit. The next morning you said they'd called Church, but... we were caught together, in the shower." My cheeks warmed in remembrance. "Scratch said congratulations, you'd just claimed me. So you see, being with me wasn't your choice. You didn't love me. You just got stuck with me. What I said earlier... I thought it was what you needed to hear. You may have felt guilty or something, but it wasn't love."

Ashes kept stroking my leg, but he was silent. He slid his hand up my hip and across my belly, banding his arm across me and holding me tight. With a slight shift, I felt his hard cock press against me and I gasped, my eyes going wide. He still wanted me? Not that he hadn't been hard that first time when we'd been caught. Just because he wanted to fuck me didn't mean anything.

"When I said I loved you, that nothing would change that…"

He left the words hanging and I tried to brace myself. Was he about to ask me to leave? Or at least move out his room?

"I meant it, Nikki. You're mine. Maybe we didn't end up together in some fairy-tale sort of way, but the woman I've come to know the last few months completely owns my heart. I hate that you've carried that with you all this time, worrying for no reason. Would it have changed things in the very beginning? Maybe. I can't say for sure."

"You're not mad?" I asked.

"No, baby. I'm not mad." He hugged me to him, resting his chin on my shoulder. "But just so you know, I still think it was hot as fuck that you knocked that slut on her ass tonight. You're welcome to do that anytime you want, as long as you plan on getting naked when we get home."

I giggled like some high school kid, but I couldn't help it. I'd been so damn worried, so scared, and it was all for nothing. Ashes slid his hand up my abdomen until he cupped my breast, tweaking my nipple between his fingers. I moaned and my eyes slid shut. I rubbed my thighs together as an ache started between my legs. He played with my breasts and nipples, teasing me.

My breath caught and held as he moved his hand down my body, not stopping until his palm cupped my pussy. I lifted my hips, silently begging him for more. I needed to come. It had been so long, too long!

"Please, Archer."

"Please, what?"

"I need you. Need… need…"

He swiped his finger over my clit and I cried out as sparks of pleasure shot along my nerve endings. "Need that?" he asked.

I nodded and whimpered as he lightly stroked the little bud. I came so fast it was almost embarrassing, but he seemed to love the effect he had on me. Before I realized what was happening, he'd stood with me in his arms. Water poured off us all over the floor, but he didn't seem to care. Ashes strode over to the bathroom counter, setting me down on the space to the left of the sink. He pulled my ass to the edge, then dropped to his knees.

My breath caught at the first swipe of his tongue, and then I stopped thinking and focused on feeling. Every stroke against my clit made my thighs tremble and my heart race. Ashes made me come twice before he stood and gripped my hips. He blinked a few times, then his gaze held mine.

"Condoms. I don't think I have any."

I bit my lip and looked around. I didn't really want to risk getting pregnant again right away, but I didn't want to wait either. I pulled open the drawers I could reach, but none of them produced a condom.

"I can run to the store and grab a box," he said.

"Or… you could see if the clubhouse has one? Or get one from someone there?" I suggested, not wanting to wait long enough for him to go shopping.

He snapped his fingers. "Prospects! I'll call a Prospect and tell him to bring some."

My cheeks warmed at the thought of the Prospects knowing we were having sex tonight. I still gave him a nod. It was better than the alternative. Ashes left and I heard him speaking to someone, then heard him walk out of the bedroom. Was I supposed to just... stay? Like this? I closed my legs and tried to ignore the chill in the air.

I didn't know how much time had passed, but I didn't think it was more than a few minutes. Ashes came back, a strip of three condoms hanging from his fingers and a smile on his face. I didn't want to know who had brought them or I might never be able to hold eye contact with them again. He ripped one off the strip, tore it open, and rolled it down his cock.

"Come on, pretty girl. We're moving this to the bedroom."

He scooped me off the counter and carried me to our bed, the other condoms still gripped in his hand. He tossed them onto the nightstand before easing me down onto the mattress. The weight of his body pressed against me.

Ashes braced himself on his hands, his gaze locked with mine. My clit throbbed and my nipples ached. I needed him, wanted him. No one had ever made me feel the way Ashes did. The heat of his gaze burned into me as he shifted his hips and slowly sank into me. I moaned as he stretched and filled me, withdrawing only to push in again. I gripped his biceps, my nails digging into him.

"Archer, please..."

He growled and thrust harder. "I fucking love hearing you say my name when I'm balls-deep in your pussy."

His filthy words made my breath catch as desire pulsed in my veins.

I whimpered and arched, lifting my hips.

"My dirty girl liked that," he said with humor lacing his voice. He leaned down until his lips were near my ear. "Do you want me to fuck you hard and deep? Want me to pound this pussy so that you feel me for days?"

I never thought I could come just from words, but with his cock filling me and his mouth telling me filthy things, I came so hard I saw stars. "Archer!"

He growled and slammed into me over and over until I felt the hot spurts of his release as it filled the condom. As he stilled, his cock twitched and jerked inside me. He panted for breath and when he his gaze locked on mine, I knew that this was going to be the first of many times tonight. I wasn't the only one who had missed the intimacy between us, and now that my fear wasn't hanging over my head, I was going to enjoy every second of being in his bed. I only hoped we didn't run out of condoms! I didn't think three would be anywhere near enough.

Chapter Eight

Ashes

Cinder had called Church early this morning, but I was only half-listening. After an amazing night with Nikki, my mind was otherwise occupied. And not just because one of the condoms had broken. Nik had freaked out a bit, but even as exhausting as Oliver could be, I'd be thrilled if we had another kid. I could understand her wanting to wait a year or two, but sometimes fate had other ideas.

Halloween was our first holiday together as a family, but Thanksgiving and Christmas were coming soon. Even though Oliver was too small for it to have an impact on him, I wanted those days to be special for Nikki. More than that, I didn't like that she was mine only in the eyes of my brothers. Even if she did wear my name across her back when she left the house, I knew that wouldn't deter every guy out there. Some were just out and out assholes, but even a wedding ring wouldn't keep those away. I'd been toying with the idea of asking her to marry me, but that was more for me than her in all honesty. I wanted her to have my last name, and the same for Oliver. I wanted her to legally be mine.

"Ashes, are you even listening?" Scratch asked, jerking my attention to the head of the table. Cinder was glaring my way, looking beyond pissed off. Shit.

"Sorry. I just…" I didn't really have an excuse. Being preoccupied with thoughts of Nikki wasn't going to fly as a reason to not pay attention.

Cinder pinched the bridge of his nose. Scratch leaned back in his chair, arms folded, and Havoc just stared me down. The only officers not making me wish I could sink through the floor, wouldn't look at me at

Harley Wylde   **Slider/ Ashes Duet**

all. Great. I wondered if I could blame my memory loss for this one. No, I couldn't. I wasn't a pansy who couldn't own up to his shit. "I was thinking about Nikki. I want to ask her to marry me," I said.

"While I'm sure that seems like the most important thing in the world, can you possibly focus on the business at hand for now?" Scratch asked. "You fuck up, and someone can get killed. Maybe even you. This room isn't the place for daydreaming."

I knew that. I wasn't an idiot, even if my memory was a giant black hole. I felt the burn as a blush climbed my neck, and I hoped like hell my face wasn't on fire too. Nothing like being chastised like a little kid at a table full of badass bikers. "Sorry, VP. Won't happen again."

No one at the table looked like they believed me. Renegade snorted and shook his head. "She wears a size six ring and she hates diamonds," he said. "Best jeweler is over on Main Street. Now focus, dipshit."

I gave him a one-finger salute, but I committed that information to memory before turning my gaze back to Cinder. He looked tired. No, more than that... it was like a heavy weight was pressing down on him. I hadn't noticed it yesterday. Had something new happened? Or was there something he'd been holding onto, something we needed to know but he'd been reluctant to tell us?

"As I was saying..." Cinder stared at me a moment before shifting his focus. "We tracked down the men responsible for what happened to Ashes."

A cough at the end of the table made Havoc place his hand over his mouth to hide the smirk that graced his lips. I wasn't sure if he was amused over me being a sap for my woman, or because I got scolded like a kid.

Harley Wylde   **Slider/ Ashes Duet**

"All right. Shade discovered who they are, with some help from Wire and Lavender. After some digging, it seems we weren't the only club hit that month. While the Dixie Reapers weren't involved, the Reckless Kings had something similar happen, as did Devil's Fury and a few other clubs spanning from Missouri to Louisiana, and from the Carolinas to Arkansas. Ashes is just the only one who has memory loss from the situation. Everyone else was knocked out, but came to without anything more than a headache."

"We're taking the assholes down, right?" asked Shadow.

"We are, but we're not doing it alone. Ashes, I'm giving you the option of going. The men responsible aren't in the area anymore. They're closer to the Reckless Kings up in Tennessee. I'm going to send three men, and Devil's Fury is sending a few as well."

I chewed the inside of my cheek. On the one hand, I'd love to get my hands on whoever fucked me up that day. But on the other... it would mean time away from Nikki and Oliver. Getting revenge wouldn't change anything. My memories wouldn't come back just because I beat on the assholes who did this to me. And honestly, I wasn't entirely sure I wanted them back.

Nik and Oliver were my life. But so was this club. I owed them a lot, especially the Pres, and the last thing I wanted to do was let them down. If Cinder thought I should go, then that's what I'd do. I drummed my fingers on the table. Ripper and Magnus volunteered to go, and I felt Cinder's gaze on me. I met and held it a moment before giving him a nod. I only hoped this didn't come back to bite me on the ass.

"The three of you will need to leave in the morning. You have about a six-hour ride. I'd tell you

Harley Wylde   Slider/Ashes Duet

fuckers not to speed, but I won't waste my breath. Just don't get your asses pulled over between here and there. I'd just as soon no one realized we're in the Reckless Kings' territory if this goes to shit," Cinder said.

"You said Devil's Fury was heading that way too. Are we just meeting there, or are we stopping along the way to ride with them?" I asked.

"As far as I know, they're leaving tonight. I believe Grizzly planned for his guys to be there before midnight," Cinder said.

"So we're going to be late to the party?" asked Ripper.

Cinder shrugged a shoulder.

"Fuck that. I say we leave tonight." Magnus looked my way. "I know you have a kid now, but the sooner we get this shit settled..."

He didn't even have to finish. I knew he was right. I gave a nod and only half-listened when the discussion changed to other business. I hoped Nikki would be understanding. It wasn't like she'd never been around bikers before. She knew how things worked in the club. Then again, the last time I went on a run, I ended up beat to hell and lost every bit of my life up to the moment I came to in the damn warehouse. If she seemed apprehensive when I told her I was leaving, then it was understandable.

Nik didn't seem like the type to cause a scene, unless club sluts were involved. I smiled a little, remembering the way she handled that woman. Still made me hot. Cinder banged the gavel and I stood, heading for the door. Before anyone had a chance to stop me, I went out and got on my bike. I roared through the compound, flying down the road. My tires

Harley Wylde   **Slider/ Ashes Duet**

spit gravel as I pulled into the driveway. I'd barely cut the engine before Nikki stepped outside.

"What's wrong?" She worried at her lower lip.

"Why would something be wrong?" I moved closer to her, but stopped a few feet away.

"You came tearing into the driveway like hellhounds were chasing you. Pardon me if I thought I should be concerned." She placed her hands on her hips, narrowing her eyes. At least she wasn't worried anymore. Well, not at the moment.

"Maybe I just wanted to see you."

Nikki pursed her lips and gave me the look that clearly said she thought I was full of shit. I was going to miss the hell out of her while I was gone. I could only hope it wouldn't take long to wrap shit up and get back to my woman and kid.

"Anything I need to know?" she asked, relaxing her stance and holding out a hand to me.

I grasped it, then pulled her into my arms. I just held her a moment, breathing in her scent. Holding her was fast becoming my favorite pastime. Well, maybe second favorite. Last night I'd tried to make up for lost time, but I still craved her. Even now, I was at least semi-hard. "I have to leave for a little while."

Nikki tensed and tried to pull away, but I wouldn't let her.

"Just listen, baby. The men who hurt me are up in Reckless Kings' territory. They fucked over a few clubs besides Devil's Boneyard. We're meeting Devil's Fury up there, and for all I know, other clubs might show up too. Cinder said this shit happened across multiple states, and he discovered who was involved. I need to go handle business, then I'll come back to you and Oliver."

- 252 -

Harley Wylde   Slider/ Ashes Duet

She fisted my shirt and buried her face against me. "You damn well better. Don't you fucking leave me, Ashes."

"Nik, you know I can't control fate. I'll die when it's my time, but until then, I'll do my damnedest to come home to you each and every time I leave the house. It's the best I can do."

She sighed and hugged me. "I know. I'm being a whiny bitch, aren't I? I'm supposed to be some tough ol' lady, and I feel like a marshmallow."

I laughed softly. "No. Not a bitch. And maybe I like that you're not some hard ass ol' lady. Besides, Meg isn't all that tough, but she belongs to the Pres. Maybe we need a little softness in our lives."

Nikki pulled away, a slight smile on her lips. "Not a bitch but maybe a little whiny?"

Yeah, I wasn't falling into that trap. Instead, I kissed the hell out of her.

"I need to pack." I caressed her cheek. "Going to miss you, Nik. Both of you."

"Love you so damn much."

"Love you too."

I kissed her again, then headed inside to visit with Oliver before I had to go. Cuddling him close, I wished I didn't have to leave. I might have told Nik that I'd die when it was my time, but what if that time was now? What if I left and never saw my son grow up? My chest felt tight as I paced the room with Oliver. This kid was making me soft, both him and his mom. I might not remember my life before the incident, but I doubted I'd patched into the club by being a pansy.

There was a knock at the door and I heard Nikki answer it. Seeing Cinder took me a little by surprise. "Pres, everything okay?" I asked.

- 253 -

He watched Oliver a moment before his gaze met mine. "Hard to leave them, isn't it?"

I looked down at Oliver and kissed his forehead. "Yeah, but I'm going. The club needs me."

Cinder moved farther into the room and sat on the couch. He stretched out his legs and crossed his ankles, arms folded over his chest. To anyone else, he'd appear relaxed, but I could see the coiled tension in him. I didn't know why he was here. I'd said I would go to Tennessee. Had he not wanted me to volunteer? Maybe I'd read everything all wrong in Church.

"Before I claimed Meg, I was always willing to put myself at the front of the line when we faced down trouble. Then we had a kid and my life changed even more. This club is still my life, but I have something else to live for since gaining a family. Same goes for you, Ashes. I offered you the chance to go in case it's what you really wanted. You're the only one who saw the men you were meeting, but since your memory is gone, there's no guarantee you'd recognize them. Hell, for all we know, you never set eyes on them."

I sat in my chair with Oliver. "What are you getting at?"

Cinder glanced around the room before focusing on me again. "You've made a nice life for yourself since you claimed Nikki. But you were distracted as shit today. As much as I'd like you to go to the Reckless Kings, I need to know you'll be focused. I don't need you getting yourself killed, or someone else, because you can't keep your mind off your woman and kid."

I understood where he was coming from, and I could appreciate his concern not just for me but for everyone handling this issue. I wanted to assure him that my head was in the game, but honestly, I didn't know if it was. Maybe I was getting soft, or maybe things with Nik just felt too new. Missing most of my life made it feel like I'd only known her a few months. And Oliver... he was still so tiny, so young.

"If you're not at the front gate ready to go within the hour, I'll tell the others to leave without you." Cinder rose. "And I won't think any less of you if you decide to stay behind."

"I want to pull my weight around here, Pres. I know I'm letting everyone down, but I just..." I shook my head, not knowing how to explain it. There were times I didn't feel like myself, like I wasn't reacting to things the way I would have before. The problem was that I had no idea who I'd been before I lost my memories.

"You don't know who you are," Cinder said. "I get that. We can't expect you to react the way you would have before when all that's gone. I've tried to be as understanding as possible, but the truth is that sooner or later we're going to need to have a discussion. About your future with this club."

And there it was. If I didn't go on this run, if I stayed behind, then it would give him even more cause to throw my ass out, which meant Nik and Oliver would be homeless too. Regardless of how I felt, or what I wanted, I needed to put them first. Being with the Devil's Boneyard was the only way to keep them safe. If that meant I had to leave them for a while and sort this shit out, then so be it.

"I'll be there. Just want a little time to say goodbye to Nik and Oliver."

"Then I'll leave you to it. And, Ashes?"

I stood and moved closer to him, Oliver clutched against my chest.

Harley Wylde　　　　　　　　　　**Slider/ Ashes Duet**

"Don't fuck up," Cinder said. "I want you and every man I send with you to come back alive, and preferably unharmed. Whatever it takes to get your head on right, fucking do it."

There was only one thing I could think that would make me feel more settled. Not that leaving Nik or Oliver would be easy regardless.

"I want Nik to be mine, and not just in the eyes of the club."

I heard a soft gasp and looked over his shoulder to see my woman lurking outside the room. Her eyes were wide and her lips parted. There was something in her gaze, hope maybe? Did she want that too?

"Nikki, you want to be married to this asshole?" Cinder asked.

"More than anything," she said.

"Then I'll have it taken care of. If Shade can't handle it, then I'll call up the Reapers and get Wire to work his magic. Or that woman of his."

Cinder walked out without another word and Nik came to stand in front of me. She tipped her head to the side, her gaze assessing but I didn't know what the hell she was looking for. Even if Shade or Wire could make us legally married, as far as paperwork went, it didn't give Nikki a ring and I didn't have time to go get one. I'd just have to make sure I brought one home for her.

"You'll be careful?" she asked. "Come home to us?"

"Yeah, Nik. One way or another, I'll come home to both of you."

She wrapped her arms around my waist and got as close as she could with Oliver between us. Our son yawned, smacked his lips, and shut his eyes. It was almost too good to be true. Would he remain asleep if I

Harley Wylde   **Slider/ Ashes Duet**

laid him in his crib? That was always the true challenge.

Nik drew back and I carried Oliver down the hall to his room. Pressing a kiss to his brow, I settled him in his crib. He squirmed a moment, but didn't wake up. As quietly as I could, I crept from the room and pulled the door mostly shut. Nik was in the hall waiting for me. It seemed we both had the same idea, since she took me by the hand and led me into our room. I shut the door, turned the lock just in case, and started stripping out of my clothes. I hadn't gotten much further than my cut, shirt, and boots before I remembered that we were out of condoms. Fuck my life.

"Um, Nik. One slight problem."

She stopped undressing and stared. "What?"

"No condoms. We used them last night."

She chewed on her lower lip. "Well, one broke, so…"

"And you want to play Russian Roulette and take a chance on me knocking you up by just not using one at all?"

I could see the indecision in her eyes. As much as I would love to be inside her, to make love to her one more time before I left, I knew she wasn't ready for another kid just yet. It was one thing for me to accidentally knock her up, and another to take the risk on purpose. "We can wait, Nikki. I'll make sure I bring back two boxes of condoms."

She sighed and came closer, cuddling against me. "Fine. But in case you forget, I'm buying some too. There's thirty-six in a box, right? So we'll probably need at least three to get through the month."

A startled laugh escaped me. Three boxes? What the hell? Did she think I was part machine? "Hey, Nik.

I know you love my cock and all, but you do realize I'm not one of those sex bots you like to read about."

I felt the heat of her blush against me. "They're androids."

"Same difference. I'm only human, and I think over one hundred condoms in a month is expecting a little much from me. That would mean at least three times a night, every night of the month."

"And we have a little cock-blocker down the hall."

I snorted. She wasn't wrong there. As often as he woke up, getting some time with her would be difficult at best. Even just trying to get some sleep wasn't all that easy, but we'd figure it out. There were nights the second my pants came off, he'd start screaming the house down. While it wasn't the worst thing in the world when I was just hoping to get a little sleep, if I was about to make love to my woman, it would suck a great deal. I loved that kid more than anything, but I wouldn't be opposed to someone in the club babysitting once a week so I could have some undisturbed alone time with Nikki.

I kissed her hard and deep. It would have to do for now.

"When I get back, we need to find a sitter for Oliver for about three hours."

"He eats every two," she said.

Dammit. "Fine. Then we need a sitter for two hours, and they need to watch him somewhere other than here. Because you and I have plans."

"I love you, Ashes. Be safe."

I kissed her once more, then pulled my clothes back on and started packing. The sooner I left, the sooner I could come home.

Chapter Nine

Nikki

Ten days. It felt like an eternity. Ashes called twice a day to check in and let me know he was okay, and I think he just liked hearing my voice. While I looked forward to every call, it wasn't the same as being able to hug him, kiss him, or know that he'd be walking through the door at any moment. He didn't talk much about what was going on with the Reckless Kings, but it didn't sound like he was coming back anytime soon.

I tried not to worry, but I hadn't heard from him the last few days. I kept telling myself he was just busy, that if anything was wrong, Cinder would have told me. But would the Pres really come talk to me? Not likely. I needed Ashes to come home, safe and sound. In my gut, I worried something was wrong.

"Are you sure about this?" I asked Meg. "He's been a bit fussier than usual. I think he misses Ashes."

"It's fine," Meg assured me. "Besides, he needs to get used to staying with other people eventually. You and Ashes are going to want some time to yourselves, and it's better to get Oliver used to everyone now rather than later."

"I won't be long. I just need to run pick up a few things at the store."

Meg waved me off. "Honey, take as much time as you need. Tanner is going to be two soon, and I honestly miss the baby stage. He's getting independent on me."

"You could always have another one."

There was a flash of pain in her eyes that was quickly gone.

"Meg, what's wrong?"

Harley Wylde   **Slider/ Ashes Duet**

"I've been pregnant twice since we had Tanner. I lost both babies. The doctor said I'm still able to have another child, but Cinder doesn't want to risk it. I asked for birth control pills after a rather lengthy discussion with him, so I don't see more kids in our future."

"Oh, Meg." I reached out and hugged her. "I'm so sorry. This club seems to have rotten luck in that department. You and Jordan... anyone else? I don't want to say the wrong thing at the wrong time. I wouldn't hurt any of you for anything."

"Just us," she said. "I've somewhat made my peace with it."

I handed her Oliver and his baby bag. "You have my number if you need anything. He ate recently, so he should be okay until I get back."

"Go, Nikki. We'll be fine."

I kissed Oliver, then walked down to my car. I waved as I pulled out of the driveway and headed for the main gate. It was a little strange leaving on my own. Usually I had a Prospect glued to my ass if Ashes wasn't with me. I was going to enjoy the freedom, even if it didn't last that long.

The store was packed, probably everyone planning their Thanksgiving dinner already. I hadn't even thought that far ahead. The club probably did something, but I'd have to discuss it with Meg and Clarity. If anyone had something on the agenda, those two would be at the head of it all. Parking what felt like three miles from the door gave me plenty of time to organize the list in my head.

I grabbed a shopping cart and started on the left, then worked my way across the store. It was a bad idea, but it was my routine. The list I always kept as a running tally in my head seemed to expand with each

- 260 -

Harley Wylde   Slider/ Ashes Duet

aisle, things I just had to have or needed to make. Like chocolate chip cookies, banana nut muffins, a three-layer strawberry cake. I really shouldn't be trusted to shop for food.

I made sure to restock the diapers and wipes for Oliver, grabbed a six-pack of beer for Ashes, then somehow managed to finish my shopping without buying out the entire meat department. Even though I'd protested rather loudly, Ashes had added me to his account, but I still winced when the clerk rang up the items in my cart and the total came in at just over three hundred.

"What the hell did I buy?" I wondered out loud.

The clerk snickered. "A little of everything?"

I nodded. "Pretty much. I'm sure I don't need half this stuff, and yet... I do. Probably a good thing this isn't one of those big box stores that carries everything from food to patio sets. I'd probably empty the account in one trip."

"Honey, it happens to everyone, especially this time of year."

Except I hadn't bought anything for the holidays. If I didn't stop eating the way I had been, or baking for that matter, my ass was going to be so big it would fit into two zip codes at once. Not that Ashes had complained about my weight. Then again, he didn't remember how skinny I'd been before Oliver. Every time I saw some celebrity in pictures within weeks of giving birth, and they were back down to their regular weight, I just wanted to scratch out their eyes. Lucky bitches! It had been two months since Oliver was born, going on nine weeks, and I was still twenty pounds heavier than before.

I pushed the cart out to the parking lot, then dug through my purse for my keys. People started to grumble behind me so I tried to walk and hunt for my keys at the same time. A horn honked, making me jump. Hastening my pace, I wanted to give a triumphant cry as my fingers closed around my keys. I stopped the cart at the back of my car and hit the unlock button on my key fob. I seriously wanted one of those new cars where you didn't even need a key, and Ashes would likely get me one if he knew, but this one still ran and worked just fine. It was still new to me, even if it wasn't brand-new, and I was grateful for it.

I opened the trunk and started to load the bags into the vehicle. As I turned to place two more into the space, a hand clamped down on my arm, jerking me off my feet. My eyes went wide when I saw the man who held me. His eyes were bloodshot and he looked past due for a hit of whatever drugs he was taking. I swallowed down my fear and tried to remain calm, but I didn't think I would be able to reason with him.

"What do you want?" I asked.

"Just you."

My jaw dropped, then snapped shut. He tugged on my cut and I suddenly understood. It wasn't that he wanted me, per se, but he wanted an ol' lady of Devil's Boneyard, and I was the only one handy. I didn't know what the club was mixed up in, or if this had anything to do with Ashes, but the fear I'd been tamping down suddenly roared to the surface.

"Please. I have a son. I can't... I need to get home to him."

"Guess your man should have thought of that before he went poking around where he shouldn't. Looks like your kid is going to be an orphan."

What? I tried to break free, kicked at him, and opened my mouth to scream. He shoved a nasty rag between my lips, then slapped tape over it before binding my wrists. The man yanked me off my feet, throwing me over his shoulder. I tried to look for help, but there wasn't a single person close enough, or anyone paying attention. Everyone was lost in their own world, fighting over parking spots or putting away their groceries. How could a woman get snatched out of the lot without anyone noticing?

When he tossed me into a trunk and slammed it shut, I blinked at the sudden darkness. This was happening. I'd been kidnapped. My heart was pounding so hard I thought it might burst from my chest. Oliver. My sweet Oliver. That man had said I wouldn't see him again. What did he plan to do to me? What the hell was Ashes mixed up in? Tears burned my eyes but I refused to cry. I'd been a helpless woman before and watched Bane die. I wouldn't be a lamb led to the slaughter again.

I twisted my hands, trying to loosen the tape binding me. I could feel my wrists getting slick as it cut into me, making me bleed. Despite the pain, I kept working toward freedom and when I finally pulled a hand from the tape, I knew that I at least had a chance. The dick who kidnapped me had taken me by surprise before, but not this time. I tried not to scream against the pain of the tape ripping off the skin on my lips, but I was finally able to gulp down huge lungfuls of air, and get the disgusting rag from my mouth. My rising panic made it feel like I still couldn't breathe, even though he hadn't covered my nose.

I dozed off a few times, then would jolt awake. My bladder felt like it was seconds away from bursting I needed to pee so bad. Something told me the man driving the car wouldn't stop and give me a potty break. Asshole didn't care if he hit every pothole between the grocery store and wherever we were

Harley Wylde   **Slider/ Ashes Duet**

going. He'd not care if I pissed myself, but I was trying really hard not to do that.

It felt like hours had passed, and I had no idea what time it was. How far were we going? I didn't even know if we were still in Florida, or if we'd left the state. Being in the panhandle, it wouldn't take long to reach either Georgia or Alabama. Is that where Ashes had gone? He'd said Reckless Kings, but I didn't know anything about them. The not knowing was the worst part, and worrying about Oliver. By now, someone would have realized I was missing. Were they looking for me? Had they found my abandoned groceries and purse? Or had someone stolen all my shit instead of calling the police like a good citizen?

Every bump of the car jostled me, and I banged my head more than once. The sharp turns made me think the ass was doing it on purpose, knowing that I was rolling around like a damn bowling ball. My stomach lurched and I fought not to throw up. With my luck, it would end up in my hair and smeared all over my face. The car came to a halt, tires screeching as the car slid. After a moment, I heard the door open and felt the vibration as it slammed shut. There were voices, deep and probably male, but I couldn't make out what they were saying, which meant they probably weren't near the trunk. Were they just going to leave me in here to suffocate? My escape plan hinged on them opening the damn trunk.

The voices grew louder, and then I heard footsteps that sounded like they were right next to the back end of the car.

"You sure this is the bitch?" someone asked.

"Had his name on her back. Unless he's got a side piece, but I don't think they mark but one woman no matter how many holes they put their dick into.

- 264 -

You know how those bikers are. Multiple whores a night."

My hands clenched into fists and my teeth ground together. Ashes wasn't like that! He was home every night with me and Oliver, when Cinder didn't have him out on runs overnight. And I knew I could trust him. There was no way he was cheating on me. He loved me!

"Get the bitch out here. He'll crack when he sees what we have planned for her. Not that it will matter," the mystery man said.

Someone laughed.

"She'll be a nice addition to the stable. Bet you have special clients just for her," said the man who snatched me out of the parking lot.

Shit. They were going to make me a whore? No. Fucking. Way. Nope. I wasn't the same woman who watched Bane die. I had Oliver to live for, and Ashes. If I was going down, I'd go down fighting this time. No more little pathetic Nikki who gets beat up and tied down.

Okay, so I'd ended up bound, gagged, and thrown into a trunk. Not the best way to start the road to the new badass Nikki. Baby steps.

I heard the lock on the trunk disengage and the lid lifted. Two men glared inside at me, and the one who'd snatched me hauled me out of the trunk.

"You didn't even gag the little whore?" the other man asked.

"I did. She somehow got it loose, but it doesn't matter. She can scream all she wants around here and no one will come looking for her."

"Time to go see your man," said the other guy.

I went with them, wanting them to take me to Ashes. I needed to know that he was all right. We

Harley Wylde   **Slider/Ashes Duet**

seemed to be in some sort of warehouse district. I still couldn't figure out where. This didn't look like any part of Florida I'd seen before, and it didn't smell the same either. Maybe that seemed weird, but to me, home had a certain scent. And this wasn't it.

They shoved me through the doors, and my jaw nearly dropped. Ashes, two other Devil's Boneyard members, and a handful of other bikers were stripped to their underwear and tied to chairs. The two idiots shoving me around didn't seem tough enough to have taken down all these hard-ass men, so I didn't think they were running things. No, someone else was helping. I wasn't sure if I should make a move before I knew more or not. What if I did manage to set Ashes free, and somehow disable these two men? What then? We could either free everyone and get out of here, or there could be others waiting.

"Nikki." Ashes' voice sounded rusty, or maybe it was more like... I swallowed hard as I catalogued his injuries. They'd made him scream in pain. "You should be at home, where it's safe."

One of the assholes behind me laughed. "Safe. That's a good one. Snatched her right out of the parking lot of the grocery. Easy as fucking pie."

"Oliver is with Meg," I said, wanting him to at least know our son was all right. "And I'm fine. A little banged-up, but otherwise I'm okay."

Well, I still needed to pee something fierce, but adrenaline was coursing through my veins and finding a bathroom seemed like the least of my worries.

"Not for long," said my kidnapper as he reached for me. I felt him grip the back of my shirt and with a loud *rip* the material gave way, leaving my upper body exposed except for my nursing bra.

Harley Wylde   **Slider/ Ashes Duet**

Knowing that all these men could see me, and that Ashes was forced to watch them hurt me, it changed something inside me. I'd been ready to fight before, but telling myself I would do whatever it took to get home, and being faced with these men, it wasn't the same. Not at all. It felt like a fire was licking its way inside me, and it was leaving blind fury in its path. I'd never been one to get truly angry, but right now, I wanted to hurt these men!

My hands clenched into fists and my jaw tightened. Before I could second-guess myself, I spun and slammed my fist into the temple of the bastard who had taken me. He cried out in shock and staggered back, but I wasn't done. I was so damn angry, and scared, and... I'd just had enough. It never even crossed my mind he might be armed, or someone else could be lurking with a gun. The thought was there, but didn't really connect in my brain. I just wanted to attack them, to hurt them.

"You. Fucking. Asshole!" I screamed each word, my fists hammering at him. The other guy was laughing as if he'd never seen anything so funny, until I turned on him next. I kicked, bit, and hit. A gun fell from somewhere inside his jacket and I kicked it toward the bikers before kneeing the guy in the nuts. Then I ran, straight for Ashes.

There was a table full of knives and other things within reach, so I snatched a knife, trying not to cringe at the blood crusting on the blade, and I sawed through the ropes binding his arms. Ashes grabbed the knife from my hand and cut his legs free, then picked up the gun and went after the two men I'd just attacked.

As much as I wanted to keep an eye on him, I knew it was better to free the others. I worked quickly, until I heard shots ring out. Freezing, my gaze darted everywhere. Had that been Ashes? No. He was frozen, gun clenched in his hand, and breathing hard. But both men he had cornered were still alive and without bullet holes. Then I saw a man in a suit standing on an upper landing. This was the man in charge. Power radiated off him.

"You were given one simple instruction. I should have known better than to hire an addict hooked on my product just because he was closer to the target. How could the two of you have fucked things up this much?" the man asked as he came down the stairs. He barely glanced my way, his focus on Ashes. Even the other bikers I'd freed didn't seem to be a concern for him.

"Who the fuck are you?" Ashes asked.

"I'm merely a cog in a much bigger machine. A worker bee, if you will. It's my boss who arranged this little meeting."

Worker bee? All the worker bees were men. Did that mean there was a queen over all this mess and not a king?

"What's all this about?" I asked.

They'd snatched me, probably to get Ashes to fall in line. But I didn't see any other women here. Did that mean the other bikers were just in the way, but not the true target? I was so confused. I didn't know why Ashes had come here, didn't have the first clue what was happening. I just knew I didn't want my son to be an orphan. We both needed to get out of here. I just didn't know how.

The man in charge eyed me up and down, a slight smile curving his lips. "You've got a smart woman on your hands. I'm thinking that she's already putting the pieces together."

Harley Wylde   Slider/ Ashes Duet

"This is about a woman, isn't it?" I asked. "I just don't understand who or why. What does Ashes have to do with any of this? Or me?"

The man chuckled. "Yes, indeed. Very smart. Your man here pissed off the wrong woman. My boss's cousin is a bit… promiscuous to put it mildly. She thought your man here was going to show her a good time, but he wasn't interested."

My mouth opened and shut several times. "What does that have to do with all these other men?"

"Nothing. Unrelated. These men are simply in my boss's way, but yours… it was just bad luck on his part that his club sent him to that warehouse. Anyone who went would have been jumped, but when MaryAnn saw the pictures of the Devil's Boneyard member who'd fallen into the trap, she went nuclear. Ranting and raving about the asshole who wouldn't fuck her, made her feel like trash."

I fought to keep any expression off my face, but from the man's laugh, I knew I hadn't succeeded.

"Yes, MaryAnn *is* trash, but she doesn't think so. She'd counted not only on your man fucking her, but she'd planned to get knocked-up. Then he shows up here, with the others bent on justice, and the opportunity was just too good to pass up. Make no mistake, anyone who came in his place would have met the same fate. The fact your man had someone at home who might make him fall in line was a pleasant surprise. MaryAnn exacted her justice on him, taking it from his hide so to speak, but I wouldn't kill him as she demanded."

"Are you telling me that my woman was kidnapped and I was beat to hell, again, because of some stupid club whore?" Ashes demanded. "Are you fucking kidding me?"

Harley Wylde Slider/Ashes Duet

"I'm afraid not, Mr. Ashes. MaryAnn is quite determined to ruin your life, the way she seems to think you ruined hers. Her plan was for you to watch as your ol' lady was violated six ways to Sunday, then dragged off to a brothel to serve out her days on her back. And you were going to be tortured and eventually killed."

My gaze narrowed on the man in the suit. "Why did you say all that in the past tense?"

"Again, smart lady. My boss has a weak spot for his cousin, but I don't give a rat's ass about the woman. She's a whore, plain and simple. But you... you're something altogether different. I believe we can come to an agreement."

I glanced at Ashes and saw that his gaze was focused on the man doing all the talking. The other two had disappeared at some point. I scanned the shadows and didn't see them, but it didn't mean they were truly gone. They could be lurking, waiting for a chance to strike out again. Or maybe they decided all this shit wasn't worth the pay.

"Tell me, are all the Devil's Boneyard women as delightful as yours?" the man asked Ashes. "Beauty, brains, and a bit of sass. I like it."

"Jordan would eat you for breakfast," Ashes said. "But yeah, we've struck gold when it comes to our women, and they're off fucking limits. The one who snatched Nikki is mine, regardless of how this shit show goes down. That fucker is going to pay in blood."

The man waved a hand. "You may have him. He's of no consequence to me. Merely muscle for hire, and an incompetent one at that. There's plenty more where he came from, as you're well aware from your time here. As for our deal... We need to run some trucks through your area. If one of the crates happens

Harley Wylde   Slider/ Ashes Duet

to fall off in your territory, you look the other way. Same goes for every club represented here."

"And if they don't agree?" Nikki asked.

The man smiled. "Then we'll have to hit them where it hurts. That's where you come in, my dear. I'm hoping the club is protective of its women. Never fear, though. Now that I've met you, I couldn't possibly let you die in a whorehouse. You're much too special for that. Don't worry. You'll learn to love my touch over time, even if I have to keep you tied down the first few months and break a little bit of that spirit I so admire."

Ashes growled and took a step closer to the man, and I fought down the bile that rose in my throat. I wouldn't take the bait, though. I had a feeling he wanted me to react, and I wouldn't give him the satisfaction.

"That's all you want?" I asked. "To run illegal stuff through the Devil's Boneyard territory and maybe lose a crate off each shipment? What happens to that crate?"

"Nik. Shut the fuck up," Ashes said.

I folded my arms over my chest and refused to look at him, maintaining eye contact with the man in the suit. He really needed to give me a name. This was getting ridiculous.

"That's all I want," the man said. "As for the crate, that's my business and mine alone. But never fear, it won't get in the way of anything the club has going on. By the time my boss figures out shit is missing, he won't be a problem anymore."

And the rest of the pieces were falling into place. At least for me. The guys from the various clubs seemed a little confused. There were nearly a dozen of them, and I wondered how they'd been taken down so easily. I was honestly amazed the others had kept their mouths shut. Then again, some of them looked a bit rough. I didn't know how they were standing. Two of them looked ready to pass the hell out.

"Why did you take all these men if you just wanted to make an agreement with their clubs? This seems a bit extreme," I said.

The man flashed me a smile. "Ah, if only their clubs had been more agreeable. A proposal was sent to each months ago, long before each club was lured into deserted warehouses in their territory. The Presidents wouldn't listen, so we tried to send a message. It went unheeded, and the next negotiation went much the same as the first."

Every man in the warehouse, everyone patched, had a blank look on their faces.

"You tried to come to an agreement with the Presidents before and after Ashes was hurt. This was just a last resort?" I asked.

"Yes. I'm sorry it came to this. We needed to make an example of them, and show them they weren't the only ones with the power. They needed to understand that my boss will do anything to see that this goes through."

"Ashes, give him what he wants so we can leave. Some of these guys don't look like they have much time left," I said.

"It's not my call, Nik." His gaze swerved to the other bikers. "And I definitely can't speak for any of the other clubs."

I looked at the others, but didn't see a single officer's patch among any of them. If these men didn't agree, if Ashes didn't agree, then we might all die. And I was *not* going to leave my son without either of his parents. There had to be a way out of this.

"Why did you take all these men if you knew none of them could give you what you wanted?" I asked the man in the suit. "Mister…"

"Ramirez. I'm Julio Ramirez, and I mean you no harm, little Nikki. I took these men in hopes their clubs would be willing to cooperate. As you can see, that was not the case. But then I realized that this one, your Ashes, had a woman at home. I could tell he has a soft spot for you, and I hoped the rest of his club might feel the same way. MaryAnn wanted you here as part of her revenge, but I had my own agenda."

Hold the fuck up. "Are you telling me that you spoke with Cinder and he knew you were torturing Ashes and did nothing?"

Mr. Ramirez shrugged a shoulder. "He could not be persuaded to see things my way."

"Do you have his number on your phone still? In the contacts or history?" I asked.

"But of course." He pulled a phone from his pocket and dialed Cinder, putting the call on speaker.

"I already told you I don't deal with terrorists," Cinder said, his voice a deep growl over the line. Mr. Ramirez raised an eyebrow as he gazed at me, as if to say, *See?*

"Cinder, it's Nikki."

Dead silence.

"Did you even notice I was missing?" I asked.

"Of course we did. Have men out looking for you right now."

"I'm guessing they won't find me," I said. "I'm with Ashes and the others. All the missing bikers are here. I'm assuming you know that Mr. Ramirez had others as well. Right?"

Cinder cleared his throat. "You have to understand, Nikki. This isn't about saving one man, or even a few men. I have to do what's best for the club as a whole. I'm not trying to be an unreasonable asshole. There are others here who need my protection, need me to make sound judgments when it comes to this sort of thing. If I agree to Mr. Ramirez's terms, what's to stop others from trying the same thing?"

I let that sink in for a moment. I could tell from the look on Ashes' face that he'd already known the answer we would get. Had he heard Cinder's refusal to the terms the first time? Had he known all this time that his club had turned their backs on him and the others? They were supposed to be a family!

"As President you're responsible for every man wearing your colors, aren't you, Cinder?" I asked.

No response. But I had a feeling he was listening, even if he didn't like what I had to say.

"Ashes and the others aren't worth less than those still at the compound. Each man in your club is equal whether they're an officer or not. Some may hold more power than others, but each and every one is your brother, your family. You don't turn your back on family!"

"Nik." There was a warning tone in Ashes' voice.

"No! I don't care if he's the big badass President of Devil's Boneyard. I don't care if he needs to make an example of me later. Right now, he needs to do whatever is necessary to bring you, me, and the others home. That's his fucking job!"

"She's right," Cinder said. "Very well, Ramirez. You may drive your shipments through my territory, but if there's an uptick in deaths from drugs or illegal firearms, I *will* come for you."

"I have no intention of harming your little town," Mr. Ramirez said. "I merely need a place to store some items from time to time, until I'm ready to make my

Harley Wylde   Slider/ Ashes Duet

move. I can assure you that I will not be taking business from your club. My interests lie elsewhere."

"Then send home my men, and Nikki."

Ramirez sighed. "Pity. I rather liked her spirit. Very well. I'll release them. But I can't let the others go until their clubs come to the same agreement. It's just business."

I looked at the other men. One wearing a Reckless Kings cut that said *Crow*. The other who looked like he was nearly on death's doorstep was from Devil's Fury. His cut said he was called *Dragon*. If their clubs didn't agree, they would die. It didn't take a medical degree to discern how far gone they were.

"Cinder, can you call Devil's Fury and the Reckless Kings and let their Presidents know that both Crow and Dragon won't make it home if they don't agree? And they need to agree *now*."

Ashes growled at me, probably worried about me being insolent to the Pres, but I was more worried about saving the men here with us than anything else. I'd take whatever punishment Cinder deemed fitting, but I wasn't going to leave without knowing these men had a chance.

"Fine. I'll call them, but I make no promises," Cinder said. "And, Nikki… we're going to talk when you get home."

At least I was going to make it home, so that was a step in the right direction. I went to Ashes, wrapping my arm around his waist and started to lead him toward the warehouse door, but he dug his heels in.

"Baby, you're not going out there in just a bra."

I huffed at him. "Really? We could be dead right now and you're worried about me leaving the warehouse without a shirt? In case you missed it, they ripped mine and you don't seem to be wearing one."

- 275 -

Ramirez came closer, pulling off his jacket, then unbuttoning his shirt. The last thing I wanted was to take anything from this man, but it was just a shirt.

"Permit me," he said, handing the garment to me. "It's the least I can do after those idiots treated you so poorly. They will be dealt with. I know your Ashes wanted to handle it, but I can assure you they will suffer much more at my hands. Take your Nikki home. You may use the car parked outside. The other two won't be needing it anymore."

"And my brothers?" Ashes asked.

"They may go as well. The others will remain here until I hear back from their clubs."

I hesitated, not wanting to leave anyone behind, but Ashes swung me up into his arms and carried me out of the warehouse. I locked my gaze on the men still held captive, and my heart hurt for them. Would they survive this ordeal? Or would this be the last time anyone saw them alive? It was wrong, so wrong to leave them.

For the sake of any loved ones missing them, I hoped they made it out of that warehouse. And I hoped this taught a lesson to every damn club out there. They weren't invincible, and it wasn't okay to leave a man behind. I wasn't even a patched member, and I knew that.

Epilogue

Ashes

Seeing Nikki walk into that warehouse had been the scariest moment of my life. I'd already heard Cinder refuse to give Ramirez what he wanted, and I didn't think he'd change his mind just to save my woman. Then she'd surprised the shit out of me and stood up for me and every man in that warehouse, demanded that Cinder do the right thing. I was both proud of her, and pissed as fuck.

But now that we were back home and standing in front of the Pres and VP, I was back to scared. I had no idea what Cinder would do to Nikki. I didn't think he'd do anything to physically hurt her, but she'd suffered enough emotional trauma already. She was stronger than anyone realized, even me, but that didn't mean she couldn't break if the right pressure was applied.

"She didn't mean to undermine your authority, Pres," I said, hoping to smooth things over. "Nik was just trying to save me and the others. She said what she did because she loves me."

Scratch snorted. "Your woman has brass balls, Ashes. Hell, hers might be bigger than yours."

I wanted to flip him off, but I refrained. Barely.

"I'm not going to do anything to Nikki, so relax. She's not only your ol' lady, the mother of the future generation, but she's also the sister of an officer. No one knows what she said, or my response, except the people in this room and the other two Devil's Boneyard members who were in that warehouse. Ripper and Magnus both think she walks on water right now and won't say a damn thing about the incident. Since she stood up for the men from the other clubs, I don't see them saying a word about it either." Cinder leaned back in his chair, the leather creaking. "Ripper and Magnus already gave me their version of what happened. Now I want to hear it from you."

I ran a hand through my hair and winced as my fingers grazed the cut on the back of my skull. Ramirez and his men had worked me over pretty good.

"I went with the others to stake out what we thought was a rival club. It was a setup. Ramirez and his men rounded us up like fucking cattle. We managed to take down a few of them, but we were outnumbered."

Scratch chuckled. "Boy, that's not what he wants to hear. He wants you to tell how little Nikki here kicked ass and saved all of you sorry bastards."

Nikki bit her lip and looked up at me, but I could see the laughter in her eyes. Yeah, she could laugh it up with the rest of them. Honestly, I was proud as fuck that she'd handled herself so well. Pissed that she'd been in danger to begin with, but seeing her go after those guys and hold her own? It had been pretty fucking impressive.

"All right. My woman saved our asses, freed us, and then talked you into bringing us home." I folded my arms and stared at the Pres and VP. "That what you wanted to hear?"

"Yep," Cinder said. "You'll both be happy to know that the other clubs also got their men back. Ramirez could be an issue, but for now we're going to monitor the situation. The fact each club had two to three men taken means that we have some work to do. Nikki was right when she called this a family. It is, and she was also right that you don't leave family behind. So, we're going to figure out where shit went wrong and make sure it doesn't happen again."

"So I'm not in trouble?" Nikki asked.

Cinder smiled, a rare occurrence. "No, darlin'. You aren't in trouble. Just don't pull that shit in front of my men, or we'll have a problem."

"Glad to have you back, Nikki," Scratch said.

"Back?" she asked.

"We know that what happened with Bane was hard on you. Instead of pushing through, you retreated into yourself. Since Ashes was keeping a close eye on you, we left things alone, but maybe we should have stepped in," Scratch said. "Renegade insisted you were fine, but you never came to any of the club events. It made me wonder."

She gave a little nod. "Yeah, I got lost for a while, but Ashes wouldn't give up on me."

"And when he needed you, you refused to give up on him," Cinder said. "You're the perfect ol' lady for Ashes, and we're proud to have you as part of this club. Now go get your son! Meg might be in heaven, but I want to get some fucking sleep tonight."

"Thanks, Pres," I said and led Nikki from the room.

We'd gotten back into town about six hours ago, and after I'd been patched up, we took a nap. I knew she'd wanted to pick up Oliver right away, but neither of us would have been any good to him. We'd been through hell.

"I thought he was going to be angry," she said as we got into the car.

"I wasn't sure how he'd react, but I'm glad to know he appreciates your strength as much as I do. I've always known that you were strong, Nikki, but you've proven it to everyone here and with the other clubs too. I'm so fucking proud of you, baby. And in the spirit of honesty…" I wasn't sure how she'd take this next bit of news, but I didn't want to lie to her, not even by omission. I pulled away from the clubhouse and headed for Cinder's house. "I think those men knocked the sense back into me. When we woke up earlier, I remembered everything."

She clenched her hands in her lap. "Everything?"

I stopped the car and reached out to clasp her hand in mine. "Everything. And, Nik, I still love you so damn much. Everything I felt after losing all my memories, all the moments we've shared, it's all still here. You're the most important person in my life, you and Oliver both. I love the two of you more than anything else."

"We love you too, Archer. So very much."

A tear slipped down her cheek, and I leaned over to kiss her, my lips brushing over hers. She was so sweet, and yet fierce when she needed to protect those she loved. Scratch and Cinder were right. She was fucking perfect for me. I was the luckiest bastard ever to have her in my life.

"Let's go get our son."

"You... you still think of him as yours, even knowing... everything?"

I squeezed her hand. "Honey, he *is* mine. I was there during your pregnancy, when he came into this world, I've changed his diapers and walked the floor with him. We might not share the same blood, but he's mine in every way that counts."

I drove the rest of the way to Cinder's house, and Meg was out front waiting for us, Oliver in her arms and the diaper bag at her feet. Nikki launched herself from the car and ran for our son, cradling him close to her. I got out and went over to them. Meg reached out like she was going to hug me, then retreated.

"I'm fine, Meg. A hug won't break me, especially from a tiny thing like you."

She wrapped her arms around my waist and gave me the gentlest hug I'd ever gotten. When she released me, I pulled Nikki and Oliver against my side. My son blinked up at me, then cooed. Brushing a kiss against his head, I breathed in his scent. I'd missed the hell out of him. "Let's take our boy home," I said.

Nikki nodded, thanked Meg, and took Oliver to the car. I started to follow, but Meg stopped me. "Ashes, can I have a minute?"

"Sure. Did something happen with Oliver while we were gone?"

"No, nothing like that. He's a complete little angel. I did have to put him on a bottle, though, and I'm not sure how easy it will be for Nikki to get him back to breastfeeding. It was that or let him starve."

"Then what did you need to tell me?"

She chewed on her lip and glanced around. "Look, Cinder is all big and tough. He has to be in his position, and I get that. But you need to know that leaving you and the others in that situation, it was eating him up inside. I watched him as he spiraled, wanting to rush in and save you, yet not knowing your exact location. When that man asked him to cooperate, Cinder's decision weighed heavy on him."

"The Pres is a good man, Meg. We all know that. He was trying to protect everyone, even if it meant sacrificing a few of us."

"I just wanted you to know how hard he took it. I'm really glad you're home, all of you, and I know he is too."

I hugged her again, then walked to the car. I'd known the decision to leave us hadn't been easy on Cinder, but I was glad that he had Meg, that she'd seen him struggling and more than likely offered him comfort. The man had my respect, and he'd earned it. "Let's get this little one home where he belongs."

Nikki smiled. "I missed him. I don't think I'll even care if he stays up all night, or wakes me every hour."

"I'll remind you of that when he wants to eat at one in the morning, then three, then five."

She smacked my arm. "Hush! You know you won't mind either. At least not this time. In another day or two, we may both be complaining about being exhausted. But at least we're here, safe, and so is Oliver. We're together again, a family, and that's all that matters."

"Love you, Nik."

"Love you too, Archer. Don't forget you owe me a wedding ring. And I expect you to wear one too. Maybe then those club sluts will back the hell off."

"And if not, my fierce little woman will kick their asses. So hot by the way. I get hard every time you start smacking someone around."

She stared at me. Unblinking.

"All right. Maybe not at the warehouse, but that's only because I'd been tortured for two days. But if I hadn't been hurting all over, then I'd definitely have been hard for you when you beat the hell out of those men. It was an awesome sight to see, even if it did give me heart failure."

"Give me time to cuddle Oliver and get him to sleep, then maybe you can show me just how hot it makes you when I start hitting people."

"Gladly, baby. Been too long since I was balls-deep inside you."

She snorted. "So freakin' eloquent."

I winked at her. "It wasn't my eloquence that snagged your attention. It was my big, long --"

She slapped a hand over my mouth. "Don't finish that sentence."

"Cock," I mumbled through her fingers. Then I licked her, making her squeal and jerk her hand back. "Admit it, Nik. You can't wait to have me filling you up again. I'll make you squirm and beg, then I'll pound that sweet pussy so good you won't be able to walk for days."

She glanced in the backseat at Oliver.

"Nik, he's a baby and has no clue what I'm saying. When he can understand more words, I promise not to say outrageous things in front of him." Then again. "Unless he's an obnoxious teen, then I may do it just to embarrass the shit out of him. Might be fun."

"It's a good thing I love you. Otherwise, I might very well run the other way."

I grinned at her. No, my Nikki wouldn't run from me. *To* me, yes. She was mine in every way that counted, just as I was hers. A perfectly matched pair. I'd never thought I'd ever have her as my ol' lady or my wife. For the longest time, she'd been in my every dream, and I'd wondered how she tasted, what her skin would feel like against mine. And now I'd get to kiss and touch her every day for the rest of my life.

I might have lost my memory for a while, might have nearly died, but I had everything I could ever want or need right here. Nikki and Oliver were my everything, and I was never letting them go.

Harley Wylde

Harley Wylde is the International Bestselling Author of the Dixie Reapers MC, Devil's Boneyard MC, Hades Abyss MC, and Devil's Fury MC series.

When Harley's writing, her motto is the hotter the better -- off the charts sex, commanding men, and the women who can't deny them. If you want men who talk dirty, are sexy as hell, and take what they want, then you've come to the right place. She doesn't shy away from the dangers and nastiness in the world, bringing those realities to the pages of her books, but always gives her characters a happily-ever-after and makes sure the bad guys get what they deserve.

The times Harley isn't writing, she's thinking up naughty things to do to her husband, drinking copious amounts of Starbucks, and reading. She loves to read and devours a book a day, sometimes more. She's also fond of TV shows and movies from the 1980s, as well as paranormal shows from the 1990s to today, even though she'd much rather be reading or writing.

Harley at Changeling: changelingpress.com/harley-wylde-a-196

Changeling Press E-Books

More Sci-Fi, Fantasy, Paranormal, and BDSM adventures available in e-book format for immediate download at ChangelingPress.com -- Werewolves, Vampires, Dragons, Shapeshifters and more -- Erotic Tales from the edge of your imagination.

What are E-Books?

E-books, or electronic books, are books designed to be read in digital format -- on your desktop or laptop computer, notebook, tablet, Smart Phone, or any electronic e-book reader.

Where can I get Changeling Press E-Books?

Changeling Press e-books are available at ChangelingPress.com, Amazon, Apple Books, Barnes & Noble, and Kobo/Walmart.

ChangelingPress.com

Printed in Great Britain
by Amazon